Praise for ***Too Close to Home***

"Engrossing . . . The fast-moving plot includes a neat twist. With any luck, [Andrew] Grant's righteous hero will have a long career cleaning up corruption and meting out his own brand of justice."

—*Publishers Weekly*

"Crisp pacing, complex plotting, and a sympathetic good guy all make for a most satisfying read. Grant has several great series going, and the janitor-in-the-courthouse theme is fodder for another."

—*Kirkus Reviews*

"This is Grant's ninth thriller, and it's a very good one, suspense tempered throughout with moral dilemmas. . . . An intelligent, exciting novel."

—*Booklist*

Praise for ***Invisible***

"*Invisible* is propulsive and engaging from the very first page. Andrew Grant has created a devilishly appealing new protagonist in Paul McGrath—the Janitor—who literally cleans up trouble and defends the defenseless in the most satisfying ways."

—C. J. Box, #1 *New York Times* bestselling author of the Joe Pickett series

"The masterful Andrew Grant outdoes himself with this deliciously twisty, magnetic thriller. Fiercely redemptive, with its clever, profoundly moving, and altogether captivating David and Goliath hook, *Invisible* is a winner."

—Sara Blaedel, #1 internationally bestselling author of *The Forgotten Girls*

"[A] superior thriller . . . Grant capably combines a riveting plot and depth of character. His best outing to date, this standalone marks Grant as a rising genre star." —*Publishers Weekly* (starred review)

"Another solid and entertaining thriller."

—*Kirkus Reviews*

"Paul McGrath is not just a janitor—he's a terrific new hero in what promises to be a fantastic and original series by Grant. Paul may be invisible . . . but his results are not in this intense mystery thriller that will leave you wanting more. In a word? Awesome."

—Allison Brennan, *New York Times* bestselling author of *Too Far Gone*

"*Invisible* is a riveting read from cover to cover. I love getting in on the ground floor of a new series, especially when it's sure to be a hit!"

—John Gilstrap, *New York Times* bestselling author of the Jonathan Grave series

"Wonderfully entertaining. Great action. Authentic spy craft. A fascinating new kind of detective, with wit and charm galore. Would that we all had someone like 'the Janitor' to help us."

—David Morrell, *New York Times* bestselling author of *Murder as a Fine Art*

"*Invisible* is the perfect thriller for these perilous and imperfect times. Buy it. Read it. You won't regret it and you won't forget it."

—Lorenzo Carcaterra, #1 *New York Times* bestselling author of *Sleepers* and *The Wolf*

Praise for ***False Friend***

"The second installment starring [Detective Cooper] Devereaux is a suspenseful action-packed drama that is sure to please fans of the series and mystery/thriller lovers alike. As a stand-alone, it will inspire newcomers to seek out the first book."

—*Library Journal*

"An incendiary thriller . . . Cooper is solid—decent, flawed, and entertaining." —*Kirkus Reviews*

Praise for ***False Positive***

"A fast-moving thriller . . . Readers who like defects in their heroes will love this guy, who knows he's not as good as he'd like to be. The final twist comes just as all finally seems well with the world. A dark, enjoyable novel. One of Grant's better works."

—*Kirkus Reviews*

"Smashing." —*Booklist*

"Engrossing . . . Action-driven, the book's pace never stops until the startling conclusion, which will chill to the core." —*RT Book Reviews* (top pick)

Praise for ***RUN***

"Breathtakingly fastpaced."

—Harlan Coben, #1 *New York Times* bestselling author of *Tell No One*

"Smart, fast, and blazing with nonstop surprises, *RUN* owned me from the first page and, man, those pages kept turning! A perfect thriller."

—Robert Crais, internationally bestselling author of *Hostage*

"Reads with the velocity of data over a high-speed line. Smart, intricate, dizzying, nothing is quite what it seems in this deftly written, twisty tale."

—Andrew Gross, #1 *New York Times* bestselling author of *No Way Back*

"*RUN* is a tightly written, expertly plotted, whiz bang of a novel with just the right dose of smartass."

—Chelsea Cain, *New York Times* bestselling author of *Let Me Go*

"*RUN* is a fast-paced, sleek thrill ride. Andrew Grant knows how to keep you turning the pages."

—Jeff Abbott, *New York Times* bestselling author of *Inside Man*

"*RUN* is an adrenaline-fueled thrill ride that will have your head spinning and your heart pounding."

—Joseph Finder, *New York Times* bestselling author of *Paranoia* and *Suspicion*

"High stakes, high tension, and nonstop action. Grant nails the world of sinister corporate scheming and big-money treachery—but don't even try to predict where this taut thriller is headed. Just hang on and enjoy this smart, original and fast-paced adventure."

—Hank Phillippi Ryan, bestselling author of *The Other Woman*

"Andrew Grant always delivers the goods, and *RUN* is his most intense thriller yet. Relentless, twisty, and blistering-fast, it's a book you don't dare start at bedtime."

—Sean Chercover, award-winning author of *The Trinity Game*

"Fast-moving . . . high on adrenaline."

—*Publishers Weekly*

"Twists and surprises abound, the pace never slows, and the writing satisfies. So go ahead, read and enjoy this one." —*Kirkus Reviews*

By Andrew Grant

Too Close to Home

Invisible

False Witness

False Friend

False Positive

RUN

More Harm Than Good

Die Twice

Even

TOO CLOSE TO HOME

A NOVEL

Andrew Grant

BALLANTINE BOOKS
NEW YORK

2020 Ballantine Books Mass Market Edition

Published in the United States by Ballantine Books, an imprint of Random House, a division of Penguin Random House LLC, New York.

BALLANTINE and the HOUSE colophon are registered trademarks of Penguin Random House LLC.

Originally published in hardcover in the United States by Ballantine Books, an imprint of Random House, a division of Penguin Random House LLC, in 2019.

ISBN 978-0-525-61964-2
Ebook ISBN 978-0-525-61963-5

Cover design: Ervin Serrano
Cover photograph: Mike Voss/Arcangel

Printed in the United States of America

randomhousebooks.com

1 2 3 4 5 6 7 8 9

Ballantine Books mass market edition: August 2020

For Gary Gutting, who made windows where
there were once walls

Chapter One

I'd known Brett Ellison for almost thirty-three minutes when we reached the service elevator. I'd already seen anger flash across his face. And surprise. And suspicion. But it wasn't until we stepped out onto the roof—which was more like stepping out onto the surface of a tiny moon—that I saw the first trace of fear.

The curved concrete shell was rough underfoot. It had been scoured and bleached by the wind and the sun until it was the texture and color of desiccated ivory, though the weather was playing nice that afternoon. The sky was calm and cloudless. There was no breeze. No birds were in sight. The streets below us were deserted, with the politicians being out of town until the next legislative session began, and the place was silent save for Ellison's ragged breathing. The sun was low in the sky over my left shoulder, staining the pointed prows of the four neighboring government towers a soft pink, and ahead the Hudson cut a dark diagonal swath through Albany's eerily empty downtown.

"I don't get it." Ellison edged closer to me and grabbed my sleeve. "Why here? What am I supposed to see?"

Ellison had been at his desk when I opened the door to his office, deep in the basement of the adjacent building. He was doing something with his cellphone. He had it at arm's length, squinting at it like his reading glasses weren't quite up to their job, and jabbing repeatedly at the screen with a rigid forefinger.

"What the actual . . . ?" His finger froze in midair and he glared up at me over his circular lenses. "Who the hell are you?"

"My name's Paul." I walked in, pulled one of his chrome-framed visitor's chairs back a couple of feet, and sat down. "I'd say it was a pleasure to be here, but it's too soon to be sure."

"Hey!" Ellison jumped up and snatched off his glasses. "I didn't say you could sit. What the hell do you want? Tell me, or haul your ass out of here, right now."

"Tell you, or haul my ass out?" I frowned. "I'm curious. Do you get many people showing up unannounced and not telling you what they want? Just hanging around, not saying a word?"

"Did you come here just to annoy me?" Ellison placed his phone facedown on one pile of papers on his desk and threw his glasses onto another. "Or do you have any other purpose in life?"

"OK, I'm sorry." I held my hands up. "Let's start over. The fact is, I came to see you. In person. I made a special trip, all the way from New York City."

"To see me?" Ellison ran his fingers through his thin sandy hair, then reversed the motion to tug his fringe farther down over his forehead. "Why? Do I know you?"

"Not yet." I conjured up a smile. "But we're going to change that. Starting now. Because I'm your new partner."

"Have you been smoking crack?" Ellison gestured toward the portrait of the governor, which was hanging at a slightly crooked angle on the wall behind his desk. "I'm a government official, dumbass. I don't have any partners. New, or otherwise. I don't know what kind of wild-goose chase you've been sent on, but—"

"I'm not talking about your day job, Brett." His phone started to vibrate, causing it to slide off the stack of papers and spin around on the chipped veneer surface of the desk like a stranded bug. "I'm talking about your other line of work. Your more lucrative one. The one you've been running with Marcus the last couple years."

"You've got some wires seriously crossed here, buddy." Ellison drew himself up a little taller and folded his arms over his chest, wrinkling the fabric of his pin-striped navy suit coat. "I don't have another line of work. And I don't know any Marcus."

"Sure you do."

"How many times?" Ellison planted his hands

on his desk and leaned forward, revealing a slight gut and bringing it into conflict with the buttons of his neatly pressed white shirt. "I don't have a partner. I'm not in any business."

"Final answer?"

Ellison didn't respond, so I took a wallet-sized photograph from my jacket pocket and placed it on a creased manila folder, more or less directly under his nose. I made sure it was facedown. He pretended not to notice. He straightened up. Glared at me. Looked at the wall behind me. Stared at the framed emergency evacuation instructions mounted on the inside of the door. Glanced at the heavy wool overcoat hanging on a bentwood stand in the corner, next to the trash can. Gazed at the coarse brown carpet. Straightened a stack of documents. Hesitated, with his right hand poised in midair. Wrestled with his curiosity for a beat or two longer. And evidently lost, because after another couple of seconds he slowly slid the picture across to his side of the desk. Picked it up. Flipped it over. Studied it for a few seconds. Shrugged. Then let it slip through his fingers and watched as it fluttered down to land on the same pile of papers as his glasses.

"I don't know her." Ellison's voice barely reached me through the stale basement air.

"No." I retrieved the picture. It was of a woman. A Latina. She was in her mid-thirties. Smiling. Beautiful. "But you will soon, right? You're planning to get to know her very well." I checked my watch. "In less than two hours. At the Renaissance. Room 2440."

Ellison didn't respond.

"In return for not reporting her husband to the INS. I believe that was the deal?"

Ellison closed his eyes and rocked back on his heels for a moment. "So. I get it now. You want to be my *partner*. By which you mean, what? You want to help yourself to heaps of my money? Well, we can talk about that. But let me tell you, before we go any further, there has to be paperwork. NDAs. Watertight ones. With shitloads of penalties for breaching them. Because I'm not admitting to anything. And if I do, when I pay for something to go away, it stays gone away. We're clear on that?"

I sighed, got up, and started toward the door.

"Wait!" Ellison's eyes stretched wide. "Where are you going? You haven't told me how much you want. Give me a chance to negotiate!"

I paused. "First, I don't negotiate. That just leads to both sides being dissatisfied. Better for one side to be happy. My side, obviously. And second, you don't get it at all. I'm wasting my time here. I had no idea you were such a wuss. You're not cut out to be my partner. I expected a man with vision. With ambition. Who was ready to grab a golden opportunity with both hands, not run and hide from shadows. But don't worry. You're not the only game in town. I'll find someone else. Someone with a backbone."

"I have plenty of backbone!" Ellison was suddenly all puffed up. "And vision. This whole business model was my creation, remember, so don't—"

"Business model?" I shook my head. "Let's not

get ahead of ourselves. You skim undocumented workers' wages and take sexual advantage of their wives. We're not talking *Shark Tank* material here, Brett. Which is why I was planning to—how do you MBA guys put it?—shift your paradigm. But now I'm not so sure. I'm not convinced you can handle it."

Ellison snorted. "I saw an opportunity. I took it. That's who I am. An innovator. An entrepreneur. This operation? It's just a small part of what I do. And for the record, I can handle anything." He stuck out his jaw. "Tell me what you have in mind. *I'll* evaluate it, and if *I* think it'll fly I'll consider letting *you* get on board."

"I don't think so." I took another step toward the door. "I don't like your attitude. Here's what you should do. Find a replacement for Marcus. Carry on the way you were. Forget about all the extra money we could have made together. And all the extra women I could have sent your way."

"I can't just forget about . . . wait." Ellison's eyes narrowed. "A replacement for Marcus? You didn't . . . is he . . . ?"

"Marcus retired." I kept my expression neutral. "On account of the accident he was about to have. Don't worry. Call him if you want. He's fine. And he'll stay that way, as long as he stays retired."

"OK." Ellison nodded. "Marcus is out of the picture. He stays out. I get it. See? I can be flexible. I can adapt. I can be a team player. But the question is, can you? Because you know what? There's something you're forgetting."

I raised my eyebrows.

"You want to work in this town, there are wheels that need to be greased. I have the connections. You don't."

I didn't reply.

"You don't." Ellison sounded confident. "I'd know. So if you want to succeed here, you need me."

I let a few seconds tick by. "Or someone like you."

"There's no one like me." Ellison switched to his warm, friendly politician's voice. "Trust me on that. So, like you said before, let's start over. Tell me your plan. The extra money. The women. How will it work?"

"OK." I paused as if I was giving his words some serious thought. "Here's what you have to understand. My proposal—the impact could be huge. Like nothing you've experienced before. It depends on a significant adjustment to your thought process, though. So realistically, for you to appreciate the full vision, you need to see a demonstration."

"Really?" Ellison put his hands on his hips. "Of what? The concept's pretty simple. It's worked great up to now."

"Maybe it has. From your point of view. But to get the ultimate result, the enterprise needs to change. There are some new concepts you need to grasp."

"What concepts?" Ellison crossed his arms. "I don't want to overcomplicate things. Or waste time. How long would a demonstration take, anyway?"

"Not long at all. Just a few minutes. It'll be the best investment of time you ever make. And you know what would be a waste of time? Looking for a replacement for Marcus. Settling for what you had before."

"Fine." Ellison held up his hands. "Then set up a demonstration. Let me know the time and place, and I'll be there."

"How about right now?"

Ellison blinked, then checked his watch.

"Don't worry. There's plenty of time before your appointment at the Renaissance."

"That's still on?"

"Of course. I drove the woman to town myself. I wasn't happy about it, but I had no choice. Not now that Marcus is a man of leisure."

Ellison opened his mouth, then closed it again without saying anything.

"It's up to you." I crossed my arms. "If you don't have the balls for this, just say so. I'll go back to the city right now, and you'll never see me again. Of course, I'll have to take the woman with me. I'm not hanging around while you get . . . acquainted, if there's nothing in it for me."

Ellison still didn't reply.

"Which would be a shame." I took the picture back out of my pocket. "She is mighty pretty . . ."

"Where?" Ellison blinked twice. "Where would the demonstration be?"

"Next door. At the Center for the Performing Arts. Nice and convenient."

"At the Egg?" Ellison frowned. "The place is huge. Who else will be there?"

"No one." I gestured to the door. "Come on. I have an area set aside. It's private. It'll be just you and me."

"Well, OK." Ellison opened a drawer in his desk. "But wait a moment. I have one more question. And don't lie to me, because I'll know. Are you a cop? Here to entrap me?"

"A cop's the last thing I am." I paused. "I was in the army, but that was a whole different lifetime."

"Then who sent you to find me?"

"That's a second question." I looked him in the eye. "But I'll answer. No one sent me. No one even knows I'm here."

"Let's make three questions a charm." Ellison's face hardened. "Are you armed? Are you carrying a gun?"

I opened my jacket. "No gun. Don't need one. Just my phone. Pat me down, if you want."

"No need." Ellison took a revolver from his drawer—a Ruger Security-Six, judging by its skinny wooden grip—and held it up at eye level. "But for full disclosure, and in case you have any stupid ideas, you should know—I'll be carrying this."

Ellison edged closer to me and grabbed my sleeve. "Why here? What am I supposed to see?"

I freed my arm and passed him a sheet of paper from my jacket pocket.

"A list?" Ellison's breath was warm on my neck. "Why couldn't you have shown me this inside? In my office? Why come all the way to the roof?"

"Just read it." I moved around behind him, blocking his way to the hatch that covered the steps leading back to the elevator lobby. "Then everything will fall into place."

Ellison paused, then scanned the page. "Are you crazy?"

"Maybe." I shrugged. "If thinking it's wrong to exploit guys who are just trying to put food on their families' tables—not to mention what you're doing to their wives—then yes, you can call me crazy. But what you call me isn't important right now. What matters is that you agree to the points on that list. Then we can both go home. Because in case you hadn't guessed, there isn't actually anyone waiting for you at the Renaissance hotel. The woman—whose name is Rita, by the way—is at her apartment with her husband. When you held her picture in your hand? That was the closest you're ever going to get to touching her."

"Screw you." Ellison's free hand balled itself into a fist. "Move. I'm leaving."

"I'll be happy to move. As soon as you agree to the items on the list. Unless you'd rather I take another route? Like maybe sharing what I know with the NYPD?"

Ellison didn't respond.

"Or maybe sharing certain details with the husbands of the women you've abused? Details like your home address? The car you drive?"

"Look. All right." Ellison relaxed his hand and massaged his temple with his fingertips. "I'll give up my cut of the laborers' wages. I'll stay away from their wives. But paying for immigration lawyers? Subsidizing their housing while they go to community college? No way."

"What did I tell you about negotiating, Brett?" I shook my head. "The whole package. I'll accept nothing less. And if you need an extra incentive, you might want to think a little harder about why we're having this conversation on a roof."

Ellison took an instinctive step away. "You think you can bluff me?" He lowered his hand until it was hovering a couple of inches from his pocket. "You are crazy. And you've picked the wrong guy. I know an empty threat when I hear one. You need to let me leave. Now."

"Let's not back each other into any corners, Brett." I kept my voice quiet and calm. "Especially as there aren't any corners up here. Only long, deadly drops on every side. So let's just take a moment. Breathe. Enjoy the location. It truly is a magnificent building, don't you think? I've wanted to see it for a long time. My only issue with it is the name. Why did they call it the Egg? It looks more like a clam, wouldn't you say? Or a mushroom."

Ellison didn't respond.

"Maybe the marketing guys felt that bottom-feeders and fungi were too hard a sell."

Ellison's eyes were dancing between my face and the hatch, behind me.

"Don't push your luck, Brett. Stay calm. Look around. Observe the curve of the roof. See how it falls gracefully away to the point where it intersects with the walls, sweeping up dramatically from below? That's the point you should focus on. Very carefully. Because there's absolutely nothing for a person to grab on to. Imagine rolling toward that edge. There'd be nothing to stop you. Then picture the plaza, all those hundreds of feet below. And ask yourself: Isn't providing a little legal aid and enabling some modest educational opportunities a small price to pay to ride down in the elevator, instead?"

Ellison didn't reply.

"Have you ever seen someone fall from this height, Brett? Onto a hard surface? It's not pretty. Not the way you want to go. And it's like catnip for reporters. You'd be all over the newspapers. And the TV. And the Internet, of course. That's not how you want your family to remember you. Or your friends. If you've got any. And don't forget, once a person's guts get spilled, their secrets soon follow."

"I can picture that scene, actually." Ellison flinched as if he was coming out of a trance, then he casually slipped his hand into his pocket. "A body rolling. Falling. Getting smashed to a pulp on the sidewalk. That's exactly what I was thinking about. Only the guy? It's not me. It's you." His hand reemerged, holding his gun, which he leveled at my chest. "And you'll be dead long before you hit the ground."

"I was wondering when you'd pull that bad boy out."

"You threatened my life. It'll be self-defense."

"Trying to talk yourself into something, Brett?

Because there's a big difference between thinking and doing."

"I fire hundreds of rounds a week." Ellison glanced down at his gun. "Don't think I won't pull the trigger."

"Where do you fire them, Brett? At a range? At paper targets?"

"What difference does it make where I shoot? Or what at? I shoot a lot is the point. And I maintain my weapon, too."

"I know you do. I can smell the oil from here. You use a little too much, if anything. But that's not your main problem."

"I don't have a problem."

"Correct." I paused. "Technically, you have two."

Ellison again glanced at his gun, but he didn't respond.

"First problem . . ." I held up my right thumb as if checking points off a list, and as his eyes tracked the movement I shot out my left hand. I grabbed his gun by its barrel and wrenched it around a hundred and eighty degrees, away from his body—and mine—so that the trigger guard broke his finger and his wrist was forced right back on itself. He screamed, and half a second later the gun was in my pocket and he was on his knees, cradling his injured hand.

"Sorry." I waited for his whimpering to subside. "I miscounted. Only one problem."

"Why did you do that?" Ellison's teeth were clenched, obscuring his words. "I wasn't really going to shoot you. I just wanted to back you off. Make you let me go."

"Then that's another way we're different." I shrugged. "When I say I'm going to do something, I do it."

"No you don't." Ellison laughed nervously. "Surely? Like, you wouldn't really throw me off the roof."

"Wouldn't I?" I looked him in the eye. "Do you really believe that, Brett? Think carefully, because your life depends on it."

Ellison looked away.

"You abuse your office, and you prey on the less fortunate in cruel and malicious ways. The only reason to keep you alive is for you to put right some of the harm you've done. If you won't agree to do that, I'll toss you off this roof the same way I'd throw a sack of garbage in a dumpster."

"Bullshit." Ellison struggled to his feet. "You don't go to jail for the rest of your life for throwing out garbage, for one thing."

"I won't go to jail for flinging you, either. Not even for a day. Let me show you something." I took out my phone, called up a video feed, and passed it to Ellison. "What do you see?"

He studied the screen for a second. "It's the plaza. The base of the Egg. There's a fenced-off area. That's new. How come?"

"So that if you do choose the quick way down, you won't land on any pedestrians. I don't want you hurting any more innocent people."

"You arranged for the fence?"

"Of course. I'm not a savage." I took the phone

and selected another source. "Now. What do you see in this one?"

Ellison stared for a moment. "Nothing's there. It's blank."

"Correct." I put the phone back in my pocket. "That's from the security camera covering the entrance I used to the building. It's out of action. All the others I passed are the same. No one saw me. There's not a shred of evidence I was ever here."

"There has to be." Ellison's eyes were flickering urgently from side to side, like he was scanning the shelves at a store on Black Friday. "Wait. Yes. The fence. People don't just carry fences around. You must have gotten it from somewhere. Or someone must have helped you. Or done it for you. There's a connection. A body gets found, the police—"

"You're right." I smiled. "Someone did take care of the fence for me. An old army buddy. From Military Intelligence. An expert in not getting found. And even if the police did somehow get their hands on him, guess what? He wouldn't say a word. So you may as well accept it. There's nothing and no one to connect me to this place."

"Why are you doing this?" Ellison sank back down on his haunches. "I don't get it. What's in it for you? Did those assholes somehow scrape up some cash? Are they paying you? Because I can—"

"No one's paying me." I scooped up the list from where it had fallen during the scuffle. "And if you have to ask, you won't understand the answer."

"That makes no sense." Ellison pressed the palm of his good hand against his forehead. "And who even are you? Paul, you said, when you first showed up? Is that your first name? Or last?"

"My name's not important." I handed the list back to him. "I'm just a janitor. Here to clean up the mess you made. One way. Or another."

Chapter Two

A CAB SWERVED TO AVOID A DELIVERY GUY ON A bike. Tires squealed, insults flew. Harried commuters swarmed around knots of camera-wielding tourists. A hot dog vendor cursed as he tried to remove a flyer for a low-rent defense lawyer that someone had stuck to his cart during the night. All around me horns honked and engines revved and men and women, old and young, from every race and creed, jostled for space on the sidewalk. Rush hour in Manhattan. I know people who would call it a scene from Bedlam. I called it home. And even though I'd only been away for thirty-six hours, I'd missed it.

I paused at the edge of Foley Square for a moment and looked across at the New York County Courthouse. My place of work. For the time being, at least. Taking a job there hadn't been a planned career move. More a response to the untimely death of my father, and the cracks in the system that had allowed the guy responsible to slide away, unscathed. Cracks I found myself obliged to fill.

A handful of people broke free from the tide of passersby and started to climb the broad expanse of steep stone steps. Some had their heads up, bursting with energy, no doubt anticipating the thrill of victory or the sweet taste of vindication. Some were dragging themselves up the dozen or so feet, seemingly reluctant to face the fate that was awaiting them inside. Others appeared indifferent to the prospect of entering. Even bored by it. But regardless of their disposition, all of them were pressed together into a single amorphous mass as they funneled through the uniform gaps between the ten colossal Corinthian columns that sprouted from the top step. They continued the final few yards in shadow, then filed through the tall brass-framed door at the center of the façade. My eyes followed the pillars up to the wide carved triangular pediment that joined their peaks. I nodded to the three statues on top, feeling welcomed by them like they were familiar sentinels, then made my way around to the back of the building.

The employee entrance is down a flight of steps, rather than up like the public's grand way in, and as I approached I saw that the glass in the right-hand door, which had been broken for weeks, had been repaired while I was up in Albany. I wondered how long it would remain intact this time. The security guard wedged behind his wooden table asked about my weekend. I asked him about his kids, and listened to a blow-by-blow account of the older one's softball game. As he talked I put my metal items in a rubber bowl, ready for their trip through the scanner. I had a bunch of keys, as usual—it was a habit never to leave home without them—and as usual he didn't notice that one was actually a disguised knife. Its folding blade was small and narrow, but it could still come in useful if you knew how to use it. I had my usual handful of coins. A phone, which was brand-new. Its connecting wire, which was the kind of thing I didn't usually bother with. And its charger. Or something that looked just like its charger, anyway. He glanced down at it, sitting there in plain sight. Passed it through the machine. And handed it back to me without question.

If you could look at the courthouse from above, you would see that it's made up of a strange collection of shapes. The front, in plan, is an unremarkable rectangle. But the main section is much more eye-catching. Despite appearing solid from ground level, it's actually a hollow hexagon with a circle in the center that is connected to the outside by rectangular corridors like spokes linking a hub to a wheel. The security station I'd passed through dumps you out in the basement of the hexagonal part, so I followed the angled passageway around until I reached the door to the janitors' room. I was expecting to see my supervisor, Frank Carrodus, there—he was usually one of the first to arrive—but no one was sitting at the round tables in the center of the room, reclining on the pair of worn-out couches nearer to the back wall, or grabbing supplies for their cleaning carts from the line of shelves along the right-hand side. I made a mental note to look for him later, then headed through to the locker room and changed into my overalls. They're the best cloaking device ever invented. Slip a pair on and you can go anywhere in the building without anyone taking the slightest notice.

I'd just turned to pull my cart out of its slot against the left-hand wall when the door slammed shut behind me. I turned and saw Carrodus standing there. His blond ponytail was looser than usual. A couple of his shirt buttons were unfastened, revealing more of his tattoos than he normally showed at work. His belt had bypassed one loop on his jeans. And there was a look of raw fury plastered across his face.

"Morning, Frank." I tried what was intended to be a friendly smile. "What's up?"

"Don't even ask," he snarled back. "I'm too mad to speak."

"Was there a problem on the subway?"

"No." He closed his eyes for a moment. "There was a problem in a goddamn jail cell. The police showed up at my house last night. The jackasses arrested me. I only just got out."

"You were arrested?" I looked at him. "Why? What did you do?"

"I didn't do anything!" Frank scowled. "The assholes wouldn't believe me. It was totally their mistake."

"What did they think you did?"

"OK, so this is completely un-fucking-believable." He crossed his arms. "They accused me of dragging a guy up to some kind of high roof and threatening to throw him off. In Albany! Which is a place I've never even been to."

"You're not missing anything. Albany sucks." I pulled my cart the rest of the way out. "It seems bizarre, though, this roof accusation. Why did they think you'd done that?"

"Let me get a coffee. I need to calm down." Frank loped across to the counter in the far corner, where fortunately someone had left enough brown sludgy liquid in the pot to fill a mug. "OK. Remember how I told you about a guy harassing some of the women at the shelter where my wife volunteers? The guy's a total douche. His thing is demanding sex in return for not reporting the women's husbands to the INS? As well as going after their money?"

"Yeah, I remember." I nodded. "You said he took a shine to your wife, too. Rita?"

"Right. The asshole tried it on with her, too." Frank's free hand balled itself into a fist. "I guess he figured she was illegal, too, the racist piece of shit."

"I also remember you making threats about the guy, Frank." I kept an eye on that fist. "I told you to go to the police, instead."

"I did go to the police." He frowned. "I thought I told you? They did fuck all nothing. What was I supposed to do next? I couldn't just stand by and let a thing like that slide. So, do you remember that guy, The Janitor? My sister who works at the fifteenth precinct kept hearing stories about him. He beat up some assholes at the projects one time. Threw some moron in a hole at a construction site in Hell's Kitchen for some reason. A couple other things like that. Well, I thought, I'm a janitor, too. Maybe I should follow his lead. Clean this up myself."

"It does all sound familiar." I leaned on the handle of my cart. "You did tell me. Weren't you planning to meet the guy behind it? Confront him?"

"Damn straight. Some scumbag named Marcus. He told Rita to meet him on Sunday night, to *discuss terms*. I figured I'd go in her place, and discuss what needed to happen for him not to get his ass kicked."

"What happened?" I straightened up. "Did you change your mind?"

"No." He shook his head. "I tried to go. I was going to take the subway then walk the rest of the way, but when I came out of my building a cab was waiting right there. In my neighborhood! You don't look a gift horse like that in the mouth, so I got in. I gave the driver the address. You should have seen this guy. Some weird dude, so freakishly tall he could hardly fit behind the wheel. Anyway, he made out like he knew where the place was. But he was full of shit. He just drove me around for two freaking hours. By the time I got to the place, the guy Marcus wasn't there. He must have gotten bored of waiting, and left. I was furious. You should have seen me, man. I made an impression on that driver, for sure. He offered to drive me home for free if I didn't report him."

"Now you're losing me." I paused. "If you didn't actually meet this guy Marcus, how come the police came after you? What was the connection?"

"It turns out that Marcus was only a lackey. It was his boss who was doing the deeds. Some government guy, based in Albany. Someone dragged him out of his office, forced him onto the roof of some weird concrete building they have up there, and threatened to throw him off if he didn't stop what he was doing."

"I can't believe a thing would go down quite like that." I shook my head. "But in any case, why would they think you were the one doing the dragging and the threatening?"

"They said the government guy was pretty traumatized, but he remembered the guy who threatened him saying something about being like a janitor cleaning up his mess. I'm a janitor. I previously made a complaint against the guy. And I may have gotten a little upset when the police said there was nothing they could do to help. I may have said a few things I shouldn't have. Thrown a few threats around. But seriously, Paul, if I was pissed then, I'm crazy now. They wouldn't listen when I asked for their help, and then they turn around and arrest me when someone finally did something about the crime they ignored? They're lazy assholes."

"How they work's a mystery to me, too, sometimes. But back up a second. The government guy. From what you're saying, his hands must be seriously dirty. Why on earth would a guy like that go to the cops? Surely he was just incriminating himself at the same time as whining about this alleged roof situation?"

"Right." Frank nodded. "But evidently the guy had some kind of a breakdown. He was scared out of his mind by whoever dragged him up there. He really believed he was going to get thrown off. And he was deadly scared of heights, or something. A hotel clerk found him wandering the streets an hour later, ranting like a madman. She dialed 911. The paramedics came and gave him some sedatives, which just made him ramble all the more. And of course the police automatically showed up and heard all these crazy claims he was spewing out."

"They can't take that as evidence, surely."

"I doubt it." He shrugged. "And given that they came after me, they can't have any real clue who did the threatening. Which is a shame, because I'd like to find him and buy him a drink. A whole bunch of drinks. But the government guy? If he isn't already, he's well on the road to being totally screwed. The cops were there when he was falling over himself to admit all kinds of shit. They heard the words coming out of his own mouth. They're bound to investigate him now. It's like he tied himself in a bow and lay down on their desks."

"I can't believe he got so freaked out. What are public servants made of these days?"

"Right? Like anyone was really going to throw him off."

"It does seem unlikely. Although, from what you told me about the things the guy was doing, he does sound like a serious asshole. You never know what might have happened. Anyway, I guess I should get to work."

"Good idea." He took a long swig of coffee. "As soon as my blood pressure's back to normal, I'll do the same."

"Oh, by the way, I found this." I took Rita's picture from my pocket and handed it to him. "That is your wife, right? I thought you'd want it back."

Carrodus snatched the picture out of my hand. "Where did you find this? I looked everywhere for it. I never take it out of my wallet. I couldn't understand how it could be gone."

I shrugged. "I saw it on the floor in the locker room. On Friday. I guess it must have fallen out."

Chapter Three

I LEFT FRANK TO CONTINUE THE PROCESS OF CALMing himself down, despite not seeing any signs that the caffeine was helping, and wheeled my cart toward the elevators. Our conversation had got me thinking about Ellison. The government guy. Had I misjudged the situation? It was good that he'd be stopped from exploiting people now. It was good that I'd prevented Frank from jamming himself up, following in the footsteps of The Janitor. It would have been better if the police had acted when Frank reported Ellison's crimes. But maybe better still if Ellison had done what he'd agreed to before I let him back into the elevator. I couldn't believe he'd freaked out so badly. I guess it was just another reminder. I was a civilian now. I had to live by different rules.

If only I could figure out what they were.

I'd been allocated to clean the third floor of the courthouse that week, but when I reached the elevator I hit the button for the fourth. That wasn't in order to avoid my duties. I actually liked cleaning things. I found its repetitive nature calming. It helped me to focus. And I enjoyed the tangible results of honest labor, which was unlike what I'd been doing for the government over the last twenty years. So rather than shirking, I started on that higher floor because another task needed my urgent attention.

I made my way around the building's inner circle with wide arcs of my dry mop, moving ten feet forward, then looping back for my cart. I continued past a pair of lawyers who were deep in conversation by a window that overlooked the roof of the central dome, then carried on along one of the narrower, spoke-like corridors until I reached courtroom 432. I listened at the gap, and when I was satisfied that the room was not in use I pushed the heavy brass-studded mahogany doors apart and wheeled my cart inside.

The courtroom was a square, maybe thirty feet by thirty. A knee-high fence divided it sideways across the center, with six hard wooden benches for spectators to sit on in the space nearer the doors. The area beyond the fence was for the officials. The jury box was to the right. There were tables for the lawyers to use in the center, in front of the flag and the judge's bench and the witness stand. On the other side, tucked away in the corner, was the clerk's desk and a pair of green metal filing cabinets.

The room had everything it needed to function, but its ambience was in complete contrast with the courthouse's exterior and first floor. Those parts of the building were grand and elegant. They looked like they could have been plucked from the center of Rome, and you could almost hear their classically hewn features proclaiming confidence in the system. But inside, the place just felt shabby and worn. It was the shop floor rather than the shop window, and a shop that clearly operated on a budget. I'd been disappointed when I first saw the condition it was in. Now I just think it's appropriate. It is the room, after all, where Alex Pardew—the guy who defrauded my father and most likely caused his premature death—should have met justice. Instead, he was allowed to walk out a free man after a mistrial was declared because a file of vital evidence had gone missing. That was the reason I'd chosen to work here. To find the file. And to bring Pardew to justice.

So far, I was halfway there.

I'd found the file. Someone had hidden it in the closet in the judge's chambers attached to that courtroom. The strange thing was, it hadn't been there the first time I'd looked. But it was the second time. Whoever had taken it must have smuggled it back after my initial search. And, I believed, removed something from it. Presumably something critical, since they'd gone to such lengths. But until I figured out what had been taken, who'd done the taking, and why, I couldn't risk involving the authorities. Old habits die hard. There were too many hallmarks of an inside job.

My current problem was that since I'd taken the file, there'd been no response to its re-disappearance.

I'd hoped that keeping it under wraps would cause some fallout that I could exploit. But no further clues had presented themselves. So I'd decided it was time to shake things up again. To do something to provoke a reaction.

I pushed my cart through the gap in the fence and wheeled it right up to the door to the judge's chamber. I parked it with my mop balanced precariously so that it would fall if anyone tried to push past it, like a makeshift early warning system. Then I slipped inside and closed the door behind me. The chamber itself was triangular, which I guessed was a product of its position within the hexagonal part of the building. It had one window, but its view was partially obscured by the back of one of the statues mounted on the portico. The figure wasn't so impressive with its rusty support visible, and at that distance you could see how its marble surface had been pitted and stained by time and pollution. I actually felt a certain affinity with the thing, given the way it did its job without complaint, regardless of its conditions. I could think of several people who could learn from it.

The leather-covered top of the judge's private desk just fitted below the windowsill. His top drawer was chock-full of opera memorabilia, which was no good to me, but in the next one down I found what I needed. A yellow legal pad. I turned to a blank page, helped myself to a pen from a grotesque Brunhilde mug, which was sitting on a Valkyrie coaster, and wrote in plain, featureless capitals:

I HAVE WHAT YOU'VE LOST. IF YOU WANT IT BACK, CALL ME:

I added the number for my new cell, a pay-as-you-go that could never be traced back to me, and crossed to the closet at the side of the judge's Chesterfield couch. The finish was heavily distressed, I guessed designers would say, but I thought it just looked ready for the landfill. I opened the closet door and saw, the same as last time, three men's dress shirts hanging on the rail. There were three ties. Two pairs of men's dress shoes on the floor. And two pairs of women's pumps. I placed the sheet of paper I'd written on behind the shoes, in exactly the same spot where I'd found the missing file, and turned to look for a convenient outlet. There was one low down on the wall, to the right-hand side of the desk. I took the phone charger from my pocket, plugged it in, stood back to make sure I was happy with its position in the room, and stopped dead. There was a sound coming from the courtroom. Right outside the chamber door. Someone was moving my cart.

I marched to the door, snatched it open, and stepped through with an almighty scowl on my face, ready to yell blue murder at whoever was interfering with my equipment. That was the correct strategy. The first rule in that kind of situation is never to show any trace of guilt. But the sight that greeted me stopped me in my tracks. There was a guy in the courtroom, standing with my cart. He was on his own. I guessed he'd be in his mid-forties, and around five feet eight. He had dead-straight, chestnut brown hair hanging limply to his shoulders and he was wearing a Yankees hoodie, jeans, and a pair of beaten-up white sneakers. He was over by the jury box. And he was busy lining up my spray bottles along its front edge. My mop was propped up in the judge's seat. My broom was in the witness box. And my metal pail was upside down on the far side of the lawyers' tables.

"Hey, you!" I waited for the guy to turn and face me. "You better not be looking for a cut of my wages."

The guy blushed beet red. "This is all yours? I'm so sorry. I didn't know anyone was here. I thought the cart had been left by mistake. I was just borrowing the things. I didn't mean any harm." He snatched up the nearest bottle. "I'll put everything back. Give me two minutes."

"There's no rush." I stepped forward and retrieved the pail. "I'll help. But you've got to tell me what you're doing. Seriously. I need to know."

The guy blushed an even deeper shade of red. "This is so embarrassing. Look, the thing is, I'm not too good at being spontaneous. I like to be properly prepared. And as this thing is so important, I thought I'd do better if I rehearsed."

"You're a lawyer?"

"No." He paused. "Not exactly."

"Then what are you rehearsing?"

"My defense."

"You're defending yourself? In a real case?"

"Yes." The guy stood up a little straighter. "It's my constitutional right."

"Maybe so. But no offense, I've heard it's not a very good idea."

The guy shrugged. "Maybe not. But it's my only option."

"What about the public defenders' office? Couldn't someone there help?"

The guy just shook his head and scooped up a couple more spray bottles.

"What are you charged with?" I took them from him and put them back in their places on the cart.

"Arson."

I whistled. "Wow. Arson's a serious crime. Are you sure you wouldn't do better with a professional on your side? I know someone who's good. His name's di Matteo. He could maybe help if cost's an issue."

"Cost isn't the problem." The guy paused. "Let me rephrase that. Cost is a huge problem. I'm flat broke, to tell the absolute truth. But there's a much bigger problem. No lawyer I've spoken to—and I've tried dozens, from the public defender to the big fancy firms—is prepared to present the case the way I want them to. They're all just looking to plead out. Try for a deal."

"Plead out? So they don't believe in your innocence?"

"I'm not innocent." The guy looked at the ground.

"Oh." I stopped loading the cart. "You did do it?"

The guy nodded.

"Look, I don't claim to know all the legal nuances, but if you did it, isn't trying to get the fairest possible sentence a sound plan? I've heard that if you try to wriggle out on a technicality, juries hate that. And if you make the judge mad, too, you're bound to come off worse."

"I'm not trying to wriggle out of anything." The guy crossed his arms. "I don't care about the sentence. That ship's sailed, and I'm going down with it. I accept that. I just want the world to know what the bastard did. I want to tell my side of the story. Then I'll take what's coming to me."

"Which bastard?" I nudged his arm. "We're in New York. You need to be more specific."

"Jimmy." The guy nearly spat the name at me. "Jimmy Klinsman."

"Never heard of him. Is he famous? What did he do?"

"He might be famous among assholes. He cost me my house. So I cost him his." The guy paused. "One of his, anyway."

"A house for a house. That seems fair, on the face of it. Want to tell me the rest?"

The guy didn't reply. He looked startled.

"Come on." I shot him a friendly smile. "It'll be good practice. Let's sit." I held out my hand. "I'm Paul, by the way."

"Len." We shook, then took opposite seats at the lawyers' table. "Len Hendrie." He was still looking a little uncertain about being there.

"All right, Len." I leaned back. "I'm listening. Tell me what this Klinsman guy did. How'd he make you lose your house?"

"He shorted the stock instead of holding it."

"Slow down." I held up my hand. "I'm lost already. I don't know what that is."

Hendrie held his head in his hands for a moment. "OK. Let's take a step back. We should start at the beginning. I run a home renovation business. Ran one, anyway. I started it out of college. We did high-end work. Quality was our trademark. We did great for the first few years. But lately everything's been harder. Our costs went up, with all the imports and tariffs. And the market for what we do shrunk like an ice cube in a pizza oven. People aren't looking for workmanship that lasts twenty years, anymore. They just want quick, superficial crap that they'll change out again in eighteen months, or flip. Long story short, my business was hurting. It was worse than hurting. It was on life support, and the banks were about to pull the plug. I was out of ideas how to turn it around. Then an old college buddy of mine gave me a tip. A sure winner. A stock that was set to rocket. But what's the problem, if you want to buy stock?"

"I don't know. I've never bought any."

"It's the same as anything else. You need money. The banks wouldn't touch me, so I went to Jimmy. He's another old college buddy. Only he's a finance guy now. He's got more money than God. So I went cap in hand and asked him for a loan. Now bear in mind, the amount we're talking about here—the amount I needed to buy the stock and make enough profit to get my business back up and running—that was chump change to Jimmy. But guess what he said."

"No?"

"Correct."

"So I'm guessing you took a loan against your house, instead?"

"Correct again. Like the dyed-in-the-wool moron I so clearly grew up to be."

"You took the loan, and the investment didn't pay off?"

Hendrie shook his head. "That's an understatement. The stock tanked."

"So you had to sell your house to repay the loan."

Hendrie nodded again.

"OK, Len." I laid my hands on the table, palms down. "I haven't known you very long so I'm not sure how best to say this without hurting your feelings, but it doesn't sound like this Jimmy guy is totally to blame for the way things panned out. Maybe, and again I mean no offense, when he turned you down for the loan that was just because he had better instincts about the particular stock you had in mind being a bad investment?"

"No." Hendrie shook his head. "The deal should have been solid gold. It was totally Jimmy's fault it went south. He made that happen."

"Slow down." I held my hands up again. "First of all, how can you be so sure the deal was that good?"

Hendrie turned away.

"Come on, Len." I waited until he looked at me. "If you can't convince me now, why would anyone else in the city believe you at a trial?"

"Well, here's the problem." He took a deep breath. "I don't want to get my other buddy in trouble. You see, the tip he gave me, maybe he shouldn't have."

"Why shouldn't he have? Was it a secret?"

"It was like this. We hadn't seen each other for months, he was so busy. Then he called me out of the blue. Said he wanted to celebrate. Hit some bars. Which we did. He was on top of the world. And I guess he could see I was in a different place. He dragged it out of me about the state my business was in. That's when he told me to buy stock. In his company. Immediately. He didn't say why. Not at first. We had more champagne. Some margaritas. Then it slipped out. You see, he works for an electronics company. He does product development. They make parts for telecommunications networks. There's some new design, a next-generation cellular Internet something. Only two companies in the world can make some critical piece of it. His. And one from China. The Chinese firm is way bigger. It's way cheaper. My buddy thought his company was bound to get steamrollered by them. But he'd just heard that the government wanted US networks to use a domestic supplier because of national security. His company was going to pick up all the big contracts. It was going to be massive. They'd have to open a bunch of new factories. It was a license to print money, he said. And as a result, their shares were going to explode when the news was released."

"So what happened? Didn't they get any contracts, after all?"

"I don't know. I'm out of the loop. My buddy's

not speaking to me. Plus I had bigger concerns to deal with."

"But the stock didn't rise?"

"No. It fell. A lot. Because of Jimmy. Because he shorted it."

"I don't know what shorting is."

"Well, normally, you make money when shares go up, right?"

"I guess I might, if I had any. But I've heard it works that way, sure."

"So shorting's like the opposite. It's a trick the finance guys use to make money when shares go down."

"How? I don't see it."

"It's a black art, I guess. The ins and outs don't matter. The fact is, Jimmy did it. The point is, why? And the answer's simple. To make money. To make more money, I should say. I offered to pay him interest on the loan, if he'd give it to me. Or to pay him a percentage of the profit I made. But instead the weasel went behind my back and shorted the stock, because that way he figured he could make more. Not that he needed it. He has six houses. Well, five now. A yacht. God knows how many cars. A helicopter. About a million bottles of wine. I needed it to eat. He didn't care about me."

"That's harsh, if it's true."

"Oh, it's true. I confronted him. He laughed in my face. Couldn't stop talking about how many more cases of wine he was going to buy with the money he'd made."

"I understand about Jimmy and the wine, but let me just circle back to the original deal for a second. The idea was that shares in your buddy's company would rocket because they were set to beat a Chinese rival to a big government contract?"

"Not quite. There isn't a government contract. The networks buy the equipment for themselves. But the government decided to prevent them from buying it from the Chinese. My buddy's company was the only other game in town. They were set to win by default."

"And this government ban was down to security concerns?" Old habits die hard.

"That's what my buddy told me."

"But if his company couldn't deliver for any reason, and the Chinese company was the only alternative, what would happen then?"

Hendrie shrugged. "I don't know. We didn't talk about that."

"Maybe the Chinese could get back in the frame?"

"I guess."

"Did the share collapse hurt your buddy's company, do you know? Did it damage its ability to deliver?"

"Like I said, I don't know. My buddy won't return my calls. He's blaming me for tanking the shares, because I asked Jimmy for the loan. I don't want to make things even worse now by mentioning him. I just want the truth to be known about Jimmy."

"I guess those things are hard to balance. How about this? Talk to my lawyer friend." I passed him Roberto di Matteo's card. "Even if you still want to do your own defense, Roberto can give you some guidance. He'll know what you can safely say, and what you can't. Give him a call. Tell him I sent you. He won't charge. You've got nothing to lose."

"Maybe I will." Hendrie slipped the card into his jeans pocket. "I'll definitely think about it. And if I do call him, your name's Paul?"

"Right. Paul McGrath. Or just tell him you were speaking to the janitor at the courthouse. He knows who I am."

Chapter Four

EVERYTHING I KNOW ABOUT MY FATHER SUGGESTS he'd been a shrewd businessman. By all accounts he was never one to leave a dollar on the table when he didn't have to. And every dollar he owned, he put to work. Every dollar, that is, except for the ones tied up in the brownstone in Hell's Kitchen that I'd inherited along with all his other assets when he died.

My father never lived in the house. He never lived in the city. If I'd known he owned property there when I was a teenager, I would have campaigned night and day to move. I loved Manhattan. I was drawn to it, compelled to spend as much time as possible in the place, and I hated the drive back to our family home in Westchester. It was only later that I really understood that my father would never have left that house, regardless of how relentless my nagging would have been. Because my mother had died there, giving birth to a sister I never saw. I was only three at the time and my mother's absence was a fact I grew up with, no different from the existence of gravity or that it got hot in the summer. But as a kid, and even as a teenager, I didn't recognize the sentimental bond that tied my father to that spot.

I don't know when he bought the brownstone. I guess I could have found out by deciphering his accounts—he was notorious for keeping paperwork way past the statutory limits—or by asking Mr. Ferguson, the lawyer who was now overseeing his businesses. More important, I didn't know why he bought the place. It seemed out of character, seeking ownership of an asset that wasn't integral to one of his companies or central to making more money. I'd heard the theory that the property came as a sweetener in some other deal. That did seem possible. My father was old school. He never disposed of anything he came upon that might be useful one day. He had no shareholders, so there was no need to worry about manipulating balance sheets or finagling ROIs or any of the other smoke-and-mirror indicators that all the Wall Street types are obsessed with. This was the trait that brought him into conflict with Alex Pardew. When he finally accepted that I wasn't ever going to join him at the boardroom table, he brought Pardew into the company as a partner. They signed an agreement that when my father decided he was ready to retire, Pardew would buy the company based on a valuation formula stipulated up front. Only it seems that Pardew didn't do his due diligence. The company had way more assets than he expected, which meant he would need way more money than he'd anticipated to meet his obligation. So he hatched a scheme to fraudulently reduce the company's value. Ironically enough the scheme came to light, according to the police, in a dispute over the brownstone.

Another thing that made the house unusual, with respect to my father, wasn't its value—it was a gold mine. It was that the gold mine hadn't been exploited. When I first looked around the property I couldn't believe the architectural features just waiting to be torn out and converted into cash. And I was very glad they hadn't been. Everywhere I looked there were throwbacks to a previous era with materials and finishes that are unattainable now. The range and variety of wood the original builders used were staggering, and it was installed and crafted using skills that are lost to the ages. It was the same story with the tile in the bathrooms and the marble in the entrance hall. Although those features look tame and restrained in contrast to the extravagance of the top floor—the entire level is devoted to a grand ballroom with a sprung floor and panoramic views of the Hudson.

I'd never imagined myself as a homeowner. I had no objection to the principle of the thing. It just never seemed to be in the cards for me. I left home when I was eighteen and I've lived all over the world, but only in two kinds of accommodation. Army barracks, and hotels arranged by my old unit—the 66th Military Intelligence Brigade—when I was sent out to infiltrate a target organization. If I'd been asked even a few weeks ago, I would have said I was as likely to own a house as I was to leave the army and come home to Manhattan. And I guess I'd have been right, only not in the way I'd have expected.

When I first came back to the city I stayed in a series of hotels. Then after a while I figured, the brownstone was there, so I might as well make use of it. There's no point in paying Manhattan hotel rates when you own a house that's just standing empty. Detective Atkinson—the NYPD's point man on my father's case—had encouraged me. And so had John Robson, another MI veteran. Our paths had crossed briefly when we were both in the service. He wound up getting sent on a mission to Azerbaijan that I was originally slated for, but missed due to a last-minute reassignment. Which was lucky for me, as it turned out. Robson encountered some moral challenges in country. His view of the best way to navigate them didn't mesh well with his CO's. Long story short, Robson was rewarded for his contribution with a Big Chicken Dinner—a Bad Conduct Discharge—and I can't hand on heart say the outcome would have been different if I'd been in his shoes. There was no contact between us for years after that until we bumped into each other again here in the city, unofficially on the trail of the same guy. We found that we worked together well. He was the closest thing to a friend I'd had in years. And given that I'd inherited a house with half a dozen spare rooms, it made sense to let him use one.

The brownstone was structurally perfect when we moved in. All the utilities were hooked up, as well, but we did encounter one drawback. There was no furniture. Not a stick. That wouldn't be a problem for long, I'd thought. It would be one of the benefits of civilian life, surely? There'd be no torturous requisition forms to complete. No cranky quartermasters to smooth talk. I'd just go to the store and pick some things out. So I tried that. I tried it at three stores, in fact. And the answer I got was the same each time. The fastest delivery on anything that wasn't grotesque was twelve weeks. Which to me sounded like eleven weeks, six days too long. So I walked out.

I figured I could take some furniture from my father's house—I couldn't stop thinking of it that way—up in Westchester, but there was a problem with that idea, too. After my father died, I promised his housekeeper, Mrs. Vincent, that she could continue to live there as long as she liked. It was the least I could do. Mrs. Vincent had moved in with us a few weeks after my father was widowed. She'd been the one who'd cooked for me. Made sure I always had clean clothes. Helped me with my homework. Made strawberry milk shakes to help mend my heart, every time it had been broken. Put an arm around my shoulder whenever I needed sympathy. Gave me a kick in the ass whenever I needed motivation, which was more often. Covered for me when I missed my curfew. And refused to condemn me when I announced I was joining the army. She'd been the most constant adult presence in my life growing up, given the amount of time my father dedicated to his businesses. She'd been more of a mom to me than my biological mother ever had the chance to be. And she'd lived in the house way longer than I had. It felt more her home than mine, so it wouldn't seem right to plunder the place for my own convenience.

We were left with one option. The camping store. We picked out air mattresses and sleeping bags for our bedrooms, which might sound incongruous for a house that was worth north of thirty million dollars, but they were luxurious compared with many places the two of us had slept in. We found a pair of lawn chairs for the lounge, which was harder than it sounds because Robson is so tall. He's at least six feet eight, though I've never heard him confirm the actual number. We finished up with a folding table and chairs for the kitchen, so we'd have somewhere to eat. After that we purchased a small dorm room–style fridge for milk and a microwave to warm up the carryout food it was fair to assume would play a major role in our futures. Our only other appliance was a fancy kettle with adjustable temperature settings that Robson had brought with him. He was obsessed with tea but had been banned from using the kettle at the last hotel he'd been bunking at. He showed me a note they'd stuck to it following an unannounced safety inspection, labeling it an *unrecognized appliance* and stating that further use would constitute grounds for eviction.

Robson was in the lounge when I got home. He was wedged into one of the lawn chairs with his long legs stretched halfway across the room, one ankle over the other. He was drinking tea out of a disposable cup and reading a thriller about an ex-

MP who'd left the service and become a wandering vigilante. It was the third one he'd gone through in a week. I was starting to think I should try the series myself.

"So, did you bait the trap?" He set his cup on the floor next to two other empties.

"Nothing to it." I lowered myself into the other chair.

"Good." He closed his book, slipping one of di Matteo's cards between the pages to keep his place. "Let's hope we get a bite soon. It would be nice to wrap this Pardew thing up once and for all. You could get some closure for your dad. And then maybe you could stop mooching around the courthouse all day long. We could hit the road. Have some fun."

"The courthouse isn't so bad." I stretched my back, struggling to find a comfortable position on the flimsy fabric. "It keeps me out of mischief."

"More like it gets you into mischief."

"Good mischief, though." I turned to look at him. "Seriously. It's all right down there. Maybe you should join me sometime."

"And this sage recommendation is based on what?" Robson steepled his fingers. "My world-renowned love of ill-fitting municipal uniforms? Or has my secret addiction to budget cleaning products somehow come to light?"

"Don't knock it till you try it." I paused for a second. "It's surprising, the people you meet. The things they tell you."

"People like your buddy Carrodus?" Robson snorted. "I can imagine the kind of things he'd like to tell me. He certainly wouldn't welcome me with open arms. He didn't seem very impressed with my performance as a cabdriver."

"Frank's all right. He'd give you a second chance, if he knew the circumstances. Anyway, I was thinking about someone else. A guy I met today. He had an interesting story. I want to run it by you. See if you pick up the same vibe as I did."

"Someone else who needs an asshole thrown off a roof? That would be cool." Robson pointed his index finger at me. "But I want to do the threatening this time. You can deal with the fence. And I'd prefer it not to be in Albany again. I hate that place."

"This guy didn't want anything. But what he said intrigued me."

"Who was it? A lawyer? A clerk? Or are you rubbing shoulders with judges now?"

"None of the above. He was an arsonist."

Robson's nose wrinkled. "Ugh. Arsonists. I hate those guys. They're all cowards. Is he guilty, do you think?"

"He's definitely guilty. He got caught, and he confessed."

"What did he torch?"

"Some other guy's house."

"Why did he do that?"

"He blames the other guy for ruining him, and making him lose his own place."

"OK, then." Robson nodded and leaned forward in his chair. "That sounds better. That's something I could maybe get behind."

"That's not the interesting part. The guy got ruined in some sort of stock scam that links back to a company that makes sensitive parts for telecom networks. The government just decided to ban its only rival—a monster Chinese corporation—leaving it the only player in the field. Then immediately after this is decided—it's not even publicly announced yet—the company gets hit by these financial shenanigans and its stock value ends up in the toilet. It's how this guy lost all his money and his house, but I'm wondering if there could be more to it than that."

"Like what? Boardroom bullshit? Insider trading?"

"No." I shook my head. "Do you remember anything about Schwarz-Meiller? There was a whole module about it at Fort Huachuca. In one of the advanced courses."

"Vaguely." Robson shrugged. "But that was years ago. Didn't it have something to do with the Mossad?"

"It did. Schwarz-Meiller was a Swiss company. It was breaking the UN embargo, selling control boards for power stations to Iran. That was back when their nuclear program was barely off the ground, and they were desperate for electricity to make more heavy water."

"OK. This is ringing a bell. The Mossad found out about the embargo breach, but instead of assassinating the top brass like they usually would, they bought the company? And then instead of closing it down, they used it to insert sabotaged components into the Iranians' supply chain?"

"Right. The plan worked like a charm. But do

you remember what the Mossad did before buying the company?"

Robson thought for a moment. "No."

"They pulled a whole bunch of financial hocus-pocus to bring the purchase price down."

"That was a smart move." Robson nodded. "Why waste money? So do you think that's what the Chinese are doing? Taking a page out of the Mossad's playbook?"

"Well, we know the Chinese are targeting telecom networks, globally. There were two routes into the States. One got blocked off—their own corporation. Wouldn't it make sense to exploit the other? The US company? As economically as possible?"

Robson rocked his head from side to side. "Maybe."

"You don't think it's possible?"

"I think it's possible, yes." He swiveled around to face me. "But I also think it's possible that something else altogether is going on here."

"Such as?"

"Listen, Paul, I don't want to speak out of turn. But are you sure you're not looking for reasons to avoid putting this Pardew thing to bed? Or to at least put off dealing with it? Could you be carrying more baggage connected to your father than you thought?"

"That sounds like psychobabble to me." I crossed my arms. "I'm fully focused. The Pardew thing is my number one priority. It's just that with this—something smells wrong. I'd hate for something to slip through the cracks that winds up hurting people and afterward for us to know we could have done something to stop it."

"That's fair." Robson softened his voice. "I'm with you. But in the same way, I'd hate to see Pardew slip through your fingers because you were too busy looking in a different direction. Imagine him lying on a foreign beach, living out the rest of his life in luxury, instead of rotting in an American jail. Or suffering whatever other fate you might have in mind for him."

"He might already be on a beach."

"But what if he's not? What if you let him get to one by taking your eye off the ball now?"

"That's not going to happen. There's a guy out there somewhere who's crapping himself over the missing file. He'll call the number on the note I left, show his hand, and whatever it is he's trying to do, we'll burn it down. In the meantime, the share guy's story should be checked out at least, don't you think? What harm could there be in that?"

"Maybe." Robson paused. "But not by you. You can't afford the distraction. What about Detective Atkinson? Why not hand it over to him. See if he thinks it has legs. And if it does, leave him to run with it."

Chapter Five

DEATH AND TAXES. THOSE ARE THE ONLY TWO things people say you can be sure of in life. But if you ask Detective Atkinson to meet for breakfast, you'll find there are two more things you can rely on. The place he'll pick will be the Green Zebra. And he'll be late.

I have nothing against the Green Zebra in itself, although its hipster Village clientele wouldn't be my first choice of people to hang out with and its food is a little too self-consciously cool for my taste. My problem is being expected to meet in the same place, over and over again. That goes against every instinct I honed over the last twenty years. Old habits die hard. But the venue was Atkinson's call, he's happy with it, and we've had no problems so far. I figured I could put up with it, despite the bizarre décor.

The place looks like it was thrown together by a bunch of drunks, in the dark, over a lost weekend. Though it was probably designed by experts and cost a fortune. Outside, it has a temporary vibe, like it's about to be closed down. Inside, the idea is that nothing matches. There are three kinds of floor covering, for example, so I chose a table in the quarry tile section, with a clear view of the door and the kitchen. The table itself had spindly metal legs and a top that was made of chessboards covered by a thick slab of slightly green glass. The boards were positioned at random so that none of their sets of squares lined up, which produced a weirdly disorienting effect. I was discouraged from looking at them, but still wished I'd brought some chess pieces to pass the time. I made do with ordering a coffee—plain black, nothing foamy—and it arrived just as Atkinson came through the door.

The detective was short and wiry and seemed to have a never-ending supply of energy. His hair had been cut since we'd last met. He was freshly shaved and was wearing a new suit with a matching blue shirt, but despite the sartorial improvements he was just as restless. He fidgeted and drummed his fingers on the table while he waited for the server, then ordered eggplant Benedict without looking at the menu.

"So, what have you got?" He let the server get halfway to the kitchen, then leaned toward me and lowered his voice. "Is it too much to hope that you've found the Pardew file?"

I shook my head, and pushed away a small pang of guilt. "This is about something else."

"It always is, when you're involved." He shook his head, but there was a smile lurking not far from his face. "What is it this time? You've discovered that ruthless merchants are fleecing the city on toilet paper? Greedy clerks are padding their overtime claims?"

"No. This is a little more serious. There could be an attempt to compromise one or more telecom networks."

Atkinson stilled his fingers and leaned in farther. "Are you serious?"

I nodded.

"Are you sure?"

"No. It's just a suspicion at this stage." I outlined what I'd learned from Hendrie, and what concerned me about it. "So you see, it could be the tip of an iceberg."

"Or it could be nothing at all." Atkinson slumped back in his chair. "A finance guy sees a way to make a buck. Hold the front page."

"He could have made money investing in the stock the regular way."

"A finance guy sees a quicker way . . ." Atkinson's fingers started drumming again.

"The guy was already rich. Why did he need to make more bucks, more quickly?"

Atkinson threw up his arms. "Did you get exposed to a bunch of weird chemicals in the army? How long were you away from the States, anyway? Don't you know anything about these Wall Street guys? They trashed the entire world economy in '08, just to line their own pockets. They left thousands of people broke. Regular folks who lost their pensions, their houses, their life savings, everything. You think these jackals would give a single shit about tanking one company or ruining one guy, if there was something in it for them?"

"I get that there are greedy assholes out there. But I still think this thing's worth a look. Will you pass it on to your contacts? Have someone check it out?"

Atkinson drummed his fingers. "If anyone else was asking, I'd walk away and delete their number. But you showed me something before. Instinct is sometimes right. I promised myself I'd be more open-minded. So OK. I will ask. But don't get your hopes up. And for the love of all that's good and holy, keep looking for the Pardew file!"

It was early enough in the fall to still be warm even though the shadows of the buildings were growing longer, so I decided to walk to the courthouse when I left the Green Zebra. I joined the flow of pedestrians surging along the sidewalk, quickly adapting to the stop-go rhythm as we paused at the cross streets and then were pulled back into motion as if by the city's own heartbeat. There was a longer delay at one intersection when a cab hit a cyclist. The driver opened his door, leaned out over the mess of splayed arms and legs and sheaves of paper blowing out of the rider's ripped messenger bag, and started yelling in Romanian. The sprawling kid just looked bemused, whether from the bang to his head or the barrage of unfamiliar words. After a moment we swept around them like a tide bypassing a fallen log in a swollen river, and we'd just got back up to a regular pace when my phone rang.

My new phone. I'd only written its number in one place. On the page I'd left in the judge's closet. I stepped to the side into a narrow alcove formed by two sets of scaffold and checked the screen. The call was from a New Jersey number, but I answered it, anyway.

"You have the file?" It was a man's voice. A New York accent. A hint of the Bronx, maybe, that I guess he'd tried to shed over the years. He was trying to keep his tone neutral, but there was no hiding the tension. It was impossible to gauge his age, and there was no background noise to give away his location.

"I may have found something fitting that description."

"You didn't find anything. You stole it." It sounded like irritation was taking hold, which was a good thing from my point of view. Anger's the enemy of good judgment.

"Well, that puts us in the same boat, so let's not split hairs. The point is, this is good news. I do have the file, and I'll be happy to give it back. All we need to do is agree on a convenient time and place, and it's yours. Though you might want to be more careful where you leave it in the future. Not everyone is as considerate as me."

"You don't understand." The man took a breath. "I don't want the file. It's important federal property. You need to put it back where you *found* it. Right away."

"No. Let's stick with my plan. I'll give the file to you. Then you can do what you want with it. Put it back. Set it on fire. Whatever."

"No dice. You took it. You return it."

"I suppose I *could* put it back, if it's so important to you. But I will need an incentive."

"There's no money in this for you. You need to be clear about that."

"Well, that's OK, because I'm not looking for money. It's information I want. Tell me why you took the file in the first place. And what you removed."

"You have some very strange ideas, my friend. I didn't take it. And I didn't remove anything. I found it. I saw what it was, and knew it was vital to get it back in the system or a dangerous criminal will be allowed to escape. Do you want that on your conscience over a half-assed shakedown? No? So do the right thing. Put the file back!"

"In the closet, in the judge's chambers?"

"Yes. On the floor. Or anywhere in there."

"Why that particular closet?"

"Because the judge will find it there. It'll be back in the right hands. And no one will get in trouble."

"Why should anyone get in trouble?"

"There was a mistrial. The case was blown. Even now with the file back it may be too late. But there's definitely no chance of putting things right if you keep it."

"Are you a clerk? Is the misfiling your fault?"

"It doesn't matter what I do. How about you? How come you have access to those chambers?"

"The judge is a family friend. I stopped by for some tea and a nice chat about the opera. He wasn't there, so I thought I'd check up on his shoe fetish. Imagine my surprise when I found the file."

"Are you serious?" There was more than a hint of doubt in his voice.

"All right. Let's draw a line under all of this. Maybe I will put the file back. It all hinges on one question. Where's Alex Pardew now?"

There was a pause on the line. "Who?"

"The guy the file is about. The dangerous criminal whose whereabouts you were just so worried about."

"Oh. Right. The suspect. How would I know where he is?"

"You took the file. You removed some information. There's a reason for that. I bet there's a lot you know."

"Is there an echo on this line? I didn't take it. I didn't remove anything. I don't know where this Pardew's at. All I know is that the file needs to be returned. So. Will you put it back?"

I ended the call, switched off the phone, reached up, and wedged it between a pair of scaffold planks. Then I slipped back out into the flood of pedestrians and continued toward the courthouse. I had work to do there. The phone call might not have been the slam dunk I'd hoped for, but it showed that the ball was back in play. There was more than one way to gain an advantage. Especially if you're not too worried about sticking to the rules.

Frank Carrodus was in the janitors' room when I arrived, shooting the shit with a couple of the older guys. They were sitting around one of the tables, with Starbucks cups in front of them and crumb-filled wrappers from Carrodus's favorite bagel place. He excused himself from the group as soon as he saw me, wrapped an arm over my shoulder, and steered me to the side of the room, near the carts.

"Great news, Paul." His voice was quiet, but he couldn't disguise his excitement. "Rita came home last night and said Marcus—the asshole who worked for Ellison, the government guy—had visited her at her work. He swore he'd retired. Said he'd learned his lesson, and was just there to deliver a message. Ellison had recovered after his shock. He'd convinced the police that nothing had happened on the roof, and they'd dropped the case. He said Ellison wasn't negotiating—he made a big point of that for some reason—and said he'd promised to stop skimming the men's wages. To cut out the *liaisons*. And to help pay for immigration lawyers and job training, just as long as *The Janitor* didn't ever pay him another visit. She asked if I'd done anything. I told her the truth—I'd tried to, but I'd messed up. And you know what? She didn't care. She was just happy I tried. She thinks I'm the best husband in the world now. I just wanted you to know, after you were so sympathetic yesterday."

I left Carrodus to the last dregs of his celebratory cappuccino, changed into my overalls, stocked my cart, and made my way up to the fourth floor.

A trial was in progress in room 432, so I mopped slowly all the way around the hexagon. I checked again and the room was still occupied, so I moved on to the next corridor. I started to sweep, and under the first bench I found a wallet. I scooped it up and made a mental note to hand it over to security before the end of my shift. Room 433 was empty, so I wheeled my cart inside. It only took twelve minutes to clean. You could hardly tell the place had been used that day. Room 434 was a different story. Coffee cups were strewn on the benches and on the floor, along with candy wrappers and used Kleenex. It was like a movie theater—a seedy one, at that—not somewhere fit for important legal proceedings. Thirty-five minutes later I threw the last piece of litter into a trash bag, retraced my steps, and found that finally room 432 was vacant.

I left my cart blocking the chamber door, and made sure the mop was in an even more precarious position after Hendrie had managed to remove it the day before. I went inside and made straight for the side of the judge's desk. To the outlet where I'd plugged in my phone charger. It was still there, only now a wire was sticking out of its socket. The judge must have used it. Civilians! A new device appears, and they're not suspicious at all. Still, as long as he hadn't obscured its tiny lens, no harm would have been done.

I unplugged the charger, dumped the judge's wire in his top desk drawer, and removed the tiny memory card. I slid it into the expansion slot of my regular phone and saw that eight files had been created. I started to work through them. The first four only showed the judge, and he didn't approach the closet even once. But in the fifth file, someone else did. It was a woman. She was pencil thin with an immaculate black bob. I recognized her immediately. I'd seen her leaving the chambers right before I discovered the file. She was wearing the same red pumps in the video. I watched as she opened the closet door. Slipped off the shoes. Made as if to place them next to one of the black pairs, then stiffened. I couldn't see her face, unfortunately, due to the camera angle. She held her position for five or six seconds. Then she set down the pumps, snatched up the note I'd left, and pushed it into the large tote bag she was using as a purse. She pulled out a pair of flats, slipped them on, and turned away from the closet. I could see her expression now. She was scared. There was no mistaking it. She bit her lower lip, closed the closet, and scurried away.

The woman had struck me as suspicious when I saw her the last time, slinking past me like a kid who's hoping not to be noticed when they've crept downstairs after bedtime. I could have grabbed her up as soon as I'd found the file, to keep my momentum and not waste any time. Part of me questioned the decision I'd made. But on balance, I figured it was better not to have acted so soon. There's nothing wrong with building tension in your enemy. Uncertainty leads to mistakes. Mistakes can be exploited. And it's always best to avoid making assumptions.

On one of our first training exercises we were

told we'd be interpreting surveillance tapes. We were taken to Prague and shown some CCTV footage that had been shot in the city. It showed two guys. One was a businessman in a suit, walking down the street. The other was dressed like a punk. He'd been in his twenties and had a 1970s throwback Mohawk, tattoos, piercings, and a bunch of chains around his neck. He was coming the other way. He saw the business guy and started sprinting toward him. The business guy held his briefcase up like a shield. The punk grabbed it, pushed him back a few feet, and finally wrestled him to the ground.

We were given a sheaf of supporting documents, told to evaluate all the available evidence and arrest the criminal. Some candidates searched the file, found the punk's address, headed to his apartment—and burst in on our training officer. Their reward was a travel order to Fort Gordon, Georgia, where they were officially returned to their units. The correct response was to note that the map we were given showed a second camera location. Footage from that position had captured a pallet falling from a construction site. It was plummeting directly onto the sidewalk. When you watched from that angle you realized that the punk was trying to save the business guy's life. And if you dug into the business guy's background, you'd notice that he held a modest position at a pharmaceutical company, which was at odds with his home in a swanky development outside the city. The Jaguar that was registered in his name. And the frequent foreign holidays he took. Further digging would uncover a receipt for a plane ticket to London, purchased with cash at short notice. But if you knew where to look, you'd also find that he'd pulled up a MapQuest route to Dresden, Germany. And if you chose the right option, you'd be able to pick him up at the border, in a car rented under a false name, with the formula for a "nerve agent" hidden in his shoe.

The point they wanted us to learn was that acting on instinct is good, if that's all you've got. But it's always better to know for certain, and to build that into a deliberate plan of action. My plan now was to pay an unofficial visit to HR, to find a particular name and address. There'd be time for some more cleaning after that. Then it would be up to Robson to earn his keep.

Chapter Six

THE CITY NEVER BECOMES ENTIRELY SILENT, HOWever late at night. The sounds just become a little slower and quieter, like the heartbeat of a slumbering beast. Softer, but still there. Letting you know it's still alive. Still dangerous. And that you should relax at your peril.

The clerk who'd taken the note from the judge's closet was named Patricia Spangler. A handwritten note in her HR file said she preferred to go by Trish. She lived in an apartment building on 22nd Street, near the Flatiron. Robson drove by a couple of minutes shy of 4:00 A.M. His car was awful. It was a cherry red Cadillac Cimarron from the mid-1980s. Its paintwork was blotched and peeling. Its interior leather—a tan, almost orange color—was cracked and hard. Its engine was small, anemic, and woefully underpowered. But we had no choice about using it. I hadn't gotten around to buying a car yet. I thought maybe I wouldn't need one in the city. Then it occurred to me that there might be one in the garage at my father's house up in Westchester. Maybe more than one. I'd figured I could check at my leisure. Suddenly, finding an alternative seemed more urgent.

We saw no red flags as the old Cadillac wheezed around the block so Robson coasted to a halt diagonally opposite Spangler's building. I settled into the passenger seat, which was surprisingly comfortable but too big for the cockpit, making the car feel cramped, and watched Robson cross the street. I was desperate to go with him and get my hands on a person connected with the scheme that had allowed Pardew to go free. Unless the guy I'd spoken to on the phone wasn't lying, and they had innocently found the file. Either way, though, I couldn't take the risk. Spangler had seen me at the courthouse and I had to maintain my cover.

I pulled out my phone and fired up the app that allowed me to view the video from the camera in Robson's lapel pin, which was forwarded via a secure website. His legs were so long it only took him a few strides to cross the street. The building's double glass doors were locked. Robson knocked. There was no response. He tried the revolving doors, to the side. They were also secured. He banged again, and swore under his breath. I was half expecting him to launch one of the metal planters lined up along the edge of the sidewalk through a window—standard practice in some of the countries we'd worked—when a guy emerged from behind the reception desk. His doorman's uniform was wrinkled. His cap was missing. His tie was loose. He rubbed his eyes, shambled across to the door, and opened it an inch.

"Police." Robson flashed his fake badge before the guy had a chance to speak. "Are you always this quick off the mark? Or are you aiming for a new record?"

"What?" The guy blinked.

"When the NYPD knocks, you open up." Robson slid his badge back into his pocket. "I don't care what time it is. Now step back and let me in."

"What do you want?"

"I want you to step back and let me in, like I just said."

The guy didn't move, but his fingers curled a little more tightly around the edge of the glass.

"Don't worry." Robson softened his voice. "I'm not from INS. You're not in trouble. Not yet . . ."

The guy opened the door all the way.

"Good decision." Robson patted him on the shoulder. "I'll leave you to get back to sleep now. I just need one piece of information. Ms. Spangler, unit 1415. Does she live alone?"

The guy nodded. "Yes. She has no husband. I've never seen any boyfriends."

"Does she have a dog?"

"No. No pets."

"That's good. Is she home, do you know?"

"I don't know. I start work at 11:00 P.M. She was probably in bed when I arrived."

"When did you last see her?"

The guy shrugged. "I don't know. Not since a

couple of weeks? I remember she collected a package."

"All right. I'm going to her apartment to talk to her now. If I get there and she's expecting me, the thing I said about you not being in trouble? That's going to change. Are we clear?"

The guy's expression went blank for a moment, then he nodded enthusiastically. "Absolutely. I won't tell a word."

I watched my screen as Robson made his way down a long hallway. It had gray carpet with darker stripes along both sides. The walls were also gray, darker at the bottom and fading to white at the top, to blend with the ceiling. There were groups of planters laid out every fifteen or twenty feet. They were of varying heights, and were sparsely stocked with ferns and bushes. After the last set there was an alcove filled with mailboxes and an ATM, then the corridor broadened out to house the elevators. There were six, laid out in two rows of three. Robson hit the call button, and the door to the first elevator on the right opened straightaway. No one was inside. I saw Robson's hand reach out and select the fourteenth floor. The car made no extra stops on the way up, and Robson stepped out into another gray corridor. He followed it around to the right. All the apartment doors were white, and they were plain except for a fixture in the middle, five feet up, that combined a bell push, a viewing lens, and a nameplate. Robson found apartment 1415. He banged on the door with his fist and stepped aside, away from the lens. I guess I'm not the only one with old habits that refuse to die.

The door was snatched open. A man appeared in the frame, his dark hair in disarray, a pillow crease on his cheek, and his white fluffy robe gaping open to reveal his stripy blue boxer shorts.

"Justice Department Investigative Division." Robson flashed another badge, flipped his wallet closed, and had it back in his pocket before the guy's half-awake eyes had time to focus on it. "I'm Agent Rasmusen. I need to speak with Patricia Spangler. It's urgent. Please step aside."

"You can't. Patricia's not here." The guy tugged the sides of his robe together.

"Who is it, honey?" A woman's voice, heavy with sleep, called out from deep inside the apartment.

"Are you sure?"

"That's not Patricia. She doesn't live here. This isn't her apartment."

Robson pointed at the nameplate on the door.

"Oh." The guy's face sagged. "Does this mean we're in trouble?"

"Well, you lied. That's not a good start. So now you have two minutes to convince me why you shouldn't be in a whole heap of trouble."

The guy ushered Robson inside, peered out into the corridor, and then closed the door. To the right of the narrow entryway was a pocket door leading to a crisp white powder room. To the left was the kitchen area. There was a small four-burner cooktop, an under-counter fridge, a drawer-style dishwasher, and a roll-up appliance garage with a stainless-steel door. The few cabinets and drawers looked like they'd cost top dollar and the breakfast bar was finished in mirror white marble. Ahead was a small living room. It had a line of low built-ins running across its whole width, with tall windows above to give an unbroken view uptown. The night sky was punctured by a million lights, while the shadowy forms of sharp-edged buildings gnawed on its lower edge. A few cabs were still out patrolling. The odd garbage truck rumbled past. Somewhere nearby a jackhammer started work on an emergency repair. I could hear it twice—live in real time, and with a momentary delay through my phone—which produced a strangely disconcerting echo like a special effect in a movie.

A woman appeared through a doorway in the far corner of the lounge. She had shoulder-length blond hair and was wearing a pink toweling robe, cinched in tight around her waist, and matching slippers. She crossed to where the guy was standing near the center of the room, touched her forehead to his shoulder, and turned to Robson.

"I want to be up front with you." She held up both hands as if she was surrendering. "This whole situation is my fault. It was my idea. I made Dave do it. He didn't want to. He said it was wrong from the start. So if anyone gets in trouble, it should be me."

"You made Dave do what?"

"Move here. With me." The woman's eyes widened. "I'm not going to lie to you. I knew it was against the rules. I just couldn't resist the opportunity. I could never afford it, otherwise. Trish said I'd be doing her a favor. This way, she doesn't lose all her rent money. No one was supposed to find out. It's a big building. Other people do it all the time. We thought no one would notice."

"Let me get this straight. You're talking about subletting? That's what's going on here?"

The woman nodded and started to chew her lip. "I'm so sorry. We'll go. We'll move out. Right away. First thing in the morning. By the end of the week."

"We can talk about timescales later." Robson took out a notebook and flipped it open. "Now, tell me where I can find Trish."

"I don't know where she went." The woman looked down at the floor. "Somewhere uptown, I guess. She didn't leave her exact address. She was still looking for a place, last time we spoke."

"If you keep lying, you won't be helping yourselves or your friend." Robson paused and waited for the woman to look up. "Let me explain. Think of my organization as the internal police service for the courthouse where Trish works. We think something bad is going to happen there, very soon. Someone has left a trail of bread crumbs that make Trish look guilty. Now we think she's being framed. We don't think she's actually involved. But we need proof. Hard evidence. So we must talk to her. Tonight. Tomorrow it'll be too late to save her. So if you want to help your friend, tell me where she is."

"Oh my God! Poor Trish. Will she be OK?" The woman's eyes looked ready to pop out of their sockets.

"Honestly, I don't know at this point. But I do know she won't be if I can't talk to her. So please, tell me where she is, and I'll do my best to keep her out of trouble. I promise."

"OK." The woman beckoned for Robson to pass his notebook, and she scribbled down an address on the Upper West Side. "Please, keep her safe. We've been friends since we were four years old."

"I'll certainly try." Robson took a couple of steps toward the door, then turned back. "There's one more thing. Something I need you to understand. There are people watching Trish. They're listening to her calls. Reading her texts. Intercepting her email. It's vital that you do not try to contact her. If you do, you'll be putting her life in danger. Is that clear? If you try to reach out and anything happens to Trish, it'll be on you."

It took Robson nine minutes to emerge from the building and join me in the car, due to the need to rouse the sleeping doorman and coerce him into erasing the recordings made by the security cameras in the lobby. It took another eight minutes on the relatively clear nighttime streets to reach the address Spangler's friend had given Robson. He drifted as smoothly to the curb as the car would allow, set the parking brake, then movement caught my eye from the side window. It was a rat. It was dark and plump, sitting on a bench by the wall bordering the park. I stared at it. The rat stared back, but lost its nerve when Robson climbed out and slammed the car door. The rat jumped back through the railings above the stonework and melted into the shadows. Robson ignored it, crossed the street, and reactivated his lapel camera as he walked. This time the doorman was wide awake. He was older than the last guy, maybe in his mid-fifties, and was wearing a neatly pressed uniform with a cap larger than those of the officers in some countries' armies. He appeared without Robson needing to knock, didn't blink at his badge, and looked mildly offended when he was told not to warn Spangler that someone was coming to see her.

The building's lobby was like a lounge in a London club. There was a cluster of deep leather armchairs arranged near a window. The gold-and-blue curtains looked heavy and stiff. The tile on the floor was richly polished, and two smaller chairs were conveniently placed near the doors to the pair of elevators. The doorman hit the call button. He'd pulled on a white glove to avoid tarnishing the brass, and the doors parted after a couple of seconds with an unhurried, graceful sigh.

Robson rode up alone to the tenth floor. The carpet in the corridor was a deep blue with a Greek key border picked out in gold. Only one door was visible without heading around the corner. The number on the frame matched Robson's information, but there was no place for a name to be displayed. Robson knocked. There was a pause, but the door opened before he had to try again. It was a woman who answered. She was wearing silk pajamas. They were pink with inch-wide white stripes. Her hair was wilder than when she was at the courthouse, but it was definitely Spangler this time. And when she saw Robson's badge, her expression was identical to the one on her face in the video of her closing the closet in the judge's chamber as she fled with the note.

"Patricia Lee Spangler?" Robson closed his wallet. "I'm Agent Rasmusen with the Justice Department Investigative Division. I'm here because we have a situation. We need to talk."

"Who?" Spangler crossed her arms. "What division? I've never heard of you. Or it."

"That's good." Robson put his wallet back in his pocket. "The kind of people who've heard of us are generally mixed up in things they shouldn't be."

"I'm not mixed up in anything." Spangler shifted her hands to her hips. "I want to know why you're really here."

"I hope that's true. I'm here because you've worked at the courthouse for six years, three months, one week, and four days. All but two of your quarterly appraisals have been rated *generally satisfactory*. However, questions have recently arisen. One in particular is serious. It needs to be answered."

"Here? Now? At 4:30 A.M.?"

"Yes. Now. Either here, or at Centre Street. It's your choice."

"Let me see your badge again?"

Robson handed her his wallet. Its leather was suitably creased and worn. The badge itself was shiny and certainly looked official. It was a little light, but there's only so much you can do at short notice with a 3D printer.

"OK." Spangler returned the wallet and stepped back into her entryway. "We can talk here. It shouldn't take long. I'm sure whatever it is, it's just a misunderstanding. We'll soon iron it out."

Robson followed her inside into a wide rectangular space with black-and-white floor tiles that were polished to such a shine it looked like liquid had been spilled on them. There was a delicate yew writing desk next to the right-hand wall. Its surface was protected by a silver tray that was holding a set of keys, some sunglasses, gloves, and a purse. The walls were finished with a marble effect, and a dozen photographs—portraits and family groups, formally posed—were hanging in heavy silver frames.

Spangler gestured to her right between two white pillars, toward the living room. "Take a seat." She turned the other way and disappeared into her bedroom. "I'll just be a minute."

Robson remained in the entryway and watched Spangler cross behind her ottoman and continue into her bathroom. The moment the door closed behind her he followed into the room. He moved fast for such a big man, and he was quiet. He headed for the bed. It was a king, with a walnut sleigh-style frame. The cream comforter was thrown back and a pink eye mask was lying discarded on the pillow. He turned to the nightstand. It was made of matching wood. There was a Tiffany lamp that was shaped like a tree, a TAG woman's watch, a retro pastel clock, a phone on a charging pad, a tin of foot cream, a hair scrunchie, and a bottle of water on a coaster. It was unopened.

I heard a metallic noise from the bathroom. Robson must have, too, because he glanced across toward the door. Then he hurried out, crossed the hallway, and went into the living room. The floor treatment changed to pale wood, which was arranged in a herringbone pattern. A deep chocolate leather couch stretched in front of a whole wall of built-in bookshelves. They were made of white wood, and were full but with no discernible organization to the titles. Robson skirted a glass coffee table and a pair of leather armchairs that matched the couch. He continued to the window and looked out over the park, directly over the car I was sitting in, giving me two simultaneous elevations of the same view. I heard shuffling footsteps approaching Robson from behind, and he turned to reveal Spangler, now wearing fluffy slippers and a red silk robe. Her face was pink and bright, like she'd just splashed it with water.

"Please." Spangler gestured to an armchair, then settled herself in the corner of the couch. She kicked off her slippers and pulled up her legs, folding them beneath her. "Would you like anything to drink? Coffee? Something stronger, maybe?"

"Thanks, but no. I'm here for answers, and nothing else."

"OK, then. Fire away."

"Tell me everything you know about the file of evidence in the Alex Pardew case."

Her face grew noticeably paler, even over video. "I know it went missing."

"Did you take it?"

"No!" Her legs shot out and she jammed her feet down into her slippers. For a moment I thought she might be about to run.

"But you did put it back." Robson didn't phrase it as a question.

"What makes you think I did that?"

Robson pulled out his phone and called up a screen shot of her stuffing the note into her bag.

"Where did you get that?"

Robson didn't respond.

"That picture. I didn't have the file. I was just holding a piece of paper."

"Correct." Robson put his phone away. "A piece of paper with a note written on it, referring to the Pardew file."

"It didn't say Pardew. It could have been any file."

"How many files go missing, and then turn up on the floor of that particular closet? One a day? A week? A year? Or one, ever?"

Spangler looked around the room as if she was searching for an answer.

"If you had nothing to do with the Pardew file disappearing and reappearing, why did you take that note?" Robson softened his voice and leaned forward. "How would you even know what it meant?"

Spangler's hands balled into fists, deep lines spread across her forehead, but she didn't answer.

Robson shifted his whole chair forward six inches. "Listen, Trish. Is it OK if I call you that? I don't think you're a bad person. I think maybe you've been caught up in something. That's probably very hard for you, and I'm not looking to make things worse. I'll help you if I can. But if you keep lying and prevaricating, what am I supposed to think? So come on. Work with me. Just a little bit."

Spangler covered her eyes with her hands for a moment, then shook her head. "OK. All right. I admit it. I put the file in the closet. But I didn't take it in the first place."

"Then why did you put it back?"

"I was trying to help."

"Who were you trying to help?"

She stayed silent and sat on her hands.

"Don't stop now, Trish. Tell me the truth. If I can fix the situation, I will."

"Josie." Spangler clasped her hands on her lap. "I was trying to help my friend. Josie Wild. She's a clerk, and she's assigned to that courtroom."

"OK, now we're getting somewhere. So it was Josie who took the file?"

"No! Josie would never do anything like that."

"Then how did Josie come to have it?"

"She didn't have it." Spangler paused, like she was trying to figure out why Robson didn't understand. "That's the whole point. She didn't have it. She lost it!"

"The file wasn't lost, Trish. It was taken by someone."

"No." Spangler shook her head. "That's not what happened at all. It was just an accident. You see, Josie—she's a mess. Her life's totally falling apart. Her husband left her because he found out she was having an affair, which she knows was a huge mistake. The whole thing's left her on the verge of a catastrophic meltdown. Her head's not in the game. Not even close. It hasn't been for months. And here's the real problem. Josie was the last person to have had the file. It was her job to safeguard it. But she forgot what she did with it. She was terrified she'd get blamed for the whole fiasco. Because the Pardew guy? Who might have killed someone? He walked as a result. It was declared a mistrial. Josie was terrified she'd get fired. What she did counts as gross misconduct, probably. Losing her job's the last thing she needed, so we all helped her look for it. All the clerks. No one had any luck. Then I found it. It was in the file room all along. On the wrong shelf."

"So you found the file in the file room. No one thought to look in there before?"

"Of course we did, smart-ass. Do you know how many files are in there? Literally millions."

"OK. So you found the file. Why didn't you just give it to Josie?"

"That's kind of what I did do. It was just, I didn't want to embarrass her. It's still a pretty sore point. And I figured, if there was an investigation, I didn't want to get sucked into it. I like my job, and mud sticks."

"Why did you pick that closet to use?"

"Because I had a good reason if I was seen in there. Returning the shoes Josie lent me. She keeps a couple of pairs in that closet. She started when she was having the affair. A saucy dress you can cover with a coat, but if her husband had seen her in four-inch stilettos, it would have been game over, there and then. And as well, because that's the closet Josie uses all the time, I knew she'd find the file in there. Or the judge would have. Either way would have been good."

"Where's the file now?"

"How would I know?"

"Why did you take the note?"

Spangler paused for a moment. "I panicked. I didn't know what to do. If the judge found the note and it came out that I'd found the file and left it there instead of following procedure, I'd have been in big trouble."

"What did you do with the note?"

"I gave it to Josie. I figured the situation was spiraling even further out of control. It was time she knew."

"What did Josie do?"

"She hugged me. She cried. She was just happy I tried to help."

"With the note!"

"Oh. I don't know."

"So who called the number that was written on it?"

Spangler paused again. "I don't know. Her boyfriend?"

Robson got up and took a step toward the door. "All right, Trish. It's late, and you've been helpful, so I'm going to leave my inquiry where it stands, for now. You're not out of the woods yet, though. I'll need to verify a few details. Speak to Josie, obviously. And when I do, if it seems like she's expecting me, I won't be happy. I'll come straight back here and arrest you for obstructing a state investigation. Then I'll see to it that your friends who you sublet to are thrown out on the street."

The Central Park rat crept back to his bench while Robson was riding down in the elevator. He held his ground this time, though, and didn't run when Robson slammed his door. We didn't hang around to observe how long he stayed. Robson cranked the engine and when it reluctantly fired he pulled a U-turn and headed back to the construction site in the Kitchen where he liked to park.

Robson wanted tea when we arrived at the brownstone, so I went to the kitchen with him. I took a seat, which felt very skinny and insecure after the saggy throne in his Cadillac, and waited while he fussed with the controls on his fancy kettle.

"What do we think?" Robson placed a cup in front of me and settled into the other chair. "Spangler. Is she guilty?"

"As sin." I picked up my cup, but the tea was still too hot to drink without milk to cool it.

"She stuck to her guns, though." Robson stretched out his legs. "There were parts of what she said that were plausible. And her story was basically consistent with the guy who called you."

"That's true. But the apartment she'd moved to? That place is way too nice for a clerk's salary. And how did she know it was a man who called my number?"

"You're probably right. I'm just making sure we see things from all sides."

"We'll find out for sure, soon." I blew on my tea. "Assuming you got it?"

"Damn." Robson frowned. "I forgot."

I turned to glare at him and Robson's face cracked into a huge smile. He reached into his pocket, pulled out Spangler's phone, and dropped it onto the table. "You seriously thought I wouldn't have? My feelings are hurt. I might have to find someone new to work with."

Chapter Seven

HOPE FOR A MORON. PREPARE FOR A MACHIAVELLI.

That was the mantra of one of my training officers. It was good advice. It's served me well over the years. You can't rely on an adversary to give themselves away, but you'd be surprised by how often it happens. Often enough to make it crazy not to check.

Spangler's phone was protected by a facial recognition system, but fortunately those are easy to get around. The NSA would never have allowed the technology into civilian hands, otherwise. Robson took a device from his keychain, about a quarter inch by a half, in space gray—because even geeks have aesthetics—which was itself not supposed to be in civilian hands. He switched off the phone. Plugged the unit into its charging port. And powered it back up. The reboot took a few seconds longer than normal. An official-looking seal swirled around on the screen before the manufacturer's logo appeared. Then the phone was switched on, unlocked, its contents free for us to view.

It usually makes sense to start with low-hanging fruit, so we searched for the number that the guy called from when he demanded that I put the file back in the judge's closet. There was no match, so next we checked for text messages starting half an hour before the time stamped on the video recording of Spangler finding the note. There was one, sent right after she left the chamber. It was to Josie Wild, thanking her for the loan of the shoes and confirming their return. I showed it to Robson.

"Is it a code, do you think? Is Wild involved?"

"I think that's doubtful." I took the phone back. "Spangler did return the shoes. That was a good cover. If Wild had originally taken the file, why wouldn't she bring it back herself? Why would she involve Spangler? Let's see what else there is between them."

My thumb got tired scrolling through the messages. There were hundreds of them. Maybe thousands. Some were from Spangler, asking about the state of Wild's marriage, and suggesting drinks or coffee. Most were from Wild. She complained about her husband. "Mr. X." Her lack of self-esteem. Life in general. Her gloomy employment prospects if she got fired. All-around impending doom. They went back years, but there was nothing after the shoes were returned on the day the note was taken.

"Can you remember when Pardew's file first went missing?" Robson took a swig of tea.

"I don't *remember* because I was overseas. Still

in uniform. But I can figure it out based on what the cops and the ADA told me."

"That's good enough. Why not plug the date in, and check comms between Wild and Spangler around that time."

I scrolled back, which was a slow process because of the number of times the cache of messages had to be refreshed, and eventually found the estimated date. There was a dense flurry of texts. At first the content was vague, with Wild blaming herself for making a terrible mistake. She said something was lost, and that it was her fault. She started to panic about getting fired, which she felt would be the final straw. Spangler was supportive. She promised to help conceal the fact that Wild was the last one to have the file. She assured her that all her co-workers would help search for it, and expressed nothing but optimism that the file would soon be found.

I handed the phone to Robson. "What do you think?"

He read the messages over several times, then shook his head. "I'd like proof. It could be the way it looks, with Spangler trying to keep Wild's spirits up. But my gut? I think Spangler played her friend for access and took the file herself. That's how she could afford to be so confident, because she knew the file would be returned when it was finished with. If I'm right, that makes her one cold operator."

"I agree with your gut. Josie Wild was most likely a patsy. We should check her out anyway, though. But assuming Spangler's involved, was she working alone, or with others?"

"Good question." Robson drank some more tea. "Hey. What was the date when you saw Spangler leaving the chamber, and you found the file?"

I told him and he tapped the screen, scrolled, and passed the phone back to me.

He'd found a message at the correct time and date. It had been sent to a number with no name attached to it. There was one word. *Done.*

I pulled out my own phone, put it on speaker, and dialed the number. The call went straight to voicemail.

"It was a burner." Robson suppressed a yawn. "Ended up in the East River, long ago. I guarantee it."

"Were there any other messages, to or from that number? Or any calls?"

Robson picked up the phone and tapped its screen. "Nada."

"Any mention of it in her contacts?"

"Negative."

"How about any other messages that just say, 'Done'?"

Robson put the phone down in front of me. "There's one. Sent the day the file was taken. To a different number."

I dialed, and got shunted straight through to voicemail again.

"This isn't looking good for Spangler." I put my phone back in my pocket. "And she clearly was working with someone—whoever she texted *Done* to. We need to flush this partner out. Or partners.

We should copy everything on her phone and go through it with a fine-tooth comb. Analyze her messages for any kind of code. Check her calls for repeating patterns. Look at the GPS log in case she's been to any suspicious places. Search her contacts and see if anyone stands out."

Robson blew out his cheeks. "That's a lot of legwork."

"It is. Are you up for it?"

"Sure. Why not?" He set his cup down and stared at the phone as if it might instantly give up its secrets if he appeared to be fierce enough. "What are you going to do?"

"Go for a second bite at the cherry." I hauled myself out of the chair. "Clone her phone, and plant the real one at the courthouse. If she doesn't have a backup, and she's in enough of a panic, she might just use it."

Robson shrugged. "Worth a try, I guess. But in the meantime—the kettle, if you don't mind."

Chapter Eight

I LEFT EARLIER THAN NORMAL THE NEXT MORNING to make sure I'd arrive at the courthouse before Spangler. The streets, already busy, grew more and more congested the farther downtown I went. The atmosphere was different than it was later in the day, too. It was dour and hostile, and during the entire journey I had a weird sensation that I was swarming in the same direction with a mass of people, but somehow still moving separately.

I reached the employees' entrance, delighted to break free from the stream of grumpy humanity, and was making my way down the steps when it struck me that it might draw unwanted attention, carrying in three phones. I needn't have worried, though, because the guard didn't turn a hair. I kept our conversation to a minimum, hurried to the janitors' room, nodded to the one guy who'd gotten there earlier than me, changed, and took my cart up to the first floor. I wheeled it across the glossy marble surface at a suitably respectful speed, skirted around the signs of the zodiac within the outer ring of the design, which matched the proportions of the dome, and wound up as planned at the main security station. I picked out one guard in particular to approach. He'd been on duty all night, so I knew he wouldn't pay too much attention to my face when I scrawled illegibly on a lost property form and handed over Spangler's phone.

The area near the elevator doors was a mob scene at that time of day, so I held back to allow some of the crowd to pass. Above my head the mural inside the dome traced the history of justice from the Assyrian period up to the founding of the United States. I realized I'd come to a halt somewhere in the middle of the Colonial era so was about to shift myself forward in time when a familiar face caught my attention. Len Hendrie. He'd just come in the main entrance and had joined the line of visitors waiting their turn to go through the metal detectors.

I went back to admiring the ceiling until Hendrie had nearly reached the head of the line. Then I wheeled forward to a spot that left me well positioned to take any of the available elevators. Hendrie emerged from the security area and started toward the first bank on the left. I followed him. The doors opened, and as usual some people were reluctant to get in alongside me and my cart full of cleaning supplies. Four of them turned away. Hendrie wasn't one of them.

He rode up to the fourth floor and I followed him from the elevator to room 432. He opened the door a crack, peeked in, then turned away and flopped down on a bench in the corridor. I pushed my cart level and paused as if I'd just noticed he was there.

"Do you mind if I sit?" I settled into the opposite corner. "Remember me? We talked a few days ago."

Hendrie looked startled, but he placed me after a moment and quickly relaxed. "Sure. I remember. Are you waiting to get in the room again? There's someone in it right now."

"It's probably a lawyer getting set up for a trial. Is that why you're back today? More preparation?"

Hendrie nodded. "You know what they say about practice. I have one shot at this. One chance to make my voice heard. I want to make it count."

"I've been thinking about that. What you told me really made an impression. I guess if they go all letter-of-the-law, some people might say you went a little too far but what happened to you was definitely unfair."

Hendrie smiled. It was small with more than a hint of bitterness, but it was the first time I'd seen him with anything other than a frown on his face. "I wish I could make everyone think like you."

"Thanks. But I wouldn't be surprised if a lot of people already do. I bet there are more than you realize. You just need to lay it all out, nice and simple. Show everyone what an asshole this guy is, for costing you your house."

"That, I can do." His smile grew a tiny bit wider.

"You can start with all the stuff about greed, right? That's bad on its own. Him caring more about his wine cellar than the roof over your head. But what else is there? The more reasons you give people to hate him, the better."

"A guy, rolling in money, ruined his friend to make a quick buck. What more do I need?"

"I don't know." I paused for a moment. "How about something political? People love a good conspiracy theory. Take the company you invested in. It was competing with the Chinese. Could there be anything there?"

"Like what?"

"Sabotage, maybe?"

"You mean Jimmy Klinsman is in league with the Chinese?" He shook his head. "I don't see it. With all the money he has, he's hardly communist poster-boy material."

"You'd be surprised what people do for money."

"Maybe. But Jimmy's just a greedy sociopath. He's not a spy. Or a secret agent."

"Perhaps not in the ordinary way. But at college, did he ever—" One of my phones beeped. It was the cloned copy of Spangler's. She'd just sent someone a text. "I'm sorry, Len, this is urgent. There's something I have to take care of right away. Good luck with your trial. I hope I'll see you again."

"You might, but only if you're up for visiting me in jail. I did it, remember. I'm guilty. I'm not looking to wriggle out of this thing."

I took a couple of steps along the corridor, then

stopped and turned back. "Are you sure your trial will be in room 432, by the way?"

"No." Hendrie shook his head. "It was the first one I found empty, the other day. I just came back here out of habit, I guess."

"Might it be worth practicing in a few others as well? You could make sure you're comfortable wherever you end up, that way."

"That's a good idea. Thanks. I'll try it."

"My pleasure. And here's another idea. Have you got a pen and paper?"

"Sure." Hendrie unzipped his folder and handed me a notepad. "Why?"

"I'm going to write down my cell number. Anytime you want an audience to practice with, call me. And give me your number, too. I hear things around this place. I'll let you know if I pick up anything helpful."

I wheeled my cart the rest of the way around the corner into the hexagonal corridor, stopped next to the window, and checked my phone. Spangler's initial message was there, along with a whole bunch more:

We need to meet!!!!!! Urgently!!!!!!

No. Too risky.

Yes!!!!

Why?

I had a visitor last night. An investigator from the justice department. He asked all about the Pardew file.

Must be the same guy I spoke to. He seem genuine to you?

How should I know? I think so. His credentials looked real. He knew a whole lot about me. Things only court officials could find out.

Good, then. Relax!

Good???????? WTF?????? How on earth can I relax?!?!?!?

Because this is better than a shakedown.

It's not better! He could come back and arrest me. I could go to jail.

You're not going to jail. They have nothing. It was just a fishing expedition.

That's easy for you to say. You didn't have a giant creepy guy in your house in the middle of the night.

That's true. But he's gone now and he's not coming back so you need to calm down.

We need to talk!

There's nothing to talk about.

There's plenty to talk about. Like, he had a picture of me taking the note in the judge's chamber. How did he get that? Does he have more? And my prints are on that file. I couldn't wear gloves, putting it back. Is there anything inside that can link us to JD? Then we'd have real problems.

I waited for a response, but none came right away. Twenty seconds ticked past without an answer, so I clicked over to Spangler's contacts to check for anyone with the initials *JD*. There were plenty of D surnames, but none with matching J first names. I'd just started searching all the J first names I could think of to cross-reference with D middle names when the phone finally buzzed again with an incoming message.

OK. Tonight. Usual time. Come all the way to the end.

Thanks. CU later ♥.

Say the place, I thought. *Say the time.*

No more texts arrived. No more were sent. *Come on! This is no time to go all cryptic.* I waited a full minute. Then another. And one more for luck. No further messages were forthcoming, so I changed tack and called Robson. He answered on the first ring. "Any luck?" I asked.

"I can tell you all about her taste in music, movies, and her preferred vacation destinations. Nothing linking her to a partner, though, and nothing else suspicious." I heard him take a swallow of tea. "I'll keep on it. You?"

"I've had a bite. There's some good news. And some bad."

"Give me the good."

"Spangler's been texting with someone. They didn't use names, but they did set up an RV to discuss what happened last night."

"That is good news. What's the bad?"

"They didn't state where or when for the meet. Only the 'usual time' and 'all the way to the end.'"

"OK." I heard him take another swallow. "So that's not terrible. It means they're talking about someplace they've used before. Where they feel safe. Which means it's probably off the beaten track. I'll go back to Spangler's GPS log and look for repeat locations that are secluded and don't correspond with any of her contacts. Leave it with me. I'll call back when I have something."

"Thanks, John. And there's one other thing. Can you also search her email and anything else you can think of for any reference to a JD? Spangler seemed worried about being linked to someone with those initials, but I have no idea who they belong to, or if it's a man or a woman."

I looked back down the corridor and saw that Hendrie had gone. I wondered if the lawyer had cleared out of room 432, leaving the coast clear for him to rehearse. I wheeled along to the end and pushed the doors open a crack to check. Hendrie wasn't there. But I could see a woman. She wasn't a lawyer. She was a clerk. At least, she was sitting at the clerk's desk. I pulled out the clone of Spangler's phone and scrolled through her contacts until I found a picture of Josie Wild. The image matched. This wasn't the ideal time to interrogate her, but experience has shown that *possible today* is better than *perfect tomorrow*.

I elbowed the doors open the rest of the way and wheeled inside. Wild glanced up, then went straight back to the papers she was studying. I continued a little farther, parked between the first pair of benches, reached for my broom, and started to slowly sweep the floor in the public area. After a minute Wild balled up a piece of paper and tossed it into the trash. It clearly wasn't her first of the morning. The garbage can by her desk was in imminent danger of overflowing.

"Let me get that for you." I smiled and stepped through the gap in the fence.

"Thanks." Wild put her pen down and pushed the garbage can closer to me with her foot.

"You've been busy." I pretended I was hardly able to lift out the liner because of all the balls of paper. "Early start?"

Wild nodded. "It's my first day back. I have lots to catch up with."

"Been away? On vacation?"

Wild didn't answer.

"Climbing Mount Kilimanjaro, maybe? Skydiving?"

"No." Wild hesitated. "Nothing so glamorous. Or fun. I was just out . . . sick."

"Oh dear. I'm sorry to hear that. Looks like you're back on your feet now, though."

"I am. Just about. Although it's not the best time to pick back up."

"No? How does that go? I'm quite new here myself. Is it seasonal, with the legal system, like in stores? Are there specials I should know about? *Fall Felonies?* Or does the full moon bring out the bad guys?"

Wild smiled. "No. There's nothing like that. Although maybe there should be. I'm just getting myself back up to speed. New procedures. Things like that. It'll take a while to adjust, I guess."

"I'm sure it will. I hate new procedures, myself. All change is for the worse, my father used to say."

"He had a point. Although these ones aren't too bad. Nothing too much to argue with."

"New ways to keep bad guys off the streets?"

"Kind of. Indirectly. It's less glamorous than how you say it, though. It's just about filing. Keeping things from getting lost."

"What kind of things? Cell keys? Police cars?"

Wild laughed. "No. Just paperwork."

I held up my bag of trash. "Does that happen often? Do I need to be worried?"

"No. You're fine. But it can be serious when it does."

"Is there anything you need me to keep an eye open for? You wouldn't believe the things people leave scattered around."

Wild paused. "Thanks. That's good to know. If I ever do need help, I'll know where to come."

"You should." I smiled at her. "I wouldn't even charge a finder's fee." I put the trash can back down by her desk. "Nice shoes, by the way."

Wild stretched out one leg. She was wearing a pair of black pumps, which were polished to an immaculate shine. "Thanks. They're my weakness. I can't resist. You should see my closet. My husband—make that my soon-to-be ex-husband—hates them."

"He must be crazy. I think they're nice. It must be hard getting to work, though. I can't picture anyone climbing subway steps in heels that high."

"I don't wear them on the subway." Wild dropped her voice to a whisper. "I keep them here. A couple of pairs. Don't tell anyone, but Judge Majumdar lets me keep them in the closet in his chambers."

"That sounds smart. If I were you, I'd—" I heard the sound of a text arriving. On my personal phone this time. I checked the screen. It was from Robson—10-30. An old military code, meaning *request assistance*. "I'm sorry. A friend just had surgery today and I need to call in and check that everything's OK. Do you mind if I leave my cart here for a moment? I'll be right back."

There was no one in the corridor outside the courtroom, so I sat on the bench and called Robson's number. As usual he answered on the first ring. "News?" I asked.

"Negative. No luck tracing anyone who could be JD. And there's a big problem with nailing down the RV. Spangler's phone is only three months old. There's nothing in the GPS log that helps us. It doesn't go back far enough."

"That can't be right. We could read her messages going back years."

"We could get her older messages because they're stored in her account in the cloud. Every time we refreshed her screen we were downloading more archived messages from the server. The GPS is different. It's specific to the individual handset."

"So we can't tell where her phone's been?"

"We can tell exactly where her phone's been. Her *current* phone. But it's gone nowhere interesting. We need to know about her previous phone. And maybe the one before that, depending on how often she changes them."

"Well, that sucks. Is there anything else we can use?"

"I was hoping her calendar might help. I can get into those older records. But there was no pattern. Nothing recurring at regular times or dates. No innocuous entries. Nothing in code. No sign of anything covert."

"So we're nowhere?"

"We've got zero of any use, at this point."

"Then how do we find out where the RV will be? And when?"

"That's why I needed you to call. To see if you had anything. Me? I'm fresh out of ideas."

I paused as two jurors went by, heading for the

bathroom. "Nothing springs to mind. Leave it with me. I'll try to think of something."

"One of us better."

"Have faith. We will. In the meantime, FYI, I just ran into Josie Wild. We chatted a little and I think we were right. I don't think she's involved."

"Are you sure?"

"It's not like she passed a polygraph or anything, but my money says she's a patsy."

"I'm not surprised. But it makes it all the more important we find Spangler's partner."

"I hear you. I'm on it."

"What are you going to do?"

"Clean something."

"No. What are you really going to do?"

"I'm serious. Cleaning helps me focus. You should try it. You could start by gathering up all those empty paper cups you leave littered around the house."

Josie Wild wasn't in room 432 when I returned to collect my cart. She could have gone through to the judge's chamber, but I didn't check. I figured there was little mileage in finding out. I was in more danger of provoking suspicion at this stage. My time would be better spent heading down to third. Mopping the corridor. Devoting myself to uninterrupted thought. I needed to locate Spangler's RV. And to do that I needed all the inspiration I could get. What I'd told Robson about cleaning was true.

I was heading for the elevator when I saw two guys slinking into one of the bathrooms. They'd be in their late teens, I guessed. They were tall and skinny with baggy jeans hanging off their asses, bright oversized sneakers, and pupils the size of pinpricks. My sixth sense flared. I've been in enough bars and back alleys in enough cities around the world to know people up to no good when I see them. I pushed my cart to the side of the corridor. Paused outside the bathroom door. And heard peals of laughter from inside, mischievous, with a nasty edge.

I opened the door and stepped inside. One of the guys had torn some lengths of towel out of the dispensing machine and was jamming them into the sinks. The one at the far end was already blocked and the faucet was running. It should have automatically shut itself off, but many of them—like that one—are broken. It was only a matter of time now before the bathroom would be flooded. And maybe the one below, as well, depending on how quickly the water was turned off.

The other guy—the slightly taller one—was standing by the side of the end stall. It was screened off with an expanse of dull cream Formica. He'd evidently mistaken it for a blank canvas. He had a red marker pen in his hand, and so far he'd managed to write, *Donny sucks coc.* He'd been about to complete his claim, but instead he turned and scowled at me.

"Who are you looking at?" He straightened up and folded his arms.

"Nobody." I kept my voice neutral.

The guy puffed up a little further.

I made an exaggerated turn to make sure he

knew his buddy was also in my field of view. "Make that two nobodies."

It took a moment for the words to register, but when they did the guy stepped toward me, his arms bowed forward like a gorilla. "Get out!"

"OK." I nodded, reasonably. "I'm going. But I'll be coming back. And if the bathroom's not immaculate when I do, we're going to have a very different conversation."

I strolled out to the corridor and paused by the door again. At first all I could hear was whooping, then there was the sound of slapping, like the guys were giving each other high fives. I crossed to my cart and selected a bottle of cleaner and a large roll of tissue. Then I went back in.

The first guy now also had the next sink in line blocked. The second guy had finished defaming Donny, whoever that was, and had moved on to making allegations about someone named Mitch's nocturnal activities of choice. According to him, they involved a narrow range of farmyard animals. He stopped when he heard the door, turned, and gazed at the spray bottle in my hand.

"I told you to get out." He waved the pen at me like it was a weapon.

"I went out. I told you I'd come back. And the place is not immaculate, which means you have work to do." I held the bottle out toward the pen guy.

Neither of them moved, but their mouths did sag open.

"Perhaps I'm being unfair. Perhaps you don't know what *immaculate* means?" I paused. "Is that the problem? Perhaps I should have said, *perfectly clean*. Which this room isn't. So take the supplies and get busy. I'll let you know if you miss any spots."

The pen guy threw down his marker, pulled a set of keys from his pocket, and positioned one in the gap between his middle and ring fingers, like a short thin blade. He threw a couple of practice jabs at me, pulling back sharply each time. I flinched anyway, as if trying to avoid getting hurt. Encouraged, he came at me with a bold lunge. I didn't back away this time. Instead I came forward, grabbed his wrist with my left hand, pushed it out to the side, and continued moving into the gap between his arm and his body. I wrapped my right leg around behind him, grabbed his hoodie with my right hand, and added just enough force to pivot him backward over my thigh. Then I helped him the rest of the way to the floor, firmly enough to wind him, but gently enough to cause no serious damage. While he was still trying to suck in some breath I jabbed my thumbnail between his middle two knuckles, which released his grip, and I relieved him of his keys. Then I let go of him, and when he finally struggled back to his feet I shoved open the nearest stall door and tossed his keys into the toilet.

"Oops." I held up my hands. "I guess I should have checked that the last guy flushed. Oh well. I hope you have duplicates. Now pick up your supplies. This work isn't going to do itself." I felt my phone buzz in my pocket. It was another text from Robson. Another 10-30. "Excuse me, gentlemen. I have a quick call to make. You—start on removing that scribble. You—find something to mop up that water. I'll be back in a minute, and I expect to see some progress."

This time Robson answered before I even heard a ring. "Paul, say, 'John, you're a genius.' "

"John, you're a genius."

"Why, thank you."

"Are you planning on telling me how this alleged genius manifests itself?"

"I've made a breakthrough. I was looking through Spangler's keychain—which is a kind of electronic notebook for passwords that you get on phones and computers—and I saw she had one for Uber. But there was no Uber app on her phone. I guess she switched to Lyft when she got her new one. So I opened Uber on my own phone and logged in as Spangler. That gave me access to her complete history. And guess what. She's only been to one place outside the city this year. And she's been there six times. A town on the coast called Rye."

"I know that place. Or I did, when I was a kid. We had a few days out there. I remember big houses. Wide streets. The beach. An amusement park. I thought it was fabulous, but my dad wasn't a fan. He thought it was too frivolous. Mrs. Vincent came with us once, too, and I don't think she liked it, either."

"Was that park called Playland? Because on each occasion, that's where Spangler got dropped off. And she always arrived within five minutes of the same time: 9:00 P.M."

"Sounds like 'the usual time.' "

"It kind of does. And I looked on Google Maps. The place has a pier."

"I remember that. An old-school boardwalk. The kind of place you could 'come all the way to the end' of."

"So what do you think? Have we found the RV point?"

"It's certainly a good candidate. Worth taking a look at. This is excellent work, John."

"You're welcome."

"How long does it take to get to Rye?"

"Say seventy-five minutes, allowing for traffic and contingencies."

"We think the RV's at 2100. I'll want to be in place by 1900. Let's allow an hour for recce, so can you pick me up at the courthouse at 1645? And bring me a change of clothes? Something black."

"You're not coming home first?"

"I have cleaning to do."

"Still?"

"I've recruited some help. Call it a youth opportunity program. These particular individuals are a little rough around the edges. They might need a little guidance and supervision. Which is where things could get interesting."

Chapter Nine

ROBSON PULLED HIS SLUGGISH OLD CADILLAC over to the side of the road where Rye Beach Avenue turns through ninety degrees and becomes Playland Parkway. I opened my door, slid out of the car, and drifted into the cover of a small stand of mature trees. The street was lined with ornate lights, like the kind of fancy lanterns you'd see in a picture of a child's fairy castle, and there was only a narrow strip of sandy beach between me and the ocean. The harsh tang of salt in the air was competing with the smell of dry soil and sun-scorched grass. The evening was still warm, but the wind was starting to pick up. I could hear the waves shifting the sand around on the beach, and the few remaining leaves were rustling above my head.

I checked for protruding roots and hidden ruts, then started moving east. I slid my phone into the bag Robson had brought, along with the clothes I'd changed out of in favor of the darker alternatives he'd provided, and stashed it in the trunk of a hollow tree. I crossed the path, hopped over a chest-high metal fence that appeared to be painted night-vision green in the soft, almost setting sun, stepped out onto the sand, and turned north. I stayed on the beach for another two hundred feet, then made my way up a ramp to a patched cement sidewalk in front of a long pavilion that runs parallel to the waterline. The building was a single story high with a castellated art deco roofline, cream-painted walls, and green wooden trim that matched the fence. Its large rectangular windows had rusting metal frames. The spaces behind them—maybe once gift stores or cafés or ice-cream parlors—all appeared to be empty and the original terra-cotta supports for the awnings were supplemented by a line of temporary-looking, dilapidated wooden trusses.

As I continued toward the main part of the park the cement underfoot gave way to diagonal planks, their wood grayed and roughened by the weather. There was a taller section of building in the center part of the pavilion, and the symmetry was emphasized by a pair of matching towers topped with white louvered cupolas and copper weather vanes that were heavy with verdigris. Beyond the building the curve of the walkway grew more pronounced as it followed the contours of the bay. It broadened to allow space for a line of benches and more fancy lights appeared, though on heftier pillars to withstand the wind.

I reached the walls of the park without incident. They were painted a crisp white, with curving green roofs rising up behind them. I could see a dome, and the bright flags waving on top of the Grand Carousel. My father had so disapproved of that thing. If he'd thought wanting to ride it as a kid was bad, he'd have blown a fuse to see what I was doing there now.

I moved on past a bizarre pair of giant blue Adirondack chairs with a gnarled old tree in between them and came to the park entrance. A tiki theme had been introduced since my childhood visits, with benches with creepy faces carved into their supports dotted around, amid conical cabanas to shelter in from the sun. There was a lone, unhappy palm tree, banners tied to the fences advertising the park's restaurants, and to the right, the pier.

All the gates at the entrance to the pier were locked. Stout cream metal railings—they looked more like prison bars—continued all the way up to the overhanging edge of the roof, so it was impossible to climb over. It was easy enough to shimmy around the side, though. The spacing of the fence rails provided convenient footholds, and their rounded tips were perfect to hold on to.

Beyond the area that was dedicated to selling things—refreshments, souvenirs, and so on—the pier was very basic. There were wide wooden slabs underfoot, like railroad ties. A chest-high wooden fence on each side, made with planks of a similar width and with equal gaps between them. After about twenty feet, behind a padlocked gate, a gangplank led down on the right-hand side to a pontoon for docking small boats. There were signs warning against swimming. And lights mounted on green swan-neck poles. They would originally have been a darker shade, but now most of their paint was missing thanks to the flaying wind.

The deck gently curved to the right and broadened out around threefold by the time it reached its end. There were groups of benches and wooden chairs, all new-looking and all bolted down. A couple of life belts, their bright red-and-white surfaces contrasting with the faded orange nylon ropes attaching them to their posts. There were bins, for trash and recycling. And a pair of assemblies like giant soccer goals, which I didn't remember being there when I was a kid.

The structures were made up of steel girders, painted black. They were flanked by mooring bollards and had red-cased electric motors mounted at the center of their crossbars. Taut steel cables led down from each one to perforated metal walkways that could be swung out for passengers to use when larger boats came alongside. Both walkways were currently suspended at a fifteen-degree angle, with their lower edges around eight inches off the ground. That made for a tight space, but I didn't care. I'd been prepared to wait with no cover, or to even semi-submerge myself in the water below the pier if that had been necessary. Being wedged under the metal mesh would be a luxury, in comparison. The only question was which walkway to station myself beneath. I wanted the best chance of hearing Spangler's conversation, but the wind was stronger out there and the water was lapping loudly against the pontoons. I thought back to the text Spangler's contact had sent. He or she had said, "come all the way to the end," so I settled on the walkway farthest from the shore. Wriggled underneath. And waited.

Two hours, ten minutes later, my arms and legs heavy with inactivity and my neck stiff from the unnatural angle, I heard footsteps. One set. Light and quick. They continued past my position, then stopped, close by. I guessed at the railing. Then a second set approached, with heavier, longer strides. They stopped in the same place.

"You asshole. I can't believe you dragged me all the way out here." I recognized the voice from Robson's interrogation. It was Spangler. "Why couldn't we have stayed by the gate? There's no one here."

"Stop complaining. You're the one who wanted to talk." I recognized this voice, too. It was the guy who'd called me in response to the note. "Either there's a security problem, or there isn't. If there is, this is no time for a half-assed response. Personally, I think we're OK. I'd have been happy to stay home and let things work themselves out on their own."

"The guy had pictures of me, Brian! Were you not paying attention? That means he has cameras hidden inside the judge's chambers. That's serious shit!"

"The guy's courthouse security, right? So he's

just doing his job. The pictures are no biggie. They prove what? You took a note? So what?"

"He was intimidating, Brian. I admitted I put the file back, too."

The man paused for a moment. "Don't worry about it. That was the right thing to do. You didn't panic. You didn't hesitate. You stuck to our story, which is exactly why we had the story already mapped out and ready to go. It's completely plausible, and it tallies with what I already said to the guy on the phone. So relax. There's nothing here for him."

"I'm not so sure." Spangler's voice was no less insistent. "How did he know to put cameras in those specific chambers?"

"Maybe he put cameras in all the chambers. Or maybe because that's where the file was found."

"How did he know where to find it?"

"Maybe it was dumb luck. Maybe he searched every closet in the building. Who knows? Who cares? We wanted the file to be found so it could get back to where we need it to be. Dumb Josie was supposed to find it. This guy found it instead. It's like we cut out the middleman, is all. The only difference is he knows you returned it. There's no way to prove you took it, too. You should get a reward for going above and beyond."

"My prints are on the cover."

"We don't know that. They might not be. The cover's rough, not like paper. Not a great surface for prints. And even if they are there, of course you touched it! When you found it and put it back. Everything's consistent. There are no red flags."

"What about inside the file? The contents? Could anything lead back to us?"

"No way. Not possible. JD went through it himself. Do you think he's an idiot? Do you think he'd leave a trail? This isn't his first rodeo, you know."

"So what do we do now?"

"We sit tight. We're golden. The only way this goes south is if you do something stupid. So relax, stay calm, and it'll all come out good. I promise."

"What about Pardew?"

"What about him? He doesn't know anything about you. He doesn't know my name. The only one who's obvious is JD. Even if Pardew got caught, there's no evidence now. So it would be *he said, JD said*. And you know who wins that contest."

"I guess."

"It's a fact. And Pardew knows the file is back, remember. He won't be stupid enough to stick around. Not with that hanging over him. Imagine the stress, crapping himself about getting picked up every time he sets foot in a grocery store? Or a bar? He'd end up shooting himself, sooner or later. Maybe we could make that sooner, if it would help you sleep."

"No! That's a terrible thing to say. I don't want any harm to come to him. I just don't want the truth to come out."

"I get that. But don't worry. It won't. Just hang tough. Do that, and we're home and dry."

Back in the car I recounted everything I'd heard to Robson, and he responded in the way I knew he would.

"I don't get it." He threw up his hands. "No one else was there. Why didn't you knock the woman out and hang the guy over the rail by his ankles until he told you everything he knew about Pardew? We could have got a jump on where he's gone."

"I was tempted. But if he'd clammed up, what then? Throw him in the ocean? Let him drown? And he seemed scared of this JD, so even if he talked, how would we know if he was telling the truth? He'd have been in the wind by the time we verified anything."

Robson grunted dismissively.

"And who is this JD? I want to know. I want to round up the whole pack. Dismantle their whole operation. You know how it works. The better the preparation, the better the ass-kicking that follows."

"I guess you're right." Robson sighed. "What do you think their operation is? Taking bribes to force mistrials? Pardew could have paid them to misplace the file. He seems like the biggest winner in this scenario. And now they could be using the return of the file to keep him out of the picture. Keep their secret safe."

"It's possible, but I think there's more to it. The way they talked, Pardew didn't sound like he was in the driver's seat. And the file didn't just temporarily disappear, either. Documents went missing from inside it. We need to figure out what they were. Why they were taken. We need a full ID on the guy Spangler's hooked up with. All I got is that his first name's Brian. And then there's JD. Could be he's the boss."

"OK. We'll start with Brian. Work our way up the food chain."

"Did you get anything on him tonight?"

"Not much." Robson frowned. "The guy's clearly experienced. I didn't pick him up until he was already on foot, approaching the pier. I followed him back to his car after the RV. A silver Taurus, maybe five years old. I got the plates, so I'll have them traced. I know someone who can handle that. I met him at Atkinson's shindig after we wrapped up the Azerbaijani thing. We'll get Brian on the hook. And we'll reel him in."

"What about Spangler? How did she get here? Uber again?"

"No. She used a car service. One that caters to celebrities. It's discreet, and she had the driver wait."

"How did she contact them?"

"I don't know."

"We should find out. It might be useful to follow her in the future."

"I'll add it to the list."

Chapter Ten

After another night when my head hardly touched my pillow, I would have liked the chance to sleep late. And if I had to get up early to go somewhere, I would have liked something hearty to eat, as compensation. The next morning, I went 0 for 2. There was a message waiting for me on my voicemail. It was from Detective Atkinson. He had news about Klinsman. And inevitably he wanted to pass it on at the Green Zebra.

I might not be the fastest student in the class, but you can't say I never learn. I remembered to take some paper, a pen, and a small scissors with me to the café. Atkinson was inevitably late. The chess table was free, so I broke a golden rule—or demonstrated a newfound civilian flexibility—and I took it. I ordered coffee, and while I waited for it to arrive I designed a set of my own chess pieces—I'd like to think they fell somewhere between Isle of Lewis and Man Ray—cut them out, and set a board. It was challenging to stop them from blowing away when anyone walked past, but I'd managed to complete the first six moves of the King's Indian Defense when Atkinson arrived. He glanced at the paper shapes, momentarily intrigued, but didn't spot the connection to his timekeeping and took the seat opposite mine. He waved to our server, ordered his usual eggplant Benedict, then called him back and added an energy-boosting kale smoothie. Judging by the intensity of his fidgeting, that wasn't strictly necessary.

Atkinson waited in silence for his drink to be delivered, then took a sip and grimaced. "OK." He briefly drummed his fingers on the table. "I asked you to come because I have news about the guy you thought possibly had links to China. I want you to know, very thorough inquiries have been made. You deserve that, given how your theories held water in the past, and I'm the first to admit that I benefited from them even when I doubted you. My contacts dug deep and what they found is, there's no connection. No cause for concern."

"Are you sure? Who did you talk to? Because it's natural for people in certain positions to deny—"

"I can't give you names, McGrath. But one guy's high up in FBI counterterrorism. One's a longtime NSA cyber task force expert, and he knows telecom inside out and backward. The other's at the Treasury Department. She's an expert in financial crimes. All of them say the same thing. There's no *there* there."

"I don't get it." I moved a random white pawn.

"The stock damage Klinsman caused only helps the US firm's Chinese rival. And as we all know, those so-called corporations are basically fronts for their government."

"That's not actually the case." Atkinson drummed his fingers. "The share thing doesn't help the Chinese at all. It's irrelevant to them. Our government hasn't lost confidence. The US company is still nailed on to win the same contracts. And its share price is already bouncing back. The official announcement was delayed, is all. Klinsman found that part out through some contact of his, and used the knowledge to his advantage. But when the information is made public, the stock will go through the roof. I shouldn't even be telling you this. I could be guilty of insider trading, myself. But the only guy Klinsman helped was Klinsman. From what I've been told, anyone else with sufficient resources and the same facts at their disposal would have made the same play. And ironically, if the arson guy had pockets deep enough to ride out the storm, he'd soon be benefiting, too."

"This smells all wrong." I moved another pawn. "My father was a businessman. A good one. And he taught me that you make money by working hard. By building things. Inventing things. Not by trading paper and screwing your friends in the process."

"Welcome to Wall Street, my friend."

"Even if he's not working for the Chinese, Klinsman shouldn't be allowed to walk away from this. He's just as guilty as Hendrie. It was a house for a house. If one guy's punished, they both should be."

"What do you want me to do about it?" Atkinson shifted in his chair. "One of them broke the law. The other one didn't. Right or wrong, that's the way it is."

"Immoral, is the way it is."

Atkinson made a show of looking at his watch. "I'm sorry, am I keeping you? Do you need to get back to kindergarten?"

"You should investigate. Find out what's behind Klinsman's golden façade. No one amasses that much money without cutting a few corners."

"Maybe so. But I can't investigate without evidence of wrongdoing. Or probable cause, at least."

"OK, then." I drained the last of my coffee, slammed my mug on the table, and gathered up my paper chessmen. "I understand. I'm not naïve. You need evidence first? I'll find you some."

"Like you found Pardew's missing file?"

"Exactly like that."

"Come on, McGrath. Focus. Prioritize."

"Don't worry." I stood up. "Another few days, you'll have Pardew's file and dirt on Klinsman. Both. I guarantee it."

I turned right out of the café, stepped into the street, and immediately had to dodge around a group of slow-moving sightseers. That just added to the impatience and anger I was feeling toward the world. Had I really spent twenty years of my life defending a system that was so inherently unfair? So frivolous, as my father would have said?

The thought of my father made me redirect my anger toward myself. The truth was, whatever good came out of my time in the service, my original motivation had not been noble. The old man was a committed pacifist. He freaked out over my reaction to witnessing a shooting and demanded I get counseling. I joined the army instead, to spite him. It was a mistake I never got the chance to correct.

I swerved around a messenger who'd stopped in the center of the sidewalk while he scanned the nearby buildings for an address, pulled out my phone, and called Robson. I wanted news about Brian—the contact Spangler had met at the pier—but he had nothing for me. So I switched tack. I tried Ro Lebodow instead. Ro was my go-to expert when it came to finance questions. The murkier the waters, the more valuable her advice tended to be. I first met her years ago when she helped me defeat a terrorist plot by unpicking a tangle of real estate transactions. I've consulted her many times since, most recently over a money-laundering case, where her insight helped me boost the local jail population, while another asshole landed himself in the morgue as an added bonus.

Ro sounded breathless when she answered. I guessed she was on her treadmill, which was one of her favorite places to work. She was the queen of multitasking, with such boundless drive it was as if she was tapped into the energy of the city itself. I asked how her schedule was looking and she said she was impossibly busy. There was no way she could see me until soon after lunch.

I decided to fill the intervening time at the courthouse. There were always floors that needed to be cleaned, and part of me was hoping that the bathroom guys might come back. They might need more guidance. I was still mulling that prospect over when my phone rang. It was Robson.

"Finally, some news. My contact at the NYPD came through. The guy from the pier last night was driving a car registered to a company. Rooney Home Security, Inc., out of Queens. I googled, and it looks legit. They install burglar alarms, things like that."

I felt my mood begin to improve. "Good lead, John. Very interesting. And you know, I was just thinking we might need an alarm at the brownstone. Maybe I should go by. Get a quote."

"I'm texting you the address now."

I knew people who refused to visit the outer boroughs, even to go to the airports, and when my cab dropped me on the Union Turnpike, half a dozen blocks west of Cunningham Park, I could see their point of view. Rooney Home Security's office was in the center of a strip mall that was set back far enough from the street to allow a single line of cars to park, as long as they stopped at an angle, like a row of fish bones. The neighboring units were identical except for signs that identified them as a church of some obscure denomination I'd not heard of before, a cellphone store, a massage parlor, and a pawnshop. Vertical blinds filled the office's window, which was otherwise blank except for a sign announcing its business hours—8:00 A.M. to 4:00 P.M., Monday to Friday—and a little clock illustration in case the numbers weren't clear enough.

Inside, there was a modest wooden desk set near the center of the rear wall. A receptionist was sitting behind it, looking stern with her metal-rimmed glasses and her gray hair up in a bun, but she was so transfixed by her computer monitor that she showed no sign of having noticed I was there. The carpet was brown with a coarse weave, like it was from a cheap hotel. The walls had wood veneer panels to waist height and were painted white above. Framed charts and graphs on one side warned of soaring crime rates across the city, and adverts on the other suggested that the only possible safeguard would be a shiny new alarm system. A washed-out reproduction of *The Hay Wain* hung by the entrance in a fading gilded frame. Three Barcelona chairs were lined up under the window, or at least cheap knockoffs covered with white vinyl that was yellowing with age and imitation chrome peeling off their plastic legs. There were two more next to the side wall and a low table with a glass top, which was covered with unruly piles of brochures.

"Is Mr. Rooney available?" I stopped in front of the desk. "I need his help. It's very urgent."

The woman peered up at me and her expression made clear that she preferred whatever she'd been looking at on her screen. "Take a seat." She spoke with the raspy whisper of a long-term smoker. "I'll see." I stayed where I was. She snatched up her desk phone with long bony fingers, wedged the handset under her chin, and jabbed angrily at its buttons. "Got a walk-in. Want to see him?" She listened for a second, then looked at me again. "What do you want, exactly?"

"A security system. For a house. A large house. In Manhattan. I want something with all the bells and whistles."

She relayed the information, listened for another second, dropped the receiver back into its cradle, and jerked her thumb toward a door in the rear corner. "Through there. Go ahead. Mr. Rooney'll see you now."

Rooney's office was roughly half the size of the reception area. The floor was covered with pale laminate and the walls were plain white. There was a gray metal desk facing away from a barred window. Two visitor's chairs with bent chrome frames and blue canvas seats. And four olive green file cabinets along the far wall, with a bunch of trophies lined up on top. Half were for bowling. Half, for shooting.

Rooney hauled himself out of his black mesh executive chair, which had a frame like a chrome exoskeleton, leaned forward, and held out his hand. He was just shy of six feet tall, with white hair cropped close to his skull; a loose, fleshy face; black suit pants; and a white shirt with the sleeves rolled halfway up his meaty forearms. He had no wedding ring, and I could tell without looking at the certificates on the wall that he'd been a cop.

"You were a detective, Mr. Rooney?" I softened my voice and added some of the mid-Atlantic overtones that were common to most of the expats I'd ever met. "I'm ex-army, myself. Paul McGinn."

We shook hands, he gestured for me to sit, and then sank back down into his own chair.

"McGinn, with two n's?" Rooney took a pad of forms from his desk drawer and sat with his pen poised.

"That's right." I nodded. It was really just a superstition to always assume another Irish surname, but it had worked for a long time so I wasn't about to change.

"Brian Rooney." He continued to scribble on his pad. "Twenty years on the job. Now at your service. How can I help?"

"That's an easy question to answer, I hope. I need a security system for my house, and I heard you guys are good."

"Thank you." Rooney nodded. "You've got to love word of mouth. It's the best marketing there is. I'm happy that people are talking about us, but do you know the real difference with Rooney Security? We're not just talk. We back our words with actions. Our motto is simple: Protected. Because if you buy a system from us, that's what you'll be."

"Straightforward. To the point. I like that in a motto."

"I do, too. I came up with it myself. Now, why not tell me a little about your situation, and make sure not to skip any problems or concerns that you may have. I'll take some notes, we'll line up an in-home survey, and I guarantee to come up with a solution that meets your needs. Sound good?"

"Sure, if you think that's the best way to do it. OK. So here's the deal. My father passed away recently and I inherited a house he owned in Hell's Kitchen. I've only just moved in. Now, you may have heard that the neighborhood's all right these days. Let me tell you, that's just not true. Not even close. Twice in the last twelve months, one of my neighbors has been burglarized while he was at work. Another was the victim of a home invasion, last summer. No one was hurt that time, but it doesn't pay to take chances. I want something done fast to keep me and my property safe. Hopefully I'm not at too much risk right now because I'm still getting set up—I don't even have much furniture yet—but this security question is a weight on my mind. I'll feel better when I've taken some action."

"First of all, let me say I'm very sorry for your loss." Rooney paused and looked down at his desktop for a moment. "I'm also sorry to hear about your neighbors' terrible experiences, but I'm sure we can make certain you can avoid anything like that happening to you. I totally get where you're coming from with this. For a first impression, I'm going to say I think you need a fully monitored, multimode system with fixed and mobile emergency triggers. I can tailor it to your exact requirements once I've been out and seen your property. Sound good?"

"I guess. As long as we can move quickly. A home visit is the next step?"

"That's right." Rooney nodded.

"OK. Sounds like a plan. How about tomorrow, 10:00 A.M.?"

"Hmm. Tomorrow's Saturday. This kind of work we usually do on weekdays. I could switch a couple of things around and do Monday? I could be there by 8:00 A.M. Or earlier? Or in the evening, if that fits better around your work schedule."

"No." I shook my head. "I want to get the wheels in motion. No delays. The home visit needs to be tomorrow."

"OK." Rooney held his hands up. "Tomorrow it is—10:00 A.M. I'll be there."

"Good. I'll write down the address. The place is easy to find, but parking can be brutal."

"Thanks. I'll manage. Any other questions while you're here?"

"Just one. How many times has your office been broken into, here?"

Rooney looked like I'd thrown ice water in his face. "That's kind of personal, Mr. McGinn."

"Not really. How can I trust you to stop burglars getting into my house if you can't keep them out of your own office?"

Rooney paused. "OK. That's fair. I'm happy to say we've never had a break-in here."

"That's good. Do you use the same kind of systems that you sell?"

"Basically." Rooney nodded. "I have confidence in my products, if that's what you mean. We use a commercial version, obviously. Less aesthetically pleasing, but just as effective."

"The same on the inside as the residential ones?"

"The technology's the same. I'm in the trade, so I buy at cost, and I've added a few extra features."

"I like extra features. I may need a few of them myself. What did you add?"

"Nothing crazy. Just a few prudent enhancements. Pressure pads, for example."

"Hence the carpet in the waiting area. I'm not sure I'd want that. My house still has its original hardwood. What else do you have?"

"Pressure pads aren't essential. Another option you could consider isn't a physical thing at all. It's a software patch. It adds very little cost, and what it does is, it gives you a six-digit PIN. That's instead of the standard four digits. It's actually genius. In theory it adds millions more permutations. But in practice it makes your PIN unbreakable. If an intruder doesn't know to try six digits, he never will."

"Now, that idea I love. I'll definitely want six digits, too. It wouldn't have crossed my mind. I mean, I didn't even see your keypad."

"Keypads should always be concealed. That's standard practice."

I paused, as if I was thinking. "I know. Behind the Constable!"

"What?" Rooney's eyes narrowed and his lips tightened a fraction.

"The painting. I thought you must have an ironic decorator—a picture of the English countryside, in Queens. Using it to hide the keypad is much better."

Rooney didn't respond.

"I might do the same when mine's installed. I'll have to think about which painting to choose. Unless you have any advice?"

"It has no bearing on the system. It's entirely up to the homeowner to pick something out. Now, is there anything else I can help you with before you go?"

"No, thanks." I smiled at him. "I've got everything I came for."

Chapter Eleven

Ro had moved offices since the last time we met. She was in the same building. She had a suite with the same footprint. Only it was seven floors higher. I suspected she'd made the change because she liked to walk up the stairs and wanted more of them. But I was reluctant to ask in case I was right. It was the kind of thing my father would have done, and I didn't want the images of the two of them merging in my mind. That's the kind of thing nightmares are made of.

An assistant showed me in and I saw right away that Ro had streamlined her furniture in the course of her move. That was quite a feat, as she had only two items to start with. A treadmill and a standing desk. Now she just had a treadmill desk. It was over by the window, where she was plodding resolutely away, wearing a sky blue velour tracksuit and keeping one eye on a FaceTime video chat with a roomful of Asian women and the other on her view over Bryant Park. The people below looked even tinier than they had from her old office, but they were still tinged with blue by the coating on the glass. When Ro saw me she clicked off her call, waved a greeting, ran her fingers through her spiky white hair, and increased her pace.

"You couldn't even get a chair?" I stood in the center of the room and stretched my arms out wide. "Not even one? You could keep it in the closet and bring it out for special guests. This place is worse than my house."

"Nope." Ro grabbed a water bottle from a holder at the side of the desk and took a swig. "Get a chair, people sit. They sit, they get comfy. They get comfy, they stay longer. Things that should take five minutes end up lasting an hour. You never get anything done that way."

"At least let me perch on the windowsill." I walked over to an empty bay and balanced on the edge. The one nearer her desk was taken up with a neat line of shoes, a purse, and a suit carrier. Ro always did like to be prepared.

"What's up with your house, anyway?" Ro reached over to put the bottle back in its place. "Marie Kondo been over?"

I shook my head. "Turns out I have a problem with furniture. I've never bought any before. It's more complicated than I thought."

"What about your other house? In Westchester. Take some from it."

"I could, I guess." I glanced out of the window.

"But Mrs. Vincent's there. It would feel wrong to strip the house around her."

"How long were you in Eastern Europe, Paul? Did you catch socialism while you were over there? Should I get you tested?" She winked. "Seriously, the stuff is yours. Use it if you want to. I'm not saying you should empty the place, but look at it this way: Re-using is good for the environment. It's certainly better than making a whole bunch of new chairs and beds and couches."

"Maybe. I'll think about it. But I'm not here to talk about home makeovers. I need some information."

Ro reduced speed, reached down for a Peninsula Spa towel from the floor, wiped her face, and nodded. "Now we're talking. What do you need to know?"

"I need you to explain a stock market thing. Shorting."

"Short-selling?" Ro sucked in a breath. "I can easily bring you up to speed. But it's a dangerous game to play. You should think twice. What shares do you have in mind?"

"None. I've never bought or sold a share in my life, and that's not about to change. This is just for research. I need to know what this thing is, how it works, and why people do it."

"OK. Well, to understand short-selling, you need to take a step back and start with regular investing. That's where you buy shares and hope that their value increases so that if you sell them again, you make a profit."

"Buy low, sell high. Everyone knows that. Even me."

"Good. Because shorting works the opposite way around. You sell high, and *then* you buy low."

"That makes no sense. How can you sell before you buy?"

"It does make sense if you start out by borrowing the shares instead of owning them."

"You borrow them?"

"Right. What happens is that you borrow a certain number. You sell them at what you hope is a high price. Then later you buy the same number of shares at what you hope will be a lower price, and return them to the owner. If the price did fall, you keep the difference and that's your profit."

"I don't understand."

"Try thinking it through with numbers. Imagine Slimeball Inc.'s shares are selling for a hundred dollars each, and you think they're overpriced. You might have done some analysis. It might be a gut feel. Maybe you read the tea leaves. But whatever the reason, you borrow a thousand of them. You sell them immediately, and make $100,000. A week later the price falls to seventy-five dollars. So you buy a thousand, which costs you $75,000. You return the shares, and pocket $25,000."

"That's fine. I get the math. But why would someone lend out their shares in the first place? Especially to a person who just wants to sell them? Doesn't selling drive down the price? Wouldn't that hurt the owner's investment? The whole thing sounds like financial suicide. And if selling's such a good idea, why not just sell the shares yourself? Why let someone else benefit?"

"Wow, slow down, Paul! There are lots of things to pick apart here. First of all, if you want to borrow shares so you can short them, you don't go directly to the shareholder and ask them. You go to a broker. You'll have to pay a loan fee, so straightaway there's an incentive for the broker to facilitate a deal. Next up, the shareholder might not even know his shares are being loaned to someone else. And even if he finds out, he might have no choice in the matter."

"I'm sorry, Ro, but this is getting more ridiculous by the minute. You're saying I could buy shares only for my broker to lend them out behind my back?"

"He wouldn't be going behind your back, exactly. It would depend on the type of brokerage account you have. The ones with the lowest fees generally give the brokers the right to do things like that. It's in the small print. No one's breaking any rules."

"It still seems underhanded."

"If you say so. But that's not the only scenario. Here's one you might like better. Say an investor thinks some shares he owns are likely to take a short-term hit, but has faith they'll eventually bounce back. In the long run, he'd gain by holding on to them. Plus he'd be picking up whatever dividends the company might pay in the interim. So, he allows them to be loaned out. He takes a fee. Maybe he charges interest. Then he gets the shares back in due course, and he cashes in when their price rises again. It's a way for him to have his cake and eat it. And avoid undue risk."

"What do you mean, risk?"

"A degree of risk always comes with an investment. Say you buy shares in the regular way, hoping they'll rise. What if you're wrong? Worst-case scenario, the company goes broke and your shares become worthless. Your whole stake is wiped out. You take a one hundred percent loss. That's bad. But it can't get any worse. You know going into the deal the extent of the risk you're taking. If you're smart, you don't invest any money you can't afford to lose. But with shorting, the danger is much, much greater. You sell a bunch of shares you don't own, so you're legally obliged to replace them within a certain timescale. You bet the price goes down. Now, if you're wrong, and it actually goes up, it'll cost you more than you made to buy the shares back. And here's the sting. The price might double. It might triple. There's no limit to how high it could rise. Your losses are potentially infinite. The promised land of quick profit can easily turn out to be the graveyard of bankruptcy. Which is why it's not a game for amateurs. It's best left to people with the experience to spot the warning signs, and pockets deep enough to take the odd hit."

"So you mean there's a chance people might lose some money? Maybe have to sell a yacht? I guess I have a different concept of risk."

"You seem very prickly about all this, Paul. What's eating you?"

I shrugged. "I don't know. This whole thing just

rubs me wrong. Look, I've got nothing against people getting rich. My father made boatloads of money. But he brought me up to believe you have to earn it. You have to make something useful. Provide a worthwhile service of some kind. What you're describing sounds fake. Like alchemy. Dishonest, even. No offense."

"None taken. I don't necessarily disagree. That's why shorting's illegal in some countries. It's controlled here from time to time, when the economy's struggling. I'm just describing the game. I don't make the rules. And don't forget, these transactions keep people in jobs. Generate taxes. Help pay for roads and schools. And soldiers."

"That's fair. But here's another question. Can shorting be used as a weapon? Could you use it to attack a company?"

"Sure." Ro sipped some more water. "It happens. There are cases where a high-profile investor doesn't like a CEO, for example, so he hits the share price to drive the guy out. Or he may think the dividends they're paying are too small, and shorts the stock to punish them."

"One investor could do this?"

"It depends on the size of the company. How big of a stake the investor has, or can borrow. How much clout he has in the industry. And he could also add some unsavory tactics into the mix."

"Unsavory, how?"

"Well, say you want to make sure a certain share price falls, and you get the ball rolling by selling your stake. Then you help build momentum by having a quiet word in the right ears. Not necessarily a truthful word, if you know what I mean. It's not legal. But it happens."

I stood up. "This could be it. How we nail him. Thank you, Ro. You're an angel."

"Wait a minute." Ro stopped moving. "Who are we nailing now?"

"Some asshole. Apparently he shorted some stock, and that ruined a guy I met. I quite like the guy, but now he's in a heap of trouble. Evidently some retaliatory fire-starting occurred, which has taken all the attention away from what the asshole did in the first place."

"Does this asshole have a name?"

"Jimmy Klinsman, I've been told."

"Oh. Well, that's interesting."

"Do you know him?"

"Not personally. Apparently he's known as Jimmy the Jester. That's partly due to the unpredictable trades he has a habit of making. And also because people who've met him say they feel like he's laughing at them, even when he's not."

"Like I said, he's an asshole."

"He most likely is. But have you considered that maybe he didn't do anything wrong? Maybe he had better instincts, and was right to bet that the price would go down?"

"No." I shook my head. "The price shouldn't have gone down. Something made that happen. I thought it was him, dumping shares. Now I'm wondering if he helped his cause by spreading a few lies."

"How can you be so sure about the price, Paul?

Have you been going to business school on the sly?"

"As if. No. But I know that the company whose shares Klinsman shorted makes sensitive equipment for telecom networks. It was about to announce that the government had disqualified its only rival—a big Chinese corporation—from bidding for a bunch of huge contracts. Its ship was coming in, big."

"And your friend—the guy who got ruined—he knew about this impending announcement? And he bought shares based on commercially confidential information?"

"He's not a friend. Just a guy I met."

"Whatever your degree of bromance, you know what this means? Your guy definitely broke the law. We don't know if Klinsman did or not."

"We don't know. But I'm going to find out."

"Why do you care?"

I shrugged. "Look. Here's a guy trying to scrape two bucks together to keep his own business afloat. He wound up losing his house because of something Klinsman did. And to what end? So that the guy could build an even bigger heap of cash. Buy more expensive wine that he probably won't ever even drink."

"None of that's illegal."

"Maybe not. But it seems like there's wrong on both sides. It's not fair that only one guy's getting punished."

"I can see that. I think you're on a hiding to nothing, though. But still, let me know how you get on."

"Will do. Thanks for your help, as always. And when I come back, I'm bringing a chair. I'm serious."

Ro stepped back from her desk. "I have an idea. You don't like the way I've set up my office. So how's this? I'll pull my old treadmill out of storage. Put it next to the new one. And next time, you can keep pace with me. I'll talk as long as you walk. Then visiting me will be good for your body as well as your mind."

"No, thanks." I shook my head. "I'm not a fan of treadmills. I knew a guy who had a nasty accident on one once."

"An accident? On a treadmill? Really?"

"Well, not really. But we sure made it look that way."

Chapter Twelve

When I was on leave from the army one time years ago, and making a rare visit to my father's—which I generally tried to avoid because he was always nagging me to join him in his business—I heard that a friend from high school had been arrested for ripping off a bunch of banks. This was back in the early days of the Internet and online accounts, and he'd found a back-door way to siphon a few odd cents from a huge number of customers, which taken together netted him a lot of cash. He'd got caught by the FBI in a sting operation and was out on bail, awaiting trial. His father was rich and influential, so he got a buddy to write an op-ed piece in *The New York Times*. He tried to position what had happened as a victimless crime. Each customer's loss was tiny, and the banks were all insured, anyway. So if no one had really lost anything, there was no harm and no foul. The argument didn't work, of course, and the book got thrown at my friend, but the concept fascinated me. I've thought about it a lot over the years. And now if Atkinson was right that there was no link between Klinsman and the Chinese, and Ro was correct that short-selling wasn't illegal, it seemed that the position had been flipped. Len Hendrie was a crimeless victim.

The same thought kept rattling around my head as I made the long trek through the tunnels in the Bryant Park subway stop, wedged myself into a corner seat on a grubby D train, then set off walking south on Lafayette. I couldn't shake the rage I was feeling toward Klinsman. He was Hendrie's buddy. Hendrie had told him about the telecom opportunity. He could have invested in the normal way. He could have passed altogether. But he chose another path, knowing it would hurt his friend. Maybe even destroy him. I was still trying to figure out how a guy could live with himself after doing a thing like that when I reached the front of the courthouse. Then I noticed a woman heading down the steps, talking on her phone. She moved with the controlled elegance of a dancer or an athlete. She had dark blond hair, which I knew was her natural color. It was shoulder length, but she was wearing it tied back, and her black Burberry raincoat wasn't fastened over her navy suit. She had on a white blouse. Navy pumps. And a burgundy purse slung over her shoulder with a matching leather briefcase.

I didn't have to guess her age. I knew it to the minute. There was no need to estimate her height. I knew it to a sixteenth of an inch. I knew the sound of her voice. What made her laugh. What made her mad. Or what had done so twenty years ago, when I thought we'd spend our lives together. Before I surprised her with my decision to join the army. After which she never spoke to me again.

Her name was Marian Sinclair. Our houses were close together, growing up, and throughout our teenage years we were inseparable. I knew she was the one for me. I never had eyes for anyone else. Her heart was set on law school, and she wanted me to go to the same one. I've spent countless hours in some of the nastiest places in the world wondering what had happened to her. Whether she followed through on her dream to become a lawyer. Now, unless she was in some kind of trouble, I guess I had my answer.

I've spent even more hours imagining a time when we could reconnect. When we could rekindle what we lost. What I destroyed, with my impulsive decision to spite my father. I've dreamed of her countless times, from thousands of miles away. Now she was within ten feet of me. My first impulse was to leap up the steps and sweep her off her feet. My second was to throw myself *at* her feet and beg forgiveness. Anything for the chance to pick up where we'd left off.

It was force of habit alone that kept me moving. Marian clearly had business at the courthouse. I had to protect my cover at all costs. That was more than instinct. It was part of my DNA now. It meant I had to make sure she didn't see me going anywhere near the employees' entrance, so I swung to my right, crossed Centre Street, and looped around behind a group of Dutch tourists that was loitering in front of the *Triumph of the Human Spirit* statue. I peered out between the tallest pair. Marian was stationary, one step lower than she'd been when I first spotted her, with her phone low down by her side. She was looking in the direction I'd gone. She stayed stock-still for a moment, like she was frozen in time. Then she brought her phone back up to her ear, continued down the steps, turned to her right, and was carried away from me by the tide of pedestrians.

The smart move would have been to abort my visit to the courthouse that day. The move I wanted to make was to chase after Marian. But when the tourists moved off—with pizza apparently next on their itinerary—I ignored both impulses. I crossed back over Centre Street and carried on around to the back of the building. It wasn't just that I had cleaning to do. There was information that I needed, and the courthouse was the only place I could get it.

Chapter Thirteen

We figured it was unlikely that anyone would actually be watching the house, but old habits die hard. Robson filled his travel mug with tea, grabbed his backpack, and was out of the door before 0800 the next morning. That was two full hours before my appointment with Rooney for the alarm system quote.

Rooney arrived at 0959, which he probably considered punctual. I considered it fourteen minutes late, but I wasn't mad. I was adapting. Rooney had brought a panel van, not the Ford that Robson had seen him with in Rye on Thursday night. It was navy blue, spotlessly clean, and shiny, and there was a gold shield–style logo painted on the side. I watched from the living room window as it pulled up directly outside and Rooney jumped down from the passenger side. He was holding a clipboard, and he waited for a guy I'd not seen before to join him from the driver's side before climbing the steps to the front door and ringing the bell.

"Good morning, gentlemen." I opened the door wide. "Thanks for coming."

"Good to see you again, Mr. McGinn." Rooney shook my hand. "I've brought an expert with me. Mike Parrie. Old houses like this one are more complex, structurally, and I like to get everything right the first time. No surprises down the road, that way."

"Sounds good to me. I don't like surprises. Not when I'm on the wrong end of them, anyway." I smiled at the new guy. "Come on in. You might want to find a better place to park, though."

"Don't worry. We'll only be an hour." Rooney winked at me. "Twenty years on the job buys a lot of slack. And the twenty-five percent blue discount I offer doesn't hurt, either. No one wants to blow that."

"How about a green discount?"

"Don't worry." Rooney mimed a salute. "I didn't forget you served. I'll look after you when it comes time for the price. I look after all my clients. You saw my office. No frills, no waste, that's my motto."

I stood aside and the others slipped off their shoes and filed past. Rooney paused midway along the hall and patted the wall, then stamped his foot.

"Nice house. Solid." He smiled appreciatively. "I used to have a license in Connecticut. No need now—I get more than enough work in New York—but I had this one client. Built himself a brand-new house. Spent a fortune on it. Wanted an alarm, and a safe. I put in the alarm for him—top of the line. Gave the safe contract to someone else. And guess what happened? The house was built for such shit, two weeks later a douche drove straight through the wall in an old Grand Cherokee. Cleaned the place out. Even took the safe."

"I don't think that's likely to happen here."

"Guess not." Rooney turned to move. "Unless they've got a tank."

Rooney's expert, Parrie, led the way. He was thorough. He went through every room, every corridor, every closet, and made detailed notes in a black moleskine with dotted pages to make it easier to sketch out diagrams. He seemed to pay the most attention to entry points, actual or potential, such as doors and windows. I also saw him plotting backup locations that could pick up anyone who'd managed to breach the perimeter. His focus seemed to be on efficiency, as he was always looking for single points that could reinforce multiple vulnerable areas. He also scanned the walls with a handheld device. It had a gauge in the center surrounded by half a dozen colored lights, and it emitted a variety of angry-sounding tones as he moved it across the surface. In some areas he made three or four passes, then scribbled furiously in his book. Rooney didn't make a single mark on the sheet of paper clipped to his board, but I guess carrying it around made him feel managerial.

"That's a clever machine." Rooney noticed me watching his guy. "Multipurpose. Gives us clues about what's hidden in the walls. Structural beams in unexpected places. Water pipes where they shouldn't be. Knob-and-tube cabling, obsolete stuff like that. Knowing in advance helps keep the installation problem-free for us, which keeps the price down for you."

Parrie finished his inspection in the basement with the electrical panel. He closed it up, scratched his temple with his pen, and turned to look at me. "Have you had any work done recently? Rewiring? TV distribution? CAT 5 cabling for a bunch of computers?"

"No." I shook my head. "I only recently inherited the place. I just moved in. I've done nothing to it. Why?"

"I was getting weird readings in some of the rooms. It was like there were all kinds of extra circuits running through the walls. The spacing was odd, too. Not like anything you'd expect. And not connected back to the panel, either."

"Will that be a problem?"

"It shouldn't be. It's just odd. I thought if you'd had work done, maybe you used a European contractor? They have different ways of cabling things there. Also, you're ex-army, right? I've seen some real botch jobs on some of the bases I've worked on. Things that wouldn't be allowed near a civilian installation. I wondered if you'd done any modifications yourself."

"I've never even picked up a screwdriver." That wasn't entirely true. I had temporarily hooked up some cameras and a microphone in the course of helping a corrupt developer find new accommodations at the Otisville Correctional Facility. But those devices were wireless, and I'd removed them before Robson and I moved in.

"OK, then." Parrie closed his notebook and looped the elastic strap around its front cover. "It's probably just something eccentric done back when the house was built. You don't usually see places this original. But nothing looked like it should get in the way. There are no red flags here, for me."

"Good news. Thanks, Mike." Rooney slapped Parrie on the shoulder. "So here's what we'll do. First thing Monday, Mike and I will confirm the technical specs and document our recommendations for the core system and the positioning of the sensors and keypads. I'll also put together three appendices. Optional extras. Monitoring packages—which will be essential based on the value of your home and what you told me about the recent occurrences in the neighborhood. And finally, maintenance support options. If I send them all on email, does that sound good?"

"Sure." I nodded. "That's better than waiting for snail mail. Like I say, I want to move fast."

"Good. In that case, there's two more things you need to know. First, I won't be the cheapest. I'm telling you now, there are half a dozen guys out there who'll quote you way less. But there's a reason for that. Those guys cut corners. They use low-quality components. Their installation guys suck. They have no experience. No local maintenance techs. And their monitoring is all done in India, or someplace like that. Their options might seem attractive when you're looking at the numbers. But trust me, it'll be a different story if you come home and find the house has been ransacked, or you're lying in bed and hear a window getting smashed or a door kicked down, and you realize no one is coming to help. Do you follow me?"

"I get the picture."

"Good. Now, second thing, I don't believe in quoting an inflated price so I can drop it later during a bunch of bogus back-and-forth. The number I give you will be the lowest I can make it, right out of the traps. I just think that's a more honest way to do business."

"I'm with you on that. I'm not a fan of negotiating, myself. In fact, in some situations, I refuse to do it at all."

"So we're on the same page." Rooney looked me in the eye. "If you like what you see on my email, do you think we can do business?"

"Let's just say, I'm pretty sure this won't be the last you hear from me."

We shook hands, then the guys retrieved their shoes and headed out to their van, which was, as Rooney had predicted, ticket free. As soon as they were rolling I checked my phone. There was a text from Robson that had arrived twenty-five minutes before—

10-18.

It was our old army code for *assignment completed*. I smiled and replied with—

10-17.

That meant *return to headquarters*. Then a moment later another thought struck me and I texted Robson again, though there wasn't a convenient code for this message—

Please stop at the liquor store and buy a bottle of wine. Anything red.

I figured I'd have some time on my hands that afternoon because Robson would have work to do. I might as well put it to good use.

Chapter Fourteen

I HEARD ROBSON COMING IN THROUGH THE kitchen door thirty minutes later. He must already have been in the neighborhood when he received my text. He was carrying his backpack in one hand and, bless him, a carryout cup of strong black coffee in the other.

"We need to get a machine." Robson handed me the drink. "Save me always having to fetch coffee for you. Stop you hogging my tea."

"One day we will." The truth is, I'd tried. I'd been to two different stores. But the choice of brands and systems was just too bewildering.

"I got this." Robson pulled a bottle of wine out of his backpack. It was a Yellow Tail merlot. "What are we celebrating?"

"Nothing." I set the bottle down on the countertop. "Yet. I'll buy champagne when we do. I have something else in mind for this. Did you get everything else we need?"

"Piece of cake." Robson took a featureless black box about the size of a paperback book out of his bag and held it up. "Cloned both computers, and was in and out within ten minutes. Those pressure pads were for amateurs. It was useful knowing about the long PIN, though."

"Shall we see what we've got?"

"Sure." Robson put the box on the table, then hustled upstairs. I took the wine bottle, put it in the sink, and ran enough water to cover its label. It had just reached a satisfactory level when Robson returned with his laptop. He sat, fired up the computer, connected the black box, and rattled a few keys.

"OK," he said. "We're in business. Want to start with Rooney's?"

"Sounds good." I sat and leaned across so that I could see the screen. "Check for anything about JD."

Robson called up a search utility and let it run for a few seconds.

"No hits." He pointed to a box that had opened in the center of the screen. "But look at this. It's an exception report. There were three files it couldn't scan. They're all big. Password protected. I bet they're encrypted, too. Forget the plain sight stuff. I'll start with them."

"Are you OK breaking into them? Harry's in town, remember. He helped crack the security on that Azerbaijani data. It's kind of his thing. I could reach out to him."

"Harry's creepy. Let me see how it goes. If I can't do it in a couple of hours, then maybe we'll call him. Meanwhile, I'm taking this upstairs. I need to focus."

"Stay down here, if you want." I crossed to the sink. "I just need two minutes to deal with the wine, then I'm heading out for a while. Let me know if anything breaks."

I took the bottle out of the sink and tested its label. The edge gave way easily enough, so I continued to pull and managed to peel the whole thing off in one neat piece. I stripped off the plastic collar. Took a hunk of wire wool from under the sink and scrubbed the glass to take the shine off its surface, paying a little extra attention to the base and neck. Then I ran down to the basement and poked around until I found a nail. I brought it back up. Scratched *Th J* in my best flowing script into the side of the bottle, an inch from the bottom. I took a cup. Filled it with tea from Robson's pitcher in the fridge. Dipped the bottle into it, upside down, so that the cork absorbed some of the liquid and lost its pale new sheen. I poured the last of the coffee Robson had brought me over the bottle itself and rubbed in the dregs so that the scratches and scuffs didn't look so recently made. Then I set it back down to dry and fetched an aluminum Halliburton attaché case that was left over from a sting we'd recently pulled on a particularly obnoxious financier. I put the bottle inside. Left the house. Zigzagged northeast, crossing 11th and 10th Streets. And finally turned north on 9th and followed it the rest of the way up to 57th Street.

Over the years, humint—human intelligence—has been in fashion in military circles. It's fallen out of fashion. It's come back in. Over and over the cycle has repeated itself. But for me, there's never been a debate. I don't care how cheap online resources can be. It doesn't matter how good at number-crunching computers are. Some things just need to be seen through human eyes. Preferably your own, or someone's you trust. Other things need to be heard by human ears. Filtered through a brain, not a microprocessor. Tested by instincts, not spread-sheets. Jimmy Klinsman was a case in point. I needed to get a proper feel for the guy. See him from all sides, like the punk from our video exercise. Currently, based on the information I'd been given, I was badly disposed to him. I could imagine all kinds of unfortunate things happening. But if it turned out he'd needed the money he made by shorting those shares to fund a private orphanage, or to sponsor clean water for some underprivileged community, or to shelter refugees, or to save an endangered species, maybe my mind could be changed. Which is why my next step needed to be to see inside his home. He had several of them. And the one nearest to Hell's Kitchen, according to the court files, was at 157 57th Street—or One57, as the marketing material billed it. The building was one of the first "super high-rises" on so-called Billionaires' Row. I heard that a single unit had sold for north of $100m. That didn't endear the place to me. But due to its proximity it did make sense to start there.

The first order of business was to determine if Klinsman was in.

I knew I was getting close to the building as I headed east on 57th and saw a cluster of S-Class Mercedes and Suburbans lined up at the curb. They were all black. All shiny. All had extra-dark privacy glass. Together they looked menacing, like a pack of predators. I approached on the south side of the street and glanced up at the building. I'd heard it was supposed to look like a waterfall, though I'd never understood why anyone would think that was appropriate in the center of Manhattan. To me the curving top, swooping through ninety degrees from vertical to horizontal, was more reminiscent of an expressionless robot from a '50s sci-fi movie.

As I drew closer, despite the height, I had to admit that the undulating stripes of silver and various shades of blue did seem to cascade down rather than soar up. The silver bands were the most prominent, plummeting down to the base of the second floor, then jutting out parallel to the sidewalk to form canopies like frozen waves. The entrance to the building's hotel was on the right, and was five sections wide. The residences' entrance, flanked by a jewelry store and a gallery with a single abstract exhibit, had three. Its pair of topiaried trees—all spindly trunks and branches with leaves shaped into pom-poms like floral versions of show poodles—was also smaller than the hotel's. I guess the designer had been aiming for an air of discretion. I thought it just looked cheap. The residences did have one feature the hotel lacked, though—a pair of security guards in gray suits and ties with white curly wires running ostentatiously from their jacket pockets to their ears.

I paced myself so that I'd remain alongside a tourist bus and then cut across the street in line with one of the Suburbans. I stayed in its shelter, helped by the darkness of its glass, and kept low until I reached the driver's door. Then I stood up straight, strode around the hood, and marched directly toward the entrance to the residences. The key in that type of situation is confidence. To project an air of absolute certainty that you're going to walk straight in, as if the possibility of being stopped didn't exist. Carrying a six-hundred-dollar briefcase into a place like that helped, too. Although if I'd been in the guards' shoes, I'd have been wondering what kind of weapon was hidden in it.

My bluff worked. The first guard stepped to the side while the second opened the door for me and gestured toward the doorman's station. It was set all the way back on the right-hand side of the lobby. The entire thing was constructed out of black marble with bold white veins—the counter, the walls, and a lowered ceiling. The lighting was subdued and the doorman himself was dressed all in black, giving a disconcerting impression of a disembodied head hovering in a box. The only other thing to catch the eye was a porcelain vase at the far end of the counter, holding a single white lily.

I paused when I drew level with the guy. "I'm here to see Mr. Klinsman. I have a delivery for him. Something special." I nodded to the doors at the side of the gold pipes. "Will you let him know I'm on my way up?"

"Hold it." The doorman reached under the counter. Stretching for a panic button? A gun? "You must have the wrong building. There's no Mr. Klinsman living here."

"Sure there is." I smiled. "He's in suite 8001, on the eightieth floor. I've been before. Half a dozen times. You don't recognize me?"

"If you've been here before, you'll know our residents take their privacy very seriously." The guy was unbearably smug. "You'll know you can't go up unless your name's on the list of pre-authorized visitors." He took a piece of paper from a shelf beneath the counter and pretended to look at it. "Mr. Klinsman hasn't listed anyone for today."

"I might not be on your list, but I'm definitely authorized. Mr. Klinsman told me what he wants. He gave *me* a list. He said I was to come by the second I found anything on it. Which is what I'm doing. Only, I haven't found *anything*. I've found his top entry. I'm giving him first shot, due to the prior business we've done together. You know about his collection, right? It's legendary. Only about four bottles short of epic. Which is why he's so desperate for what I've got in this case. Trust me, if he doesn't snatch it out of my hand, someone else will. There's no way I can keep this baby under wraps. And if Mr. Klinsman misses out . . ."

The doorman shuffled on the spot and ran his fingers through his hair, but he didn't speak.

"OK." I nodded resignedly. "I'll show you. But

don't tell anyone you've seen this." I laid the case on the counter and worked its combination. Then I took out the bottle and set it down like it might break if anyone breathed on it too hard. "Here. Look at this. Do you know what it is?"

"A bottle of wine?"

I rolled my eyes and snorted. "No. Not *a* bottle. *The* bottle." I lowered my voice. "The last remaining bottle of Chateau Margaux 1787 in the world."

The doorman looked blank.

"This wine? Think of it as the holy grail, only in liquid form. Only rarer than that. Do you know where it came from?"

"France?"

"Well, obviously. But where, specifically, in France? And how did it come to the United States?"

"I'm going to guess, a vineyard? And a ship?"

I shook my head and looked away for a moment. "It came from Thomas Jefferson's personal cellar. Look." I pointed to the initials I'd scratched into the glass. "Jefferson's personal mark. His handwriting. Which means that not only is the wine inside the bottle unbelievably rare, so's the bottle. It was touched by Jefferson himself."

The doorman shrugged.

"You know who Thomas Jefferson was, right? Third president? Founding Father?"

"Of course I do."

"Good. But did you know as well as those things, he was once US ambassador to France? And while he was in Paris, he built up the most amazing collection of wine. He had exceptional taste. But because this was so long ago, it was thought that there was none of this particular kind left. Do you know who drank the last bottle?"

The doorman shook his head.

"No one drank it. The guy who owned it wanted to. He was going to. The wine was so special and so rare that the guy arranged for a private dinner at the Four Seasons. The bottle was the star of the evening. It was given pride of place at the center of the table. The sommelier opened it, so it could breathe. But before it could be poured, a waiter knocked it over. It broke. The wine gushed out all over the floor. It was an utter disaster. The guy sued the restaurant. They had to claim it on their insurance. And do you know how much was paid out in the end?"

The doorman shook his head again.

"The guy sued for $500,000. He got $225,000. That's what the insurance company said that bottle was worth then. This bottle's worth way more now. There's inflation to take into account. And the rarity factor. It's literally a once-in-a-lifetime ownership opportunity. Buyers will be lining up for it as soon as they know it exists. Do you think Mr. Klinsman would be happy to lose out?"

"I'm sure he wouldn't." The doorman crossed his arms. "But I still can't let you go up, if you're not on the list."

"OK." I held up my hands. "Rules. I get it. But I'm trying to do the right thing by a very important client, here. How about you call him? Explain the situation. Be sure to say, 'Chateaux Margaux. 1787.' The date's important. See what he wants to do."

"I can't do that, either." The doorman shook his head. "It's against the rules as well."

"Again with the rules!" I took a deep breath. "Look. These are exceptional circumstances." I pointed to the initials again. "Thomas Jefferson. The guy who deprived the last owner of one of these bottles from enjoying the wine—the waiter—got fired. He never worked in New York again. What do you think would happen to you if you deprive Mr. Klinsman? I'm telling you, that's a story that won't end well. Unless you're harboring a secret desire to work on the door at the only brick structure in Ulaanbaatar."

"All right. I'll call. What's your name?"

"McGarry. Paul McGarry."

The doorman took a slim cordless handset from its cradle under the counter. He called up a number from its memory. Hit Dial. Listened for a few moments. Then hung up, looked at me, and shook his head. "You're not going to believe this. It went straight to voicemail. Mr. Klinsman's message says he's in England on business until next week."

"Wait a minute. Was that his regular number you called? His work cell?"

"I guess."

"Well, how does that help me?" I slapped my forehead with my palm. "I could have called that one myself. Try his other number."

"What other number?"

"His unlisted number. Oh, come on." I closed my eyes and breathed out slowly. "We both know that guys like Mr. Klinsman always have a separate personal phone. In case there's anything discreet or under the radar he needs to know about. Say, his mother shows up and he has an apartment full of hookers. Or his dealer swings by with a fresh batch of fishscale. I know you have it. He knows you have it. What happens if this deal slips through his fingers and you didn't even try to call?"

The doorman sighed, snatched the handset back up, and dialed a number manually. I shifted closer to him. For a moment I couldn't hear anything. Then I picked up the sound of a double ring. The phone was connected to a network in a place with a different tone. A place like the UK. The call rang eight more times, then tripped through to its mailbox. "This is the Jester. Leave a message, and I probably won't get back you." The doorman hung up.

I put the bottle back in the case, closed it, and spun its locks. "Well, then. Now we know. It's his loss. Thanks for trying."

"Wait, you're going?" The doorman stepped closer to the counter. "Hold up. At least leave the bottle with me."

"Are you joking? I'll have gotten rid of it by the end of the afternoon."

"But Mr. Klinsman?"

I shrugged. "Klinsman snost and lost. Or whatever the international business traveler equivalent is. He can cry me a river."

"He won't be happy."

"Don't tell him, then."

Chapter Fifteen

I READ A STORY ABOUT ONE57 IN A MAGAZINE AT an airport in Dubai shortly after the plans for the building were announced. It was more of a puff piece than a serious article, and one of the claims it made was that the residences on the higher floors and the Park Hyatt hotel lower down would be completely physically separate. I remember thinking that sounded like bullshit. Management wouldn't want an arrangement like that. The maintenance guys wouldn't. And the emergency services would definitely be against it. The only people with an interest in spreading a perception like that were in sales and marketing, as they tried to extract every last dollar from the deep pockets of their privacy-conscious clientele. Back then I'd wondered if that view made me cynical. Now it was time to see if I was right.

I made my way across to Seventh Avenue, walked one block north to 58th Street, then looped around until I found the loading dock for the Park Hyatt. I climbed up onto the concrete slab, found a path through the storage area, and followed the sound of voices. They were coming from behind a door marked *Auxiliary Plant Room.* I knocked and a sudden silence descended. I tried the door. It opened with a piercing shriek from its hinges, and inside the room I saw four stocky guys in overalls playing cards around a table fashioned out of upturned milk crates and a *Store to Let* sign from a commercial real estate agent. There were a dozen carryout cups on the table, with lids. It could have been coffee in them, I thought. Or it could have been something else.

"Excuse me, fellas. Sorry to interrupt your game." I pulled out a business card I'd pinched from Rooney's office and handed it to the nearest of the guys. "I'm here to check the security door between the hotel and the apartments. Someone reported faulty contacts. It's probably nothing, but a thing like that, I've got to check. No one wants an alarm going off in the middle of the night."

The guy I'd given the card to glanced at my aluminum case and nodded. "You need the service elevator. Go right, right again, then all the way to the end of the corridor. You'll see twenty-five buttons set out in a square. Two basements. Twenty-one guest floors. And two that are blank, like spares just filling the space. Hit the one on the right and hold it for ten seconds. Then it'll take you where you need to go. Only, you'll come out in a kind of closet. It'll be locked. You'll need a key to get through to the apartment side, so you'll have to go see Pablo and sign one out. He's our supervisor. But do us a favor? Don't tell him you saw us."

"Thanks for your help. And don't worry. I won't tell a soul. I won't even need to disturb Pablo. I've got a kind of passkey that should do the job just fine."

I once read in a different magazine that a house is a machine for living in. If that's true, then Klinsman's apartment was a machine for flaunting wealth in. I opened the main door—the alarm wasn't armed and the lock took fifteen seconds to pick, which proves it's true that there's nothing more dangerous than thinking you're safe—and stepped into a foyer that must have been thirty feet wide. Its floor and walls were finished in black-and-white marble, like zebra hides that had been petrified and polished. I continued through a squared-off arch into a living room—or great room, as the sales brochure probably called it—which was thirty feet deep by sixty wide. That was the whole width of that part of the building. It was like stepping into a designer furniture store. There were pieces by all the big guns—van der Rohe, Le Corbusier, Breuer, Noguchi—everywhere I looked, all jumbled in with no rational organization or division between living room and dining items. The space itself was completely open except for six massive circular pillars arranged evenly around the perimeter. There weren't any walls—just full-height windows with narrow, delicate frames on all three sides. Central Park was laid out to the north, a deep green canyon carved out through the angular cliff-edged buildings. The Hudson flowed languidly past on the western side, and the East River balanced things up on the right. The room was so high up it was like looking at a model of the city, a sanitized facsimile, not the real thing. It was fascinating to gaze out for a few minutes, but I knew I could never live in a place like that. I didn't see the point. If you want to live in New York, then live *in* New York. Not perched above it. A city should be a thing you participate in, not look down at through a triple layer of self-cleaning glass.

I left the living room, moved back across the foyer, and started down a corridor that took me past a giant kitchen with an attached breakfast room. Next I came to a bedroom, about fifteen feet square, not counting its full bath. My attention was drawn because it was completely dark. I went inside and switched on the light. The windows were covered with blackout blinds, and in place of a bed and a dresser and the normal bedroom things, this room was fitted out with a pair of floor-to-ceiling cabinets along the full length of the north and south walls. Each had glass doors, digital thermometers with displays built into the frames, and racks and racks of wine bottles were lined up inside. Each slot was numbered, and the bottles were lying with their corks facing out so I couldn't see their labels. They wouldn't have meant much to me anyway, but I'd scanned the file at the courthouse and seen the list of the ones that had been destroyed by the fire at Klinsman's mansion. I wondered if I'd recognize any of the same kind here. And I wondered if any of them were worth more than an apartment, like the one I'd pretended to find.

The next door led to another bedroom of the same size, also dark, with an identical setup for storing wine. The next room, which was in the southwest corner, was laid out as a home office. Two whole sides were made of glass, with more stunning, sterile views. There was another giant column set just in from the angle of the windows. A large antique yew desk with a riot of ornate carving took up much of the north wall. An iMac with a giant screen was sitting on top of it, so I took a black box out of my case—the same kind Robson had used at Rooney's office—and hooked it up. While it took care of copying everything on the computer, I searched the desk drawers. They were full of the normal kinds of clutter—pads of paper, pens stolen from hotel bedrooms, a letter opener, loose AA batteries rolling around, chargers for obsolete phones, operating instructions for a first-generation Blackberry—but nothing significant.

The wall above the desk was covered with framed pictures. There was a large one in the center with eighteen small and medium ones clustered around it, giving the impression that someone flung them toward the top corner of the room and they somehow got stuck in motion. The focus of the biggest one was a guy in fake fatigues with the name *Klinsman* taped to his chest, a hunting rifle in his hands, and an elephant at his side. It was lying on the ground with half its skull blown away.

The guy was smiling. He was in most of the other pictures, too. Some with the dead elephant. Others, in a Jeep, or standing in the bush, or near a lake, or by some scenic vista. But regardless of these other shots, my eyes kept getting drawn back to the first image. Regardless of any Chinese government connection, and whatever lay behind the share-shorting deal, Klinsman and I were going to have a conversation before this thing was over.

There were two armchairs by the east wall, angled toward each other. They were covered with tobacco leather, heavily distressed, I'd guess artificially. A campaign chest with polished brass corner protectors and locks sat between them for use as a table. A large shell sat on it, apparently serving as an ashtray based on the way it was stained and the trace of cigar odor that lingered around it. There were framed images on this wall, too. Seven of them. They were all the same size, set out in two rows with four above and three below, and a blank space at the bottom right denying the symmetry. They were all graphs. Their titles were company names. Their vertical axes showed values in millions of dollars. Their horizontal axes, time. In all of them the values had declined, rapidly. Each one had a sticker applied inside the glass, at the top right where there was space above the plot line. They were star-shaped. The first two, starting at the top left, were gold and were embossed with *#1*. The next was a yellowy *#3*. Then a silver #2. The lower row started with another silver #2. Then there were two more gold *#1*s. It was very strange. The opposite of a glory wall. More of an homage to disaster. The financial equivalent of a chauffeur hanging photographs of wrecked limousines. I could see why Klinsman wouldn't want to display them at his office. Why he wanted to display them at all was still a mystery. Maybe they were some kind of masochistic motivation device. Maybe he thought that being confronted by his failures would drive him to do better. Or maybe they were someone else's failures—some bitter rival—and he had them there to gloat over. Either way, it was weird.

I moved on to the drawers in the wooden chest. The bottom two were empty, but in the top one I found a blue folder. There were two items inside it. The printout of a graph, with the same kind of drastic downhill profile as the framed ones but with dates from only a few weeks ago. And a star, embossed with a gold *#1*. Whoever's performance he was immortalizing, it evidently hadn't improved of late.

There was a subdued *ping* to my left. The process of copying Klinsman's computer files was complete, so I dropped the file back in the drawer, collected my black box, and continued my recce. The next room, heading east now, was around fifteen feet by ten. It was lined with built-in wooden bookshelves. Made of alder, by the look of them. They were beautiful. The work of a true craftsman. I could inspect every detail, because there weren't any books on them. There was no furniture of any other kind, either. Just a pallet in the center of the floor, made to support twelve narrow wooden crates. The kind that valuable paintings are transported in. There were numbers stenciled on the sides, but no indication of the artist or the work.

The final area—the toe of the boot-shaped floor plan—occupied about a third of the overall space. It was the master suite, with a door that could be locked to keep any family members or visitors at bay. It had two full baths on the right-hand side of its private corridor. On the left there was a walk-in closet. It had two doors, and the storage options suggested it had been laid out with his and hers sections in mind, but the room wasn't segregated inside. One rail was in use at his end. Five suits were on it, hanging in monochrome order from black to pale gray. There were a dozen shirts, all white with monograms, and two pairs of khaki pants. One drawer contained underwear. Four pairs of shoes were jumbled on the floor. The rest of the rails, drawers, shelves, cupboards, nooks, and display cases—there seemed to be acres of places to hold things—were empty. The only other items in there were suitcases. There were two of them at the far end, leaning against the wall. They were full of women's clothes, along with the musty smell that comes from being closed up for too long. I shut the cases again and was about to leave through the second door when it struck me—I was in a place about twenty-five feet long by twelve feet wide. That's three hundred square feet. More than three times the net living area a soldier gets in a barracks. And it was a closet. Which wasn't even being used.

The bedroom was at the end of the corridor. It

was twenty feet by thirty, with floor-to-ceiling windows providing views to the north, the east, and the south. There was only one piece of furniture. A bed. It was circular, and had been set in the center of the room like an island. I sat on the edge and looked out. I could see shrunken versions of some of my favorite buildings dotted around the toylike city, way below. The Citicorp was there. Rockefeller Center. The shiny top of the Chrysler. The sight reminded me of all the times as a kid I'd go with my father to the observation deck at the Empire State Building. He'd quiz me on what had changed as visit by visit we watched the city evolve. The memories are still there, fused together like a time-lapse movie in my head. The perspective this place gave was very different, though. And not just because I was looking south, not north.

I gazed out until the shadows began to lengthen, then hauled myself up, grabbed my case, and started toward the exit. I was halfway there when, on the spur of the moment, I ducked into the first of the bedrooms that had been fitted out as a wine cellar. I opened the door to one of the cabinets. Picked out a bottle at random. It was a red. A Bourgogne, Domaine Leroy Richebourg. I checked the label and found its date: 1949. I googled it and saw that a bottle of that vintage had just sold for $6,000. A bargain, compared to the Chateaux Margaux. I put it in my case, and set the doctored Yellow Tail in its place in the cabinet. Then I retraced my steps out of the apartment, through the locked door, and down in the hotel's service elevator. I found my way back to the auxiliary plant room. The same guys were inside, playing the same game.

"Thanks for your help, fellas." I stopped just inside the door. "They did need a little adjustment, but those sensors are fine now. Shouldn't hear any more about them for a long time. But before I go, I have something for you." I opened my case and took out the bottle of Richebourg. "Enjoy. Just do me one favor. If Pablo catches you, don't tell him it came from me."

Robson was sitting cross-legged on the living room floor when I got home. His laptop was open in front of him, and he was surrounded by half a dozen uneven stacks of paper.

"I got us a printer." Robson scowled. "You owe me."

"Sure." I reached for my wallet. "How much was it?"

"Not for buying it. For getting it set up. The damn thing's possessed. I had to take it upstairs and threaten to throw it out of the window before it bent to my will."

"That sounds tough. How about if I make it up to you with Chinese food?"

"That might work."

"Do you fancy going out?"

"Not really."

"Well, that's good. Because I have carryout waiting for us in the kitchen."

We ate our food quickly—old habits—while I outlined what I'd found in Klinsman's apartment.

Then we tossed the trash and headed back to the living room to confront Robson's piles of papers.

"What have we got?" I was trying to make sense of his stacking scheme.

"Not much. Just a bunch of stuff about Rooney's security business." Robson pointed with his foot. "We've got accounts. Lists of clients. Lists of employees. Contractors. Suppliers. Sample proposals. Standard letters—follow-ups, price-rise notices, service reminders. It's all totally boring. There's nothing about Pardew, his file, why it was taken, returned, or what was removed from it. Nothing about Spangler. No mention of any JD. I'm just hoping this whole exercise doesn't turn out to be a bust."

"What about the locked files?"

"I haven't got into them, yet. I hate to do it, but maybe it's time to ask Harry."

"I can do that. I'll call him, set up a meeting for tomorrow. If he's free." I retrieved my case and took out the black box. "In the meantime, I have some files of my own to check. I want to see what secrets Klinsman is hiding on his home computer."

Chapter Sixteen

Easy, like Sunday morning.

It was Sunday morning. And if by *easy* the song meant tired because I got so little rest—sleep being no match for the thrill of finding an interesting little nugget in Klinsman's computer files—then I guess that was true, too.

There wasn't much data to sort through. I guessed it was Klinsman's secondary machine. He probably had another computer—most likely a laptop, as he traveled so much—for everyday use. A lot of his records were synced, using a cloud service to keep them up-to-date. His calendar was. So were his contacts and his personal email account. There were only three documents saved exclusively on that hard disc. They were all spreadsheets. Inventories, listing things that he owned. One was about art. One, cars. The other, wine. Each had a table that recorded the individual items, the date and place they were purchased, the price he paid, their location, and their current value. He had an extensive portfolio, as he probably thought of it. A staggeringly valuable range of possessions. Taken together they painted a stunning picture. But it was when I focused on the details that things became really interesting.

I first noticed something fishy in the spreadsheet that cataloged Klinsman's wine collection. In the court documents that he filed, Klinsman claimed to have lost 261 bottles in the fire. His spreadsheet showed that only 197 were stored in that cellar. I went back to the records of his art. He'd claimed that four paintings had been destroyed. Only one, the least valuable of the group, was supposed to have been hanging at the house. He'd claimed that six of his cars were written off. I remember, because the list included long-lost American brands like Studebaker and Duesenberg that I'd been desperate for my father to buy when I was a kid. It's possible that he had room for all of them in his garage—but four were listed at a storage facility in White Plains.

Was it conceivable that the differences in the records were simply clerical errors? Or that Klinsman had moved some of his things around and not updated his files? Sure. But when all the discrepancies were in his favor, and he stood to gain hundreds of thousands of dollars as a result, I wasn't buying it. I decided that unless Robson had found a lead to Pardew since the night before, Klinsman's Westchester mansion—or the remains of it—would be the next place I'd visit.

Robson was already in the living room when I

came downstairs. I guessed he'd been there for a while. He was in his pajamas—his favorite blue silk pair—and his teacup was down to the dregs. He was sitting in the same spot on the floor as yesterday, but I was pretty sure the piles of papers had all been shifted around.

"Morning." He looked up when he heard me at the doorway. "Put the kettle on."

"How's it going?"

"It's a pain in my ass." He shook his head. "I'm still looking for the devil."

"Do you think it's likely you'll find him in the house?"

"In the details. I'm thinking something must be hidden in all these files. Even if it's nothing to do with Pardew directly, there might be something we can use for leverage over Rooney."

"Sounds like a plan. And maybe there's something in the locked files, also, if Harry can get in. I'm seeing him in an hour. I'm going to give him Klinsman's contacts, too. Maybe he's mixed up with someone we can lean on. He actually had a buddy with the initials *JD*. I thought it might be our lucky day. Two birds, one stone. Then I googled the guy. He died a year ago."

"A long shot, but worth taking. Anything else interesting on his computer?"

I told him about the spreadsheets. "His calendar was on there, too. Shows him being away in the UK for another few days. Lots of business meetings penciled in. I'll ask Harry to look at everyone he's seeing. He seems like a dull boy, though, our Jimmy. All work, and not very much play. The only social thing listed is a dinner club that gets together every two or three months. Hopefully we'll be done with him before the next one. If not, I might have to see if they have room for an extra member."

No one knew what had happened to Harry Hamilton to make it so he wouldn't work in the field anymore. More accurately, no one I knew well enough to talk to could tell me. All I did know was that he still did a good enough job for the 66th to be happy to let him stay at home in New York and handle some of the murkier analytical tasks that came along. And fortunately for me he was sometimes happy to deploy those skills, off the books, when I was in need of help.

I was still half a mile from the place we'd agreed to meet, making slow progress up Eighth Avenue and finding out the hard way that the semi-seized clutch in Robson's Cadillac was not well suited to stop-and-go traffic, when Harry materialized out of the crowd waiting at a set of lights. He glided across a couple of feet of asphalt and was sitting in the passenger seat with the door closed before I'd barely registered movement. And I couldn't put my finger on how, because he wasn't slouching or pressing himself back in his seat, but when I looked across I got the impression I could see straight out of the window, like he wasn't really there.

"Are we on TV?" Harry's body was completely still. "Is there a new show, *Badge Engineering Gone Wrong*? I thought this was a Pontiac when I saw it coming. It was only because of the hideous color I knew it was you."

"I'm not sure there'd be much of an audience." I reached across and shook Harry's hand. "There aren't too many of these left, I'd guess. Which is a good thing. Though Robson seems to like this one. Remember him? He lent it to me for the day."

"He's not doing you much of a favor. He's probably hoping you'll have a crash and write it off. Let's face it, there's no chance of it getting stolen."

"Even if someone did steal it, in a moment of madness or desperation, they'd soon regret it. Probably fill it with gas, get it detailed, and bring it back."

"They'd do better taking it to the crusher. Is that a cassette player? I haven't seen one of those since a rental I had in Albania."

"Did that one work?"

"No."

"Neither does this."

"OK. Let me propose a deal. If I get you what you need, you never make me set foot in this car again."

"Done."

"There are only three files you have a problem with?"

I took a thumb drive out of my pocket and passed it to him. "Right. They're locked. Password protected. Robson thinks they're encrypted, too. I need to know what's in them."

"Shouldn't be too big of a deal."

"Between you and me, I've copied all the other files we acquired from our suspect onto there, too.

Robson thinks they're just business records. I was hoping maybe you could check for anything hidden in them? Any unusual patterns? Things like that."

"Can do."

"And there's one other thing. I've also included the contacts of another guy I'm looking at. He's kind of a sideline. Lower priority, but could you do some digging, anyway? And if you find anything fishy, let me know?"

"Sure. Anything else?"

"No, I—" Then an impulse hit me out of nowhere. "Actually, yes. Let me give you one other name. Marian Sinclair. I think she's a lawyer in Manhattan. I could really use a full background on her. Her address. Where she works. Whether she's married. That kind of thing. But I need total discretion. I'd rather not know than make her suspicious."

"Roger that. Leave it with me. I'll be in touch."

I slowed to avoid a taxi that jumped a red light and Harry took the chance to bail out. His door closed without a sound and he'd melted into a stream of pedestrians before I'd even shifted gear.

It's no surprise that a car equipped with a cassette deck didn't have a satellite navigation system, but even if it did I wouldn't have used it. It wasn't necessary, because I grew up in Westchester and knew the area by heart where Klinsman's mansion was built. And it wasn't wanted, because I didn't care about saving a few minutes by taking some other route. I wanted to take the Saw Mill River Parkway. That was my father's favorite. I hadn't cared when I was younger. I never wanted to leave the city at all, so coming down in favor of one undesired route rather than another seemed pointless. But I remembered how much he liked the gentle sweep of its curves. The occasional glimpse it offered of the river. The contrast between the different shades of green in the various species of trees that lined the road and filled the space between the halves of the highway. My father saw these things as a reward for taking the time to seek out beauty. I wasn't ready to go that far. But I do have to admit, they're pretty.

I stayed on the parkway until I reached the turn for the Mount Kisco Country Club, then rolled through the tree-lined streets south of the town and headed toward Bedford. It wasn't strictly necessary to go that way, but it's an old habit. From the time I was old enough to drive, I had an ulterior motive. That route took me past Marian Sinclair's house. I had no idea if she still lived there, but after our close encounter at the courthouse, my memories of her were bubbling near to the surface. I slowed down as I reached the tight bend before her house. The entry was on the left. I glanced into it, as I'd done a million times before. The driveway was long and straight. There were more weeds poking through the gravel than I remembered, but the house was just the same. It was wide and low, in the classic ranch style. There was a porch all along the front. We used to sit there in the evenings and talk about everything, and nothing. The bugs always ignored her, but they feasted on me. I didn't mind, though. Not too much. It was worth it, to spend time with her.

A car was coming the other way around the curve. A black Mercedes SLK. It was moving fast, but braking hard. Its turn signal came on. I caught a glimpse of the driver. It was Marian. I stepped on the gas—the car barely responded—and I checked the mirror. Had she seen me? It was impossible to say. No one was behind me, so she could complete her turn right away. I imagined her speeding to the end of the driveway. Executing a swift three-point turn in the dusty fishtail. Roaring back to the road. Then she'd bury the accelerator. The supercharger would whine. And she'd catch me in seconds. Instead of talking romance, she'd demand to know why I was stalking her. Two *chance encounters* in three days. That wouldn't look good.

Ten seconds crawled past, and there was no sign of her in my mirror. Ten more, and she still hadn't appeared. I relaxed my right foot. Maybe she wasn't coming. There was no need to risk landing the unwieldy Cadillac in a hedge. I doubted that Robson would be happy if I wrecked his car over a woman. The best plan would be to continue to Klinsman's neighborhood. Focus on business. And forget about Marian. Well, see what Harry could find out, first. Then forget her.

At least until all the urgent matters were squared away.

Klinsman's house hadn't existed when I lived nearby, and now it didn't exist again. That wasn't necessarily a bad thing. I guessed it had been one of the properties that had crept in to fill the gaps between the older neighborhoods. They were generally nearer to the roads. Bigger. More expensive. And built in a vulgar mishmash of styles that did nothing but call attention to themselves. Any architectural failings that Klinsman's place may have had were moot now, though. The building was totally destroyed. Len Hendrie had done a serious number on it. If that's what he was capable of when he turned his mind to something, maybe he could make a decent fist of his defense, after all. On the other hand, all the prosecution would need to do was show the jury a photo of the devastation, and the game would be over.

The perimeter of the site was still cordoned off with swaths of yellow police tape. In some places it was wrapped around the trunks of the trees that had survived the inferno, and in others it was hanging from posts that had been driven into the ground where the gaps were too big. Now the tape was swinging in a breeze that was strong enough to kick up traces of oil, burned plastic, and a bunch of other foul-smelling chemicals that lurked in the rubble.

And the damage wasn't restricted to the trees and the house. The land had taken a major beating, too. The countless gallons of water used to fight the fire had scoured the dirt, cutting channels deep into the ground and forging its way to the street. Stones were strewn all around. Layers of rock were exposed. Huge slabs of mud had dried to form tortured Dali-esque shapes. All around the imprints of the fire trucks' giant tires were pressed into the soil, while ripped-up grass and shredded shrubs lay scattered near the remnants of the structure.

There wasn't much left of it. I could see two sections of wall, not much more than a single story high, bravely pointing at the sky. A stone stump that could have been the base of a chimney. A flatter area to the right that had probably been the garage floor. A concrete pad jutting out on the far side that perhaps had been part of a terrace. There was also a crop of orange-and-white posts sticking up at various points, with numbers attached to them. I guessed they were markers left by the arson investigators to show where their samples had been collected. There was no hope of salvaging anything else. Not without special equipment and access to a laboratory. Maybe the experts could tell if wine bottles and oil paintings had been consumed by the flames, but there was no way I could. I'd wasted my time driving out from the city.

I turned back to the car, impatient to get home and hoping that the stench from the scene wouldn't linger in my clothes, when I heard footsteps behind me.

"Can I help you?" It was a man's voice, and it didn't sound friendly.

I summoned a rueful smile and turned to face whoever it was. "I wish you could. Do you ever get the feeling you've been sent on a fool's errand?" I took another of Rooney's cards from my pocket and held it out like a peace offering. “The insurance company asked me to come out here. They wanted to know whether the site needed to be secured. They were worried that if any valuable items had survived, they might be vulnerable. It’s standard practice for claims above a certain threshold. This one was way above. I guess the homeowner—a Mr. Klinsman—must be an avid collector?”

“I wouldn’t know.” The guy was tall and slender, maybe sixty years old, with close-cropped white hair and a matching beard. He glanced at the card, then handed it back. “We’re not close.”

“Are you guys neighbors?”

“To an extent.” He offered me his hand. “I’m Peter Rourke. My family’s lived here for generations. He—Klinsman—showed up a decade or so ago. Built his huge monster Shangri-La palace. It took three years, start to finish. Damaged the road. The trees. The power lines. Caused carnage before it was done. And he didn’t get the right permits, always. There were rumors about bribes. Anyway, after all the chaos, he didn’t even want to live here full-time. He just comes and goes as he pleases. He has no interest in being part of our community, that much is clear. He screeches in and out, all hours of the day and night, one fancy car after another. And he has his giant parties. His city guests leave, drunk, and get in accidents. If you read about a DUI in the police blotter, you can guarantee it’ll be someone connected with Klinsman.”

“According to the paperwork, Mr. Klinsman had quite a wine cellar.”

"I guess he'd have to, the amount he and his buddies drink."

"Did he ever talk to you about how many bottles he had, approximately?"

"He never talked to me about anything."

"Nothing? Not art, for example? I read he was a real connoisseur, and I've never met one of those guys who didn't love to ramble on about what painting he had here, what sculpture he had there."

"No. Nothing like that."

"What about guy stuff? Like cars? You said he had a bunch of fancy ones he used to show up in."

Rourke shrugged. "Didn't discuss them. He had a four-car garage. Sometimes the doors were open. I never saw more than two cars inside, though. And I never saw the same car twice."

"Did he ever park them, not in the garage?"

"There were cars all over the place when he was having parties. Days at a time, more than once. No idea which ones were his and which were his drinking buddies'."

"Can you remember how many cars were there the night of the fire?"

"Didn't see any. Klinsman wasn't here when the place burned down."

"Were you home that night? Did you see the fire?"

"Oh, yes." Rourke nodded. "Couldn't miss it. The flames were twice as high as the house. It was like a volcano. Brighter than daylight. I couldn't get out of my driveway the next morning because half the fire trucks were still there, blocking the street. The runoff water flooded my basement. It went in my pond and killed my fish. And do you know what? Klinsman hasn't even bothered to come out and see the mess for himself. I've left him a dozen messages about my fish—koi aren't cheap, you know—but he won't return my calls."

"He sounds like a real asshole." I slapped my hand over my mouth. "I'm sorry. I shouldn't have said that, after the bad luck the guy's had."

"It wasn't actually down to luck." Rourke stepped closer to me and lowered his voice. "It was arson. A guy from the city did it. The police arrested him. The full story will come out at the trial, I guess, but think about it. You don't come all the way up here to torch a random house. The guy had a reason. And I'm telling you, Klinsman had it coming. It's good for the cops that the guy confessed or they'd have been here for weeks, there'd have been so many suspects. Dozens of people would have been happy to do it. It would have been like *Murder on the Orient Express,* only with matches instead of knives."

Back in the car, I watched Rourke saunter down his own driveway, then I checked my phone. There was no word from Robson or Harry. I thought I'd return to the city anyway, but on the spur of the moment I decided on a different plan. To go see Mrs. Vincent. I hadn't been in contact in any meaningful way since she told me about my father's death. I guess I'd been associating her with the bad news, and I knew that wasn't fair. She was just the messenger. Now. But growing up without a mother, she'd been a huge influence on my life. Bigger than my father had been in some ways, given the amount of time he spent working. Now that he was gone she was the closest person to a relative I had left. I felt a pang of guilt that it had taken a bunch of talk about using furniture from the house to spur me into visiting her.

Ten minutes later I heard the familiar crunch of gravel under my tires as I pulled up in the parking area at the end of the path that led to my father's—Mrs. Vincent's—front door. Last time I'd been there I was surprised by how old the house looked. The cedar siding had been more silvery than I'd remembered, and the sharp angles of the walls and the roof had looked dated. It didn't seem that way now. Maybe the sun was warmer, softening the color and smoothing the lines. Maybe the anticipation of how my father would receive me after so long away and so few words between us had hardened my perception. But whatever the reason, I climbed out of the car, took a breath of the warm air, which was heavy with a welcoming blend of flowering shrubs and aging, sun-bleached wood—pure nectar after the residual fumes at Klinsman's fire scene—and followed the uneven cracked bricks up to the front of the house. I pulled the thick iron handle that rang the bell and listened to the deep *clang* echo around inside the house. I stepped back and waited for Mrs. Vincent's thin face to appear as she hauled open the heavy door. A ladybug was bustling over a frond of flowers that was overflowing from one of a pair of terra-cotta urns, the petals even brighter than the insect's scarlet body. It reached the end of the blooms, its wings unfolded, and away it flew. I rang the bell again. There was still no answer.

I moved to my left and looked in through the living room window. The white fabric couches were immaculate. The books were perfectly lined up on the shelves within the tall built-ins my father had designed with profiles that resembled his favorite buildings in the city. There was no sign of Mrs. Vincent, so I continued around the side of the house, stepped up onto the deck, and tried the dining room window. The room was narrow with a long oak table running along the center and four high-back gray suede chairs on each side. They were set up in perfect alignment, like soldiers on parade. My father wouldn't have liked that image. Looking at them from that angle made me realize I'd only ever seen three of them in use, despite their having been there all my life. I wondered if my mother had liked throwing dinner parties. That was something else I'd never know about her.

The deck wrapped around to the back of the house, so I followed it as far as the kitchen window. Inside, the countertops looked pristine. There was a bowl upside down on the draining rack, along with a spoon, a cup, and a saucer. The dishwasher's door was open a crack, and I smiled when I remembered how Mrs. Vincent had never quite trusted those machines. She'd been convinced they'd fill with mold if they were left closed, even for a day.

Mrs. Vincent was nowhere to be seen. I was sorry about that, so I thought about going inside and waiting for her. I could have done. It was legally my house. I had a key. But I decided against the idea. It seemed intrusive. And potentially pointless. I had no idea how long it would be before Mrs. Vincent came back, and without her the house was just the place where my mother had died. The thought of the room where her life had drained away was suddenly oppressive and unwelcoming. Perhaps if I was really honest, my love of the city wasn't the only reason I'd chosen to live in the brownstone.

I made my way back to Robson's car, but before I left I strolled the rest of the way down the drive until I reached the garage. My father had always been obsessed with reliability. He tolerated nothing that could possibly delay his departure or obstruct his route to the road. He even parked facing out of the garage, which left an exhaust stain on the rear wall. That was the only place he ever allowed anything to make a mess. So when I looked in through the side window I expected to see something sensible, like a newer Cadillac. I hoped to see one, or maybe even two more fun cars, like the classics I'd always pestered him to buy. But I was surprised by what I did see. Nothing. All four stalls were empty.

That made sense, though, when I thought about it. Mrs. Vincent had to go out from time to time. Of course, she'd use my father's car. She used all the other facilities and amenities he'd provided. It was still unexpected, though. A vehicle was a personal thing to a man of my father's generation. I'd never pictured anyone else driving it.

Chapter Seventeen

SECRETARIES DON'T ALWAYS TELL THE TRUTH. Friends don't always know the facts. Husbands and wives don't always care. But if you have access to a guy's personal calendar you can be reasonably sure when he's going to be around. Which is a useful thing when you want to start your week with a covert visit to his workplace.

Jimmy Klinsman's company—Klinsman Asset Management—was based, predictably enough, in the financial district. Its offices were on the sixteenth floor at 120 Wall Street. The building was made of pale stone. It was studded with symmetrical windows and rose straight up for fifteen or so floors before tapering in, ziggurat style, to a flat rectangular peak. It was classically elegant as far as it went, but to me it looked stunted. It was like someone had taken a prototype of the Empire State Building, removed its top quarter—minus the spire—and planted it near the river to see if it would grow.

The executives and their visitors entered through a row of shiny brass doors at the top of a short flight of steps from the sidewalk and emerged into an extravagant pink marble–lined lobby. Aside from its garishness, the area had a number of other disadvantages. There were security guards watching everyone who came in. Receptionists, checking IDs. And automated barriers blocking the way to the elevators. That's why I continued around the building until I came to the loading dock. The access is on Pine Street, which is really more of an alley that far east, where it's dwarfed by a tall black glass building, all angles and points like a kid's drawing of a space rocket.

The security guard was in his booth. He was leaning back in his chair. His collar was open, his tie was loose, and he had his phone propped up on the narrow shelf beneath the window, with a TV show playing on it. He saw me, ran his fingers through his wild curly hair, slid the window a quarter of the way open, and grunted an incomprehensible greeting.

"Morning." I held up a driver's license in the name of Paul McNulty and gestured to the overall I'd borrowed from the courthouse. "It's my first day. Can you tell me where the janitors' room is?"

The guard picked up a clipboard and scanned the sheet of paper that was attached to it. "You're not on the list." He dropped the board and turned back to his phone.

I rapped on the glass to make sure I had his attention. "I didn't ask if I was on some list. I asked where the janitors' room is. I need to get to work."

"You're not on my list"—he twisted his neck around and glowered up at me—"you don't work in this building. Now get lost."

"You wait just a minute, pal." I crossed my arms. "This building's managed by Silverstein Properties, correct? Well, Josh from Silverstein's head office sent me. He screwed up the paperwork, that's not my fault. I can't help who is or who isn't on your dumb-ass list. And what do you think, anyway? I came down here to clean other people's bathrooms for fun? Because let me tell you, they might wear smart suits and fancy dresses, but those people upstairs live like animals. The mess they make? You wouldn't believe it. And if I don't clean it up, who will? Your list? Will it magically sprout arms and legs and pick up a mop? Or will you do it? Because if no one does, there'll be hell to pay. Someone will have to answer."

"What's your name again?" The guy struggled a little more upright in his chair, picked his clipboard back up, and reached for his reading glasses.

"McNulty." I split it into three slow syllables and held out my ID. "Paul. I should be on there. If I'm not, just write down my details. Or if it's easier, copy my license. Use your phone. Take a picture. That way, if there are any questions, you're bulletproof."

He took my license and squinted at it. "This picture doesn't look much like you."

I shrugged. "What can I tell you? It was taken

when I'd just got out of the army. I've maybe put on a little weight since then."

"You were in the service?"

I nodded. "Twenty years. Logistics. All over the world."

"And now you're a janitor?"

"It's an important job. The world couldn't function without janitors. All those people upstairs, with their high-powered jobs and their Porsches and their summer homes in the Hamptons, they wouldn't have any of that without us. The same goes for security guards, if you think about it."

"I guess." He looked at his watch. "It's early. No one's here yet to show you what's what."

"Don't worry." I slid the license back into my pocket. "I know what I'm here to do."

The janitors' room in that building was smaller than the one I was used to at the courthouse. There was no space for tables and chairs or couches. The ceiling was lower, giving it the air of a large closet. Minus the amenities, though, it had the same general layout. Only it was reversed. The supply shelves were on the left, and the carts were lined up on the right. Rather than using numbers there were names stenciled on the wall. That was a nice touch. I thought I'd maybe suggest it to Carrodus.

There were ten bays in the room. The first eight were occupied. Some of the carts were customized in familiar ways, with cloth holders slung around the bins to carry bottles and brushes, or trash bags twisted into ropes to support mops and brooms.

The ninth bay was empty. The final one had no name attached, but it was home to an empty cart with a broken wheel. I guessed it was awaiting repair, or disposal. I pulled it out and gave it a test run up the center of the room. It was a pain to keep straight and it squealed like a spoiled toddler being dragged out of a toy store, but I figured it was good enough for what I needed. I pulled my overalls on top of my clothes, grabbed a few bottles of polish, some dusters and a mop, and set off in search of the service elevator.

Klinsman's suite was at the northeast corner of the building, above the level where it narrowed. The area outside its doors was set up for visitors to wait in. There was a brown leather couch in a generic mid-century style facing a pair of cube armchairs with a coffee table between them. It was made of rough reclaimed wood and held stacks of magazines about golf and yachts. The walls were plain white, but they had no need of adornment due to the views from their four windows. Two looked out over the river toward Brooklyn. The others, up toward Midtown. I paused and watched a long, low boat loaded down with garbage steam steadily beneath the bridge, trailing seagulls in its wake. Then I turned, pushed open the doors, and went through, towing my cart behind me.

A woman in her early twenties was sitting behind an L-shaped reception counter by the right-hand wall. She had scarlet hair. Her skin was so pale it was almost transparent. She was so thin and so studiously disinterested in her surroundings that I figured she must be either a wannabe fashion model or a heroin addict. Or both. I nodded vaguely in her direction and continued into a corridor. There was a line of offices on the right—four of them—which would be against the outside wall, and therefore have river views. To the left—with no view—there were three cubicles. I guessed they were for the admin staff, or people who were not yet fully fledged in the black art of making money without making things. Beyond them, at the far end of the corridor, a glass-walled conference room took up the full width of the suite.

Each office had a blond wood door flanked by a pair of vertical obscured-glass windows. All the doors were closed, and the first three had brass nameplates mounted at chest level. The one on the nearest door read *James J. Klinsman*. I was about to open it when the receptionist zipped past me with a file in her hand and went inside. I didn't want an audience for what I was planning to do, so I continued along the corridor. There was a light on in the next office, so I kept going. The third was dark, but when I paused to listen my eye was drawn to the floor outside the final office. Something was lying there near the foot of the door. A strip of metal. It was facedown, surrounded by sawdust and slivers of wood. I wheeled my cart past, bent down, and flipped it over. It was another nameplate. It read *Trevor W. Francis*. The typeface was the same as Klinsman's, but the font was a few points smaller.

"Wait!" The receptionist closed Klinsman's door and scurried down the corridor toward me. "What are you doing? Don't clean that up."

I thought it best not to tell her I had no intention of cleaning anything in that place. "What happened?" I straightened up. "Did this Francis guy throw a tantrum?"

"What?" She stopped moving. "No. How do you figure that?"

"Well, it looks like someone slammed the door and the nameplate fell off. So I'm thinking, one, you need a new carpenter. Two, this is Francis's office, so he probably did the slamming. And three, you're leaving the mess for him to clear up to make sure he learns his lesson."

The receptionist turned her head halfway to the side and looked at me out of the corner of her eye as if she was trying to decide if I was joking. "You can clear it up another day, OK? After Trevor's seen it. Otherwise, how will he know he's been fired?"

"Francis has been fired?"

She nodded.

"And he doesn't know it yet?"

She shook her head.

"This is how he's going to find out?"

She nodded again. "This is how Mr. Klinsman does things. *If you don't help earn it, you can't help spend it.* Everyone knows that. You carry your weight, or you're out. And you know you're out when you arrive in the morning and find your nameplate on the floor."

"For real? That's barbaric."

She put her hands on her hips. "Really? Is that right? Who are you to judge? Have you ever had to end someone's career?"

Actually, yes, I thought. *Several people's. Some of them permanently.* "Hey, don't bite my head off." I held my hands out, palms first. "You're right. What would I know? Still, I was just thinking, maybe Klinsman could have sat down with the guy. Explained what he was doing wrong. Given him the chance to put things right. Helped him, if he needed it. Given him some training. Some encouragement. And if he still couldn't make the grade, thank him for his service. Wish him well for the future. And look him in the eye when he did it."

She started to smile as if she thought I might be joking, then her lips curled into a frown and she shook her head. "No. That wouldn't work for Mr. Klinsman. He's far too busy to waste time on losers and flakes."

"I guess he must be. But tell me, what did Francis do wrong, anyway?"

"He missed his quota, two months running."

"Ouch." I nodded gravely. "I guess he had to go, in that case. Where is he now? Did he see the writing on the wall and decide to use up his vacation days?"

"Associates at KAM don't take vacations." She rolled her eyes. "No. Trevor's still in the hospital. He should get out later today. The doctors said it wasn't a heart attack, after all. Just a panic thing. He should be back at work this afternoon. Tomorrow morning, at the latest."

I was sorry to hear that Francis was due back so soon. The way Klinsman was acting reminded me of an incident at a company I was sent to infiltrate in England one time. It was a startup ISP that we thought had been compromised by the Russians to launch a bunch of denial-of-service attacks on US utilities. It turned out we were wrong, but anyway, the startup bubble soon burst. The company needed to cut costs, so it decided to lay off half its staff. The task of breaking the news fell to the Human Resources director, and being the warm, empathetic character he was, he chose to do it by sending a group email. And not just to the people who were getting fired. He sent it to everyone. Not the smartest move when you're dealing with the nation that invented soccer hooliganism. The staff rioted. Literally. They tore the place to pieces. Smashed the furniture. Wrecked the computers. Broke the windows. Tore up the carpets. There were a couple of medium-sized fires. The directors feared for their lives. They locked themselves in a bathroom and waited for the police to rescue them. Which they did. Several hours later. I was thinking that if Klinsman was around when Francis learned his fate, he could see if Francis had the same kind of backbone as the Brits I'd worked with. And if Francis wasn't up for full-scale civil commotion, he could at least give his boss some pointers about improving his office etiquette. Which I'd be more than happy to help hammer home . . .

"Good, then." I stepped closer to my cart. "I'll be back on this floor tomorrow. I'll check in with you first thing. See whether the sword of Damocles has swung, or if its thread is still intact."

"What?" She tipped her head to one side.

"It's not important. Just janitorial humor."

"What—" Her phone started to ring. She looked at the screen for a second, then hit the answer button and pressed the phone to her ear. "Yes. Not yet. I will! Don't worry. I know they're coming. I know how big it is. I have. There's plenty of time. I know how you like to rehearse. Look, I'm doing it now." She hung up and jammed the phone back into her pocket. "I'm sorry." She held up a memory stick and started moving toward the conference room. "We have an important client coming in. I have to get the slides ready." She turned back for a moment and glared at the door next to Klinsman's. If looks could shatter wood, there'd have been more to clear up than a nameplate.

I watched her go inside, open a cupboard in the left-hand wall, and plug the memory stick into a machine in a rack of AV equipment. She reached for a keyboard, and as soon as she was busy tapping away I retraced my steps toward the entrance until I reached Klinsman's door. I pushed, and it opened.

His office was fitted out with fairly standard executive fare—a single pedestal desk, a chair with wheels, a couch under the window, a coat stand. It was all pretty bland, except for the crocodile. It was silver, standing with its legs planted solidly in the center of the room, six feet long from nose to tail. It had rubies for eyes. Diamond-studded teeth. And an irregular slab of greenish glass that flowed all around the creature's body to form the surface of a table. I looked more closely to see what was causing the opaque effect, and I realized it was etched with the image of hundreds of twenty-dollar bills. I ignored the urge to drop something heavy on it and wheeled my cart back so that it was blocking the door.

There was a charging wire protruding from a grommet at the center of the desk, but no sign of a laptop. The bottom drawer was full of gun brochures. Mainly ones that specialized in big-game hunting rifles. At one time I'd thought seriously about moving to Africa when my final tour was up, and hunting elephant poachers. Maybe it wasn't too late, now that reconciliation with my father was off the table. I pushed the thought away and moved to the next drawer. It was fitted with a wire mesh organizer separating a bunch of pens, pencils, paper clips, and elastic bands. There was also a wooden cigar box that contained two business cards from every job he'd had from high school to the present. I wondered if he was saving them up, ready to put in a frame. He did seem to like displaying things. I put the box back and moved on to the top drawer. There were three folders inside. Each one had a printed label stuck to its top corner. The first, *For Signature*. Next, *Correspondence*. And last, *Filing*.

The signature file contained two bundles of papers. The first was at least twenty pages thick, and seemed to relate to a company that Klinsman was purchasing. The other was even bigger. Maybe sixty pages, about all kinds of assets he was planning to sell. It wasn't clear if there was a connection, so I took out my phone and photographed the key pages so I could figure it out later. The correspondence file was mostly full of invitations to fundraisers from politicians. There were also some requests for support from alumni groups and smaller museums and galleries, but one page at the back of the file really grabbed my attention. Klinsman's company name and address were stated in Arabic. But the rest of the letter was in Chinese. I photographed that, too, then checked the final folder. It was empty. I guess the receptionist wouldn't last long if she didn't keep the filing up-to-date, even if she didn't have a nameplate to pry off.

I returned the files and checked for hidden compartments in the desk, but there weren't any. I examined the walls. There was only one thing hanging on any of them. It was a fluted gold frame, like the kind you'd expect to find around a priceless renaissance oil painting in a dusty Italian gallery. Only this one held just an ordinary piece of letter paper, yellowing slightly with age. It had three words emblazoned across it, in bold handwritten capitals—DO IT NOW!!!—with the initials *JK* inscribed below and to the right. A museum-style brass plaque screwed to the lower edge of the frame proclaimed, *James Klinsman, 1995*. I looked behind it, thinking its job must be to conceal a safe. Why else would it exist? But there was no steel door. No keypad. Klinsman must have hung it there for sentimental value. Or to guard against the risk of procrastination. All of a sudden a picture formed in my mind of the guy Francis. I'd never met him. I had no idea what he actually looked like. But somehow I could see him staggering home from the hospital and dragging himself straight into work, only to find he'd been discarded with no more regard than a cheap strip of brass.

I took the frame off the wall and carried it to the desk. Laid it facedown. Unpicked the metal tags that held the back in place. Removed the paper. Set it the right way up. Fished a pen—the thickest I could find—out of the middle drawer. And wrote in the space below Klinsman's words, REGRET IT LATER, PM^C^. Then I reassembled the frame. Replaced it on the hook. Moved my cart, and left the suite.

Sometimes their attempts were clumsy. Sometimes they failed. But when I was at the courthouse, I felt like I was surrounded by people who were at least trying to do the right thing. Whose work was necessary. As the inscription along the base of the portico said, THE TRUE ADMINISTRATION OF JUSTICE IS THE FIRMEST PILLAR OF GOOD GOVERNMENT. It was refreshing to be there, after spending time at Klinsman's office. I felt like I was cleansing myself, not just cleaning the fabric of the building. I started with the octagonal corridor on third and continued all the way around, slowly and thoroughly. Then I moved on to room 310, and I'd almost finished when my phone rang. It was Harry.

"I'm thinking, a Jaguar. British Racing Green."

"Have you been overdoing the caffeine again?" I put my broom back on my cart.

"Did you forget our deal? I break into your

files, and there'll be no more of that gross Cadillac. Wait, Robson isn't there, is he? Unnaturally tall people bother me."

"No, Robson's not here. And I hadn't forgotten our deal. A Jaguar? Maybe I could do that. So tell me. What did you find?"

"I think our boy Rooney is branching out. Dabbling as a private investigator. Particularly when it comes to adultery cases. Those files are full of pictures of people caught in the act. At least I presume that's why he has them. He could just be a garden-variety pervert."

"So the files were locked because of the explicit pictures?"

"That would be my best guess. The pictures in the first two files were obviously taken from a distance, through windows, from a car, that kind of thing. They're super enlarged, grainy, really poor quality. Then it's like he moved up a league. And maybe stacked the deck, too. The later pictures are clear. They're all close-ups, and they kind of look staged. I think he rigged a place and started luring people there. And get this. The final six are of the same girl, but different guys. So either someone has a very enthusiastic soon-to-be ex-wife, or Rooney's set himself up a honey trap."

"That's really interesting, Harry. Thanks. Good work."

"Will it help, do you think?"

"I'm going to say it's more exclusionary at this stage. I'm not sure how it's linked to finding Pardew. Did you have a chance to look at the other files? See if there's anything Robson might have missed?"

"I did look, yes. There was nothing else raunchy, that's for sure. We definitely switched from the R section to the G. One thing Robson might not have seen in there—I retrieved Rooney's Google Maps history. I've found it useful in the past. People sometimes go where they shouldn't and think no one will know because they deleted the search. But it never goes away, if you know where to look. Even if it's not connected to the Pardew thing, it might kick-start some interesting conversations with Rooney. I'll email it to you. As for the rest, Robson's probably right. It's just a bunch of regular records. Quite boring, honestly. Rooney's business looks legit. It's quite healthy. He has a decent customer base. Multiple revenue streams. Acceptable growth. It's not all plain sailing, though. He's spending a fortune on legal bills. The nature of the business, maybe? Do alarm companies get sued a lot? People install a system, get burgled anyway, and want their money back?"

"I don't know. I'll look into it. How about my other project? Klinsman? Anything in his contacts?"

"There wasn't anything specific to latch onto. But it was like you must have dropped that memory stick in the sewer. I feel gross, just reading about the names on it. If they were baseball players and you were picking the all-asshole team, this is the pool you'd want to be fishing in. It's foul, but I'll keep looking."

"Thanks. And Marian Sinclair?"

"Yes." Harry paused. "About that. Are you sure you want me to do anything? The way you asked, I kind of got the sense it was something personal. That's not the way to get a relationship off the ground, Paul. Trust me. You're guaranteed to crash and burn. My advice? Do it the old-fashioned way. Take her to dinner. Have a conversation. If there are things you want to know, just ask her."

Chapter Eighteen

THE HOUSE WAS DESERTED WHEN I GOT HOME. There were two more disposable tea mugs abandoned in the living room. Both were empty. The papers were still there, though the piles had been rearranged again. But there was no sign of Robson.

I hoped he'd get back soon. And I hoped he'd bring food. In the meantime I decided to check the documents I'd photographed in Klinsman's office. I pulled out my phone. The process seemed too easy. The device, too mundane. In some ways I wished we could go back to the days when there was more panache to our business. And better gadgets. Cameras miniaturized in secret laboratories and built into rings and belt buckles. And before that, into briefcases and purses. It was a lost art, casually positioning the hidden lens and holding still long enough to get the proper exposure. Then there was the tension of not knowing if you'd captured a vital gem or the inside of your sleeve. The only bespoke thing now is some software that hides your pictures in an obscure folder that looks like it's part of the phone's operating system. It does you no good at all if some zealous customs official opens your photos app and finds all kinds of illicit images there.

I scrolled to the correct location and opened the first picture. It's easy to photograph documents with a phone but not so easy to read them on the small screen. It's better on something with a larger display. And better still, on paper. I went into the kitchen and woke the printer that Robson had bought. He'd installed it on the kitchen counter, next to his kettle. I tried to connect, but discovered I needed to join the Wi-Fi network he'd also set up. I found the router in the pantry, where the phone line comes in. There was a plate underneath where the passcode was printed. I entered it into my phone, and got rejected. Had I typed it wrong? No. That was a stupid question. Robson had obviously changed it from the manufacturer's default setting and didn't write the new password down. Old habits.

There was a noise from the kitchen and I saw Robson in the doorway, a smile on his face and a large paper sack in his hand.

"Is Thai good?"

"Thai is excellent. I'm starving. But first I need the Wi-Fi code."

"Sure. I have it right here." He pointed to his head. "What are you trying to do?"

"Print some documents I copied at Klinsman's office. Make them easier to read."

"No problem. Here. Give me your phone." He entered a long string of letters and numbers, hit a couple of other keys, and a minute later the printer whirred and pages started to appear in the slot at the front. "What did you get?" He handed me the phone back and pulled out a handful of papers.

"A couple of things. One of them's in Chinese. I wanted you to take a look."

Robson started to read the top page, and as he went along his eyes grew wider and his mouth sagged open. "Paul, this is amazing. You've cracked the whole thing wide open. This is a letter from President Xi. He says, 'Dear Jim, Thanks for sabotaging that corrupt, decadent Western telecom company, on behalf of the people, with your brilliant short-selling scheme. I don't know what that is, being the world's foremost communist, other than Bernie Sanders and AOC, but great job, anyway. Your next mission, should you choose to—' "

I grabbed the papers out of his hand. "Very funny."

"Come on." He grinned. "It was a bit funny. But I'm sorry, my friend. You're barking up the wrong tree. The letter's really from an investor from Hong Kong who wanted to set up a meeting with Klinsman on Thursday. The guy won't even be in town that day. No smoking gun there, I'm afraid. So. What else did you get?"

"Bunch of contracts, waiting for him to sign. Looks like he's buying some company. RevoTek? And selling some other stuff."

"RevoTek? Can I see?"

I handed the papers back to Robson, and as he leafed through them his expression grew darker and meaner until it reached the point where, if you came across him in a dark alley, you'd shoot yourself just to get the inevitable over with. "I'm sorry, Paul. To be honest, at first I thought your obsession with this dude was unhinged. I was wrong. We need to deal with Pardew first, obviously. Then Klinsman? We're taking the asshole down."

"What have you found?" I took the papers back and glanced at them. "What changed your mind?"

"I've heard of RevoTek before. When I was in that cab, driving your buddy Carrodus around for you. There was a segment about it on Taxi TV. On a loop. It nearly drove me crazy. It's like there are only three news stories a day, according to those guys. But one of them was about that company. It's family owned. Based in Hackensack. They used to make bicycles. Now they just make the wheels. They specialize. They're the best in the world, apparently. All the Olympic teams go to them. All the world records have been set with their wheels. They just brought in a new product line, for racing wheelchairs. Then they hit a snag. The owner died, and the son's not interested. Sound familiar? Anyway, they only employ like fifty-five people, but they were worried the company would have to close. There are no other manufacturing jobs up there, especially for people with such narrow skill sets. But the report on the TV said a buyer had been found. They promised there'd be no job losses. Said they planned to invest. Grow the business."

Robson pointed to the paper at the top of the stack. "See that name? That's the new owner. It's a holding company, evidently owned by Klinsman. And the other papers? They show he's selling the land where the factory is to a developer. The machines, to competitors in China. The patents, to a rival in Germany. He's a two-faced lying sack of shit. If he was here right now, I'd kill him with my bare hands. Cut up his body. Dissolve it in acid. And flush it down the toilet."

Another reason to wish Klinsman's trip to England had been a few days shorter. "Why would he do that? Don't answer. I can guess. To make more money, more quickly."

"Unless he just likes getting hurt. Either way, he's going to find out how that feels. Shall we eat?" Robson opened the bag, unloaded the cardboard containers onto the table, and tore down their sides to form makeshift cross-shaped plates. Then he handed me a pair of chopsticks. "Have you heard from Harry?"

"He called a while ago." I took a bite of Sam Rod Duck. "This is good. Anyway, Harry did get into those files. He thinks they were locked because they're full of explicit pictures."

"A porn stash? Has Rooney got a wife? A girlfriend? Maybe we can use that."

"Harry thinks it was more likely Rooney was moonlighting as a PI. Cashing in on straying husbands and wives. He thinks the files were locked because the material was so gross. It struck me it might be because Rooney doesn't have a license. Or because the investigations weren't initiated by his clients."

"You think Rooney was freelancing? Our boy's an entrepreneur?"

"It seems that everyone wants as much money, as quickly as possible. So who pays more? A heart-broken spouse confronted with proof of their partner's affair? Or a guy with kids and half his worldly goods on the line?"

"Paul, you cynic!"

"Plus there's the fact that in one of the files, you have the same woman in the same place with a bunch of different guys."

"It could be a wife with more than one lover?"

"True. But either way, I can't see a link to Pardew. You?"

"Not immediately." Robson sucked up a rebellious glass noodle. "Not like the thing I've been working on."

"You've found something?"

"I was wondering when you'd ask. The answer's yes. Something big. A major piece of the puzzle, I think."

I paused with my chopsticks midway to my mouth. "So? Are you going to tell me?"

"In a minute." Robson's voice was languid. "I'm eating."

Robson scooped up the last of the Shrimp Massaman, cleared away the detritus, fetched a set of his papers from the living room, and laid them out on the table.

"I told you the devil was in the details." He shuffled the papers until a particular page was on the top. "At first Rooney's records all seemed legit. Then I started going through them with a fine-tooth comb. And when I got to his client list, guess who I found?"

"Elvis Presley?"

"Alex Pardew. He bought a brand-new, top-of-the-line system from Rooney's company. A coincidence? I thought. So I took a drive to Pardew's address. A nice place, out in Armonk. And guess what? There was no system at Pardew's house. Which raises the question, what did he pay for?"

"And the question, when did he pay for it?"

"Good. We're on the same page. He made the payment the week before his DUI charge was dropped."

"So alongside his legit business, Rooney runs a conduit to channel bribes to a judge."

"That's the way I read it. He uses the business to conceal the flow of cash."

"This is a big piece, John. It's massive. It explains why the file was taken, and why some of Pardew's records were removed. Rooney heard his client had been caught again, and that his finances would specifically be coming under the spotlight, and was worried about the scheme coming to light."

"Right. And when they were done with it, they were happy to return the file because they weren't looking to deliberately derail your father's case. That was just collateral."

"Agreed. At the pier I heard Rooney say that Pardew knows the file is back and won't be stupid enough to stick around. It sounded like Pardew running was a by-product, not their aim. He's in the wind, not off the hook."

"This does raise another question, though. Why not hit Pardew up again? Businesses usually like repeat customers. Especially illegal ones."

"There could be a lot of reasons. The case could have been given to a different judge, who isn't bent. Pardew could have been broke. Or too tight to meet their price. The case could be too high profile. They could have weird moral scruples, where they don't mind helping drunks but draw the line at potential killers?"

"Could be any of those."

"Maybe we'll figure it out if we can put more pieces in place. Like, how did Rooney know to approach Pardew when he got busted for the DUI?"

"He's a retired cop. He probably still has contacts in the department. And the woman, Spangler—she works at the courthouse. The information could be coming from that end."

"Either of them could have found out about Pardew getting arrested. A better question is, how did they know he'd be open to paying a bribe? Approach the wrong person and they make a deal by reporting you. Could it have been the other way around? Could Pardew have approached Rooney?"

"That's the same question, but backwards. How would Pardew know who to go to?"

"There are other questions, too. How's the judge connected?"

"How does he get paid?"

"Is there more than one judge involved?"

"This whole thing's turning into a Pandora's box. Is it time to be sensible, Paul? Should we hand it off to Detective Atkinson?"

"We will do that, but not yet. Because here's the biggest question of all. Where's Pardew now? How well is he covering his tracks? If he hears that Rooney's been arrested and he figures more dirty laundry could see the light of day, he might go deeper underground. And I don't want him getting any harder to find than he already is. The guy's responsible for my father's death. We're still due a little private time, before the police get involved."

Chapter Nineteen

MAYBE OLD HABITS DIE MORE EASILY THAN I'D thought.

Pardew knows the file is back, remember. He won't be stupid enough to stick around.

During training they taught us to use all kinds of devices to monitor people and record their conversations. There were wires to wear. Bugs to conceal. Parabolic microphones to train on subjects from crazy long distances. But more important, we were taught to listen. To everyone. All the time.

This point was hammered home during one exercise in particular. We were told the purpose was to ensure that we didn't become too dependent on technology. The scenario was that we were to wait in a bar for a pair of businessmen to show up and discuss the project they were working on. Our task was to eavesdrop without being detected, memorize what the business guys said, and report the key points. We were warned that the conversation would be heavy with technical details, and that at the debrief we'd be pressed for the specifics. It was vital that we get all the jargon exactly correct.

When it was my turn I made sure to arrive early, figuring I'd be less suspicious if I wasn't seen walking in. I ordered tonic with ice and a slice, and tipped the barman extra to serve me the same thing all evening without being asked. It looked like a regular drink but had no alcohol to dull the recollection and insufficient volume to prompt urgent bathroom breaks.

The place was busy. It was noisy, too. All the tables were taken, and there was a throng of couples and groups of friends at the bar. There were only three seats left. I took one next to a pair of women who looked about my age. They were wearing cocktail dresses and getting ready for a night on the town. After half an hour the guys I was waiting for walked in. They were wearing suits and carrying briefcases. They slid onto the final empty stools, ordered beer, and chatted constantly for the next couple of hours. There was more talk about baseball than business, but I did my best to memorize all the important topics. I was fairly confident going into the debrief the next day. Which turned out to be much harder than I expected. But also, much more useful. Because the instructors didn't care about what the businessmen had said, after all. They only grilled me about the women. What the two of them had said. What implications could be drawn about their jobs. Their relationships. Their families. Schools. Qualifications. Financial stability. The kind of conclusions you could only make if you didn't just hear things. You had to absorb them. And think about them critically.

Pardew knows the file is back, remember. He won't be stupid enough to stick around.

Robson was wide awake the instant I walked into his room, even though it was only 4:00 A.M.

"Is the house on fire?" His voice was completely calm.

"Rooney knows where Pardew is. Or he did. They were in contact. They may still be. And Pardew may still be in town."

"Are you sure?" Robson sat up. "How do you know?"

"Rooney told me. At the pier. Only I wasn't listening right. He said, Pardew *knows the file is back*. How could he know what Pardew knew if they weren't communicating?"

"You're right. Rooney couldn't know. He must have been observing Pardew, at least."

"And there's this. When he was trying to reassure Spangler, he said that Pardew *won't be stupid enough to stick around*. 'Won't be.' Not 'has already left.' So he's still here. Maybe."

"It's possible." Robson swung his feet onto the floor. "Shall we head over to Rooney's house and convince him it's in his best interests to share his buddy's location?"

"That's tempting. But it's too risky. I'm thinking it's time for me to plant a seed. Can you be outside Rooney's office at 0800, in case it grows?"

At 0801 I was in the shelter of a dumpster at the east end of Pine Street, dialing Rooney's office number on a pay-as-you-go phone. My call was answered after two rings.

"Brian Rooney. Help you?" His voice was full of morning rust.

"Good morning, Mr. Rooney." I'd decided on an English accent for the occasion. "I'm calling to let you know that your houseguest is becoming extremely unruly. I happened to be passing and I heard him yelling and screaming and banging on things. It was hard to follow everything he said, but I definitely heard him mention the police."

"Who is this?" Rooney coughed. "I don't have any guest. I don't know what you're talking about, you limey weirdo."

"Well, that's very strange. The person clearly stated your name and business. He claims he's part of a bribery ring involving you and a corrupt judge, and says he wants to confess."

"You must be insane. Don't call me again."

I didn't really have a good reason to go back to Klinsman's office. It was unlikely that any useful information would have surfaced in the last twenty-four hours, with him being away in London, but I needed to fill the time until Rooney showed some kind of reaction to my call. And I also wanted to know how things panned out with Trevor Francis. The guy who was getting fired. In the event that he discovered his inner hooligan, I wanted to be a witness. And to cheer him on. So I took out the battery, tossed the phone in the dumpster, and made my way to the rear entrance of Klinsman's building. The same guard was on duty. He seemed less hungover and this time he waved me through, if not cheerfully, at least without giving me as much grief as the day before. I took the same cart from the janitors' room, despite the damaged wheel, which made it hard to push. I took the elevator to the sixteenth floor. Stepped out. And got no farther. The waiting area was crammed full of people. At least two dozen of them. Men and women, mid-thirties to early seventies. All were on their feet, milling around, muttering and chuntering and adding to the tension and hostility in the air. After a couple of minutes a guy, short, with ginger hair and a soccer jersey from a team I didn't recognize, stepped forward and banged on the door.

"Come out!" He banged again. "Francis, we know you're in there. We saw your car in the parking garage. So come out. Face us. Or are you a coward as well as a backstabber?"

A woman's voice answered from behind the door. I recognized it as belonging to the skinny receptionist. "Mr. Francis is not coming out. You all need to leave. Right now. I've called security. They're on their way. We'll bring the police into this, too, if we have to."

"We're not leaving till we talk to Francis." The short guy banged on the door again. "Let us in. Send him out. We don't care which."

"Neither of those things is going to happen." The woman's voice was strong and steady, if a little muffled by the wood. "You all need to leave before this gets out of hand."

"It's already out of hand. It got out of hand when Francis betrayed us!"

I eased my cart across to a woman at the edge of the group. "Everyone seems pretty upset. What's going on?"

The woman shook her head and sighed. "It's probably a mistake to be here. It won't change anything. I know that. It's too late. All we can do now is look him in the eye. Make sure he knows how we feel about what he did to us."

" 'He' being this Francis guy? What did he do?"

"Stole our kids' soccer field."

"He stole a field? How?"

"He tricked us. We're all from White Plains. Our kids play for the White Plains Wanderers. It's a small club. We had our own field, but not much else. Other teams, in other towns, they have much better facilities. Places to change. To shower. To get snacks and hang out. It's hard to attract kids to our club. And hard to keep them. But it's so expensive to develop, we didn't think we could do it until Francis showed up with his proposal. He offered to broker a deal with a client of his. They would buy the land for a dollar. Keep one half and build houses on it. Pay for pitches on the other half, proper ones with drainage and nets and a clubhouse. They were to set up a trust so it could run as a nonprofit. The club would have been set for life."

"Sounds like a good arrangement, if there was enough room on the half they didn't build on."

"You know what people say. If something seems too good to be true, then it generally is."

"So the deal didn't happen?"

"Francis's buddy getting the club's land for a dollar, that part happened. Nothing else did."

"If he's dragging his feet, couldn't you sue him? Force him to keep his obligations?"

"Turns out he doesn't have any. The original proposal was fine. It was clear, straightforward. But as time passed it all got super complicated. There were amendments. Riders. Qualifications. Conditions. Caveats. All manner of things that totally changed the picture. The upshot was, he gained, we lost. The final deal was watertight. It was legal. It just wasn't fair."

"I'm sorry to hear all that. Isn't there—" Someone banged on the door from the inside, then a man's voice called out.

"This is Trevor Francis. I'm coming out. I want to talk. I owe you an explanation. I know you're upset, but please move back, give me a chance to speak."

The door opened a few inches and a guy slid out sideways through the narrow gap. He'd be in his late thirties, with thinning sandy hair and a charcoal suit that was only marginally more gray than his face. The door slammed behind him. The crowd surged forward, babbling and yelling. The guy was pressed back against the wall, but he just held up his hands and stayed still until the noise subsided to a background murmur.

"OK." His voice was quiet but steady. "I'm

here. I'm not hiding. And I have four things to say."

"Apologize to us, you freak!" It was a woman's voice, somewhere in the center of the crowd. "Give our kids their field back."

Francis paused to let that pass. "First thing. You're right. All of you. I did betray you. And your kids. You're right to be angry, and I don't blame you for hating me. Second. I didn't want to do what I did. I was forced to by James Klinsman, to keep my job. I get how that sounds like a lame excuse, but you don't know what the guy's like. He's an animal. Third. Partly as a result of what happened with you guys, and the Wanderers, I no longer work for Klinsman. I no longer work for anyone, in fact. Which is OK. It was my decision. I don't expect sympathy from you, or anyone else. Fourth. Finally, and most important, I'm sorry for everything that happened. You don't deserve it. Your kids don't deserve it. I don't know if there's anything I can do to make things right, but I give you my word that I'll help in any way I can with any legal challenge you guys choose to mount." Francis took a moment to scan the faces around him. "Now, if you'll excuse me, I have to go and tell my wife that as of this morning her husband is among the ranks of the unemployed."

Francis waited a moment, then launched himself forward and made for the elevator. The crowd mainly parted, though he did have to step around a few people. He got jostled a couple of times but he kept moving, his eyes fixed on the sliding doors. Someone whistled. A few guys hurled some insults.

When Francis had made it halfway I edged back and hit the call button. The doors opened just as he reached the threshold. I could hear his breathing as he passed me. It was sharp and shallow, and I could see beads of sweat dotting his forehead. He stepped inside and the elevator doors closed. I was happy he'd escaped the mob, but couldn't help wondering if the conversation he was due to have with his wife would take place at their home, or back at the hospital.

The crowd continued to mill around, but it felt like there was less air in the place, somehow. The common purpose was lost. The anger had evaporated, leaving the general mood sad and confused. A couple sat on the couch. Others drifted to the windows and stared out. Some slowly formed into ragged groups. No one showed any sign of wanting to leave, though, so I hit the call button again. There'd be no point in trying to get into the office. They'd be crazy to open the doors with the mob still there. Plus I had no desire to pick up Francis's nameplate. I hoped he hadn't done that himself. It should be left for Klinsman to deal with, himself. Though I doubted he would. He struck me as the kind of guy who expects others to clean up after him. And if I was going to clean anything that day, it would be at the courthouse. I had time before I was due to relieve Robson, unless he called to say Rooney was on the move first.

There was no word from Robson while I took the short walk from Klinsman's building to Centre

Street. Nothing while I got changed. Restocked my cart. Rode up to the third floor. And cleaned two corridors and three courtrooms. I was tempted to head up to the fourth and put some work in there, but I knew that would make it tough to reach Rooney's office by the agreed time. Specially with the extra stop I'd decided to make. It would partly be in the best interests of the operation—ensuring that the same vehicle didn't have to be parked outside Rooney's office all day—but my motivation was mainly selfish. I didn't want to have to sit in Robson's mangy Cadillac for hours, let alone potentially have to chase another vehicle in it, so I stopped at a car rental office on Lower Broadway and picked up a silver Chevy Impala before heading over to Queens.

I ground my way through the silted city streets until I reached the strip mall that housed Rooney's business. I pulled off the main drag to access the row of parking spaces and rolled past Robson's Cadillac. That left me with two options. Stopping outside the church, or the pawnshop. I chose the church. It was a little farther along the strip, but offered a better angle to watch Rooney's door. I reversed into the space and adjusted the rearview mirror so I could see the office. There was less chance of Rooney catching a glimpse of my face if he walked by, that way. And it would be easier for me to pull out quickly and follow him, if it became necessary.

Robson took off after six minutes, so it wasn't too obvious that he'd been waiting to be relieved. I watched him go, then settled in to wait. The driver's seat in the Impala was actually less comfortable than the one in the old Cadillac. That set my mind wandering. Form versus function. Cause versus effect. Intention, result. The abstract thoughts were welcome, helping me to quickly reach the state I was trained for. A small portion of the brain remains hypervigilant, alive to any change in the target, and the rest of the mind and body becomes languid and relaxed, able to stay on post for hours. For as long as necessary.

That day it was only necessary to stay there for forty-seven minutes. Then two things happened simultaneously. A blue van with a gold shield emblazoned on the side turned in to the parking area, moving fast so that its tires gave a slight squeal as it stopped opposite Rooney's door. And Rooney emerged from the office, pulling on a suit jacket as he strode forward and jumped up into the passenger seat. Then the van was moving again before the door had even closed all the way. I let it pass me, then pulled back out onto the street, surging into the traffic and joining the stream, three cars back. That was a workable distance, given the size of the van and the weight of the traffic. The vehicles around me ebbed and flowed, but I made sure to maintain a position no fewer than two cars behind the van, and no more than four. We weaved through the streets, an unwelcoming blend of residential and commercial, for just shy of twenty minutes. Then the van pulled over to the side and stopped. I continued, made the next right, pulled a fast U-turn, and took up a position the moment I regained visual contact.

Rooney and a guy who I'd not seen before were standing in a small yard in front of a modest, tidy row house. Its door opened and a man emerged. I guessed he'd be in his late sixties, and he walked with a stick. He refused Rooney's hand. It looked like he started yelling. His body was stiff and hostile. He was doing lots of gesticulation with his free hand. After a minute he turned and pointed at an alarm box on the wall between the first- and second-floor windows. Rooney seemed to be trying to calm the situation down. For several minutes he had little effect. Then gradually the other guy became less aggressive. Eventually the wind dropped from his sails altogether and he grudgingly accepted Rooney's hand. They talked for another minute, then he started back toward his door. Rooney and his driver made for the van. I figured I could safely discount the encounter—if Rooney had Pardew stashed in the older guy's basement, I doubted he'd be dumb enough to yell about it on the street—but I was left with a decision. Should I head back to Rooney's office independently, so that I could get there first and avoid any risk of being spotted tailing him? Or continue to follow, in case he had another destination lined up? One that might be of more interest? I was leaning toward following when my phone rang.

It was Robson. "I just slotted another piece into place. I've found the link between Pardew and Rooney."

"Excellent. What is it?"

"Isn't Pardew's lawyer a guy named Steven Bruce?"

"He is. I saw his name in Pardew's file."

"Well, get this. I found a payment from Rooney's company to Bruce four days after Pardew paid for his nonexistent alarm system. And the amount? Exactly fifteen percent of Pardew's payment."

"Makes sense. Who knows a client better than their lawyer? Bruce could test the water, and when he's satisfied, put his guy in touch with Rooney. The fifteen percent must be a kind of finder's fee. Any sign of how they pay the judge his cut?"

"Not yet. I'm still looking. But I did find something else. It could be big. Or it could be nothing."

"What is it?"

"I figured with a scheme like this, Pardew can't be the only client, so I looked for other payments to Steven Bruce, assuming they're also finder's fees. I found thirty-two in the last three years. Then I had to figure out who in Rooney's books paid the corresponding original bribes. I couldn't drive by all his customers to see which ones didn't have systems installed. There are too many. So I hit on a different idea. See which ones Rooney visited. I figured they'd most likely be genuine. And people who paid without a visit from Rooney, they'd be the ones to be suspicious of."

"That's a good theory. But how could you find out which clients Rooney visited?"

"It's not ironclad, but I did it by checking the addresses he searched for on Google Maps. Evidently it's his go-to system for getting directions."

"I didn't realize you knew how to get that search history."

"I don't. Harry found it."

"Wait a minute. He said he was going to email that file to me."

"Right. And it's lucky he did. It was very useful."

"You read my email?"

"Duh. You left your laptop in the kitchen. I figured that was an invitation. What kind of Intel officer would I have been if I ignored things like that? Don't you read mine?"

"OK." I let Rooney's van pull one vehicle's length farther ahead. "Moving on. What did you find on the map searches?"

"In the same period that he made thirty-two payments to Bruce, there were thirty-two customers that Rooney didn't look up on the map. I started googling their names. Did the first ten. And guess what? All of them had been arrested. And all were acquitted."

"Atkinson will need to join the dots, but it's sounding pretty conclusive. He'll probably get a promotion off the back of it. It doesn't help find us Pardew, though."

"No. But another thing I found might. As well as addresses for his legitimate customers, Rooney also searched three other places. All of them two days before the file went missing and Pardew walked."

"So what? They could be friends' houses, where he'd been invited to dinner. Or prospective customers who didn't like his quotes and signed with other companies. Or changed their minds. Or couldn't scrape enough cash together to go ahead."

"No. They're all addresses for stores. And

what's weird is when I googled them, I found that they're all out of business."

"Maybe he's sick of his crappy office in Queens and is thinking of relocating."

"That is possible. But Rooney lives in Queens, remember. Manhattan's way less convenient for him. He'd gain a pain-in-the-ass commute, every morning and evening. It would be more expensive. There'd be nowhere for him to park. Or for his customers. And his business is doing fine where it is. No. I think this could be something else. Imagine you're Rooney. What if you don't just worry that your bribe operation might come to light during Pardew's trial? What if you know it will, because Pardew decides to spill the beans? What would you do, aside from taking the file and removing the evidence?"

"No question about it. I'd disincentivize Pardew."

"Right. In some places we've worked that would mean two in the head and a shallow grave. But this is New York, and that kind of thing might attract unwanted attention. So why not put Pardew on ice until you're done sanitizing the file? Then you could safely let him go. Because as Rooney said, he wouldn't be stupid enough to hang around once he knew the file was back. All you'd have to do would be open the door, remind him his leverage has gone, and the proof of his guilt is back in the hands of the court."

"It's possible. Rooney was desperate for the file to be put back. That much fits. But it's not a lock."

"Look, I'm not saying it's a sure thing. It's just

a theory. But the beauty is, it's so easy to prove or disprove. There are three addresses. One in the Village. One in SoHo. And one in the Bronx. We check them out, and we'll know immediately, one way or the other. A tiny effort, but a huge reward if Pardew is at one of them."

"And not much to lose if he's not."

"Agreed. Which is why I'm on my way to the first place now. You stay on Rooney, and I'll keep you posted."

"Negative. Text me the address. Rooney just got in a beef over an alarm system with a guy who can't walk without a cane. I can't see him standing around and getting a walking stick shoved in his face if he believed Pardew was freaking out somewhere and yelling for the cops. Either we're way off the mark, or Rooney knows the story isn't true for another reason. Like he has a partner in place, sitting on Pardew and keeping him quiet. In which case, it would be better for the two of us to go."

Chapter Twenty

THE ADDRESS ROBSON SENT FOR THE FIRST DERELICT property was on Bleecker Street, which surprised me. The last I'd heard, the area was booming with all kinds of high-end fashion stores opening up alongside gentrified versions of legendary music clubs. I soon saw how much things had changed.

I crossed the river via the Queens Midtown Tunnel, which was its usual bottleneck, and headed west along 42nd Street. I glanced up at Ro's building as I passed Bryant Park, where the usual unruly crowd was spilling out onto the sidewalk, and kept going all the way to Ninth Avenue. Then I swung south to Hudson Street, continued to the part of the city where the grid starts getting messed up by the corner of the island that's been snipped off by the river, and forked left into Abingdon Square. From there I followed Bleecker southeast until it crossed Sixth. I was moving slowly—there was no choice in that traffic—and in fifteen blocks I counted twenty-nine vacant storefronts. I couldn't help but wonder what had forced so many previously healthy businesses to close. They looked like rotten teeth in a once white smile, or diseased victims of a deadly commercial plague that had swept through the area.

I saw the familiar cherry red Cadillac parked on the street near University Plaza, so I drove past and made a right onto Mercer. I found a spot midway down the block and dumped the car. Then I walked back and joined Robson, who was pretending to browse the window of a hat store.

Robson nodded to me in the reflection in the glass. "Behind us, three to the west, no awning."

I located the storefront he'd been watching and saw that its entrance and window had been covered with separate roll-down metal shutters. Both were covered in graffiti, with big balloon initials overlapping one another in a garish rainbow of unwelcome colors. Above that, in the space that would normally have been covered by the awning, the rusty frame of an air conditioner was jutting out from a band of weathered, uneven brickwork. Over the store there were three windows, too filthy to see through. I guessed they were part of the apartment where the owners would originally have lived.

"No one's watching it from the street," Robson said. "And not from any vehicles, or on foot. I can't tell about the other buildings."

"Safe enough to take a look inside?"

"Safe enough." Robson nodded. "I already walked by. The padlocks on the shutters are rusted solid. They haven't been opened in months. But the door to the left? The lock's brand-new. Probably leads to the apartment on the second floor. That makes more sense than the store itself as a place to hold someone. We should try there."

"Got it."

Robson stood and obscured the view from the street while I picked the lock. It was much more substantial than I'd expected, given the overall state of disrepair the place was in. It took almost two minutes to get it open. Inside, there was just enough space for the door to swing open before the stairs began. The walls had once been painted cream, but now they were covered with chips and stains, and there was a diagonal series of holes where the banister rail had been torn off. The carpet, which had maybe once been burgundy, was now filthy brown and threadbare. It gave off a damp, musty smell with an overtone of something vaguely biological. Whether the origin was human or another kind of animal, I couldn't say.

We started up the stairs, keeping to the sides, where the treads were less likely to creak, but it was hardly a covert entry. At the top there was a landing that opened onto four rooms. The first one at the front of the building would have been a living and dining space. It accounted for two of the unit's three windows, though each of them was now barred and nailed shut. The walls were beige, with lighter patches where pictures would once have hung. A wire was hanging limply from a broken ceiling rose. The wooden floor was blotchy and sticky, like a carpet had recently been removed along with all the furniture.

The next room was the kitchen. Its window was also barred and nailed shut. There were cabinets all along one side with dated fake-wood fronts. The countertop was made of aged Formica with a random swirly pattern and dozens of deep parallel scratches. There was linoleum on the floor, made to look like quarry tiles but now pocked with cigarette burns and covered with stains around the space where the stove would have been. There was a single stainless-steel sink, scratched by years of washing dishes and stained by countless pots of tea and coffee. Robson tried the faucet, and it released a feeble stream of yellowish water. He turned, and pointed to the space behind the door. There was a black trash bag, its top bunched up but not tied. He unfurled it and peered inside, keeping it at arm's length. Then he tipped the contents out all over the floor. There were a dozen or so empty water bottles and packets of the kind of food you can heat in the microwave.

"Look. Civilian MREs." He poked the heap with his foot. "There's oatmeal for breakfast. Pasta and stew for lunch and dinner. What can I say? I've got by on worse."

The door opposite the kitchen led to the bathroom. There was a sink, a tub, and a toilet, all with cracks and stains in their porcelain, but all with working surfaces that showed signs of scrubbing. There was a bleach bottle on the floor. A shower curtain attached to its rail with cable ties, which looked fairly new. It depicted a map of the world, though some of the countries were labeled incorrectly and some were misspelled.

Robson shrugged. "Usable, if your vaccinations are up-to-date. And you don't have a geography quiz to study for."

The final room had been a bedroom. Its window was nailed and barred in the same way as the others, but it was covered by a heavy gray curtain. The bare boards on the floor were sticky and a rectangle in the center, about eight feet by five, was covered with wispy bluish fluffs. The remnants of psychedelic turquoise-and-brown wallpaper were clinging in patches to the walls. A bare lightbulb was lying on the floor at the end of a wire that stretched all the way to the ceiling and still left ten feet of slack. Robson picked it up and took a closer look.

"Only twenty-five watts. That's not much light. Why's it on this crazy long cable? And what are those?" He was pointing to a pair of small shiny round hooks that had been screwed into the ceiling, four feet either side of the lighting rose.

"There are more, down there." I pointed to the skirting. "Four on each side wall. Maybe this place was a kennel for the world's smallest dogs. The craze for pocket pooches, taken to the extreme."

"No." Robson shook his head. "They were for guy ropes." He pointed to the fluffy patch with his foot. "Someone laid out a blanket on the floor, and pitched a tent over it. Like an indoor camp. All they'd need is a mattress and a sleeping bag. Then the cable would stretch all the way in and they could read or whatever without the light being seen on the street. It's an interesting setup."

"It is. But was it set up for Pardew?"

Robson shrugged. "And if it was, where is he now?"

The next address Robson wanted to check was on West Broadway, in SoHo. It was one of five derelict storefronts on a single block. In terms of size and age it looked similar to the one in the Village, but it had a wider set of shutters that covered both the door and the window. These also had graffiti on them, though different tags had been sprayed, coming more from the red end of the spectrum. And this one still had its awning. Faded and frayed at the edges, but clinging on with an air of forlorn hope.

I persuaded Robson to leave his Cadillac a block away, so we sat in my rental, diagonally opposite the store, and looked out for watchers for half an hour.

"I never realized it was so hard to run a store." I shifted a little in my seat. "I figured as long as you don't set up in some completely inaccessible place, you open at least some of the time, your merchandise isn't terrible, you don't rip your customers off too badly, or yell at them when they come in, then you're good to go."

"The McGrath philosophy of retailing." Robson nodded. "I like it. You should write it out by hand in big copperplate letters and frame it. And then one day it'll take pride of place in your corporate global headquarters. New recruits will be required to learn it by heart, and recite it whenever they're asked by management. Any hesitation and they're fired. Word will spread, you'll be invited to lecture at business schools . . . You know what, though? You probably wouldn't be too far off the money, if it wasn't for the landlords. Those assholes are worse than drug dealers."

"It can't be all their fault, surely. They wouldn't drive people out of business on purpose. It can't be in their interests to have their properties sitting empty."

"You'd be surprised. It all comes down to the holy trinity. Greed. Stupidity. And the tax code. I'll give you an example. My cousin in Chicago wanted to open a clothing store. He found a great storefront and the landlord offered it to him for three months, rent free. The next nine, the rate was reasonable. During that time his store took off. So the next year? The landlord tripled the rent. Tripled it. My cousin couldn't pay. He went bust. Then the storefront sat empty while the asshole claimed a tax loss. And he did exactly the same thing to six other businesses on that street."

"That makes no—" Robson put his hand on my arm, cutting me off. He gestured to the other side of the street. A guy was approaching the store. He slowed down. Stopped at the door. Pulled out a key. And worked the lock. I couldn't see his face, but he was the right height for Pardew. He had the right hair color. The same slacks and jacket I'd seen in a picture in Pardew's file.

"Is that . . . ?" Robson raised his eyebrows.

"I've never met him in person. He matches the photograph, though. What I can see of him, anyway."

"This guy's not being held against his will. He has a key. He's letting himself in. So what's going on? Have we got this ass backwards, somehow?"

"I don't know." I opened my door. "There's only one way to find out."

Robson blocked while I picked the lock. It was the same kind as the one I'd just dealt with in the Village, which helped. It looked new, too, although it showed a few more signs of wear. I had it open in just over a minute. I eased the door back and stepped inside, testing each footstep for sound before committing my full weight. I waited for Robson to follow. He nursed the door back into place and we started up the stairs. They were old and there was no carpet, so we couldn't avoid a few creaks. We reached the landing and saw that here the front half of the apartment was all one room. The doors and internal walls had all been removed, creating an open space that appeared to still have been in the midst of a renovation when it was abandoned.

There were three doors to the rear. Two were open. The one on the right led to the kitchen. The center, to the bathroom. And as we stood I heard a click from the one on the left. Someone had just worked the lock. We made our way around to it and I knocked, then dodged back so I wasn't in front of the door for a second longer than necessary.

"Alex Pardew?" I paused. "We know you're inside. We need to talk."

"Go away." It was a man's voice, muffled and distant.

"Mr. Pardew—open the door."

"I'm not Pardew. I don't know who that is."

"If you're not Pardew, who are you?"

There was no answer.

"Open the door. We need to talk. Right now."

"Go away." The man's voice was higher-pitched now, and sounded more desperate. "Don't come any closer. I've got a knife. I'm warning you. Try to come in and I'll cut you."

"I understand. Now just listen. No one's going to try—" I drove the ball of my foot into the door just below the handle. It flew open, swinging around, hitting the wall, and raining pieces of shattered frame down all over the floor. I moved aside again and waited. No bullets came my way, so I risked a peek. The space inside the room was dominated by a tent. It was made of orange-and-brown nylon, and was held up by ropes attached to circular hooks in the walls and ceiling. A cable snaked its way down and disappeared inside. Behind it the window was closed and barred. There was no sign of any person.

"Go away." The voice came from inside the tent. "I'm not coming out."

"No?" Robson stepped past me, leaned down, tugged the zip that fastened the entrance of the tent, reached inside, and hauled a guy out by his ankle. "Are you sure about that?"

The guy curled himself into a tight ball. "Let me go!"

"Why would I do that?" Robson didn't relax his grip.

The guy straightened out, kicked at Robson's hand, and tried to crawl back to the tent. Robson used his other hand to grab him by the lapels of his jacket, haul him upright, and press him against the wall. The guy was at least sixty. He had sunken cheeks, his left eye was stitched closed, and the top of his ear was missing.

"OK." Robson glared at the guy. "You're not Pardew, but you're wearing his clothes. Why?"

The guy started to wriggle, trying to free himself, but he didn't answer.

"Where did you get them from?" Robson tightened his grip.

The guy didn't answer.

"What's your name?"

The guy shook his head and wriggled more frantically.

"Any weapons on you?"

The guy gurgled and kept on wriggling.

"If you won't answer, I'll have to search you." Robson pressed the guy against the wall a little harder. "And you know what they say. It's easier to search a man's pockets after he's dead."

The guy sagged in Robson's grip. "All right. Please, don't kill me. I'm sorry. I'm not used to people. Are you here to make me leave?"

"No." Robson let the guy go. "Why would we do that?"

"That's what happens when you find a good place."

"Well, we're not going to do that. We're happy to leave you here, alone. We just need to know, when did you last see Alex Pardew?"

"I keep telling you, I don't know who Pardew is."

I pulled out my phone and called up Pardew's picture. "This guy. You have his clothes. So tell us. When did you last see him?"

"Him?" The guy scratched his temple. "He's Pardew? Yes. I've seen him. Of course I have. He gave me this place."

"He gave you the place?" I lowered my voice. "Come on. I need more."

"The guy, Pardew, he lived here for a while. With an asshole."

"Pardew lived here with someone else? There were two people?"

The guy nodded. "The asshole was different. He came, he went, he was in, he was out. Pardew, he was here all the time."

I showed him another picture on my phone. "Is this the asshole?"

He nodded. I showed Robson my phone. A picture of Rooney was on the screen.

"You saw the asshole come and go? How often?"

"Every day. He never stayed long." The guy shook his head. "He must be crazy."

"How do you know all this?"

"I was," the guy looked down, "having an outdoor spell. Staying at the Sidewalk Sheraton, if you know what I mean."

"We know." I nodded. "But if you were outdoors, and Pardew never left, how did you know he was here?"

"I saw him come in one day. I didn't see him come back out. Not like the asshole. He came in and went out every day."

I didn't feel like disputing his logic. "Well, if he never left, how did he come to give you the place?"

"One day the asshole came. He didn't shut the door. Usually he did. It was raining, so I went inside. He came upstairs. I followed, like, halfway. I stopped when I heard him talking. To Pardew. He said he had to go. Because of his tools."

"What tools?"

"His lever. That was gone. His file. That was back. Like that. Weird stuff. Then I guess I must have sneezed or coughed or something, because the asshole ran over and found me. He kicked me down the stairs and threw me out into the street. I tried to fight him, and I grabbed him and spun him around and tried to cling to his coat, but he punched me in the face. I stayed down till he'd gone. Then I got up and saw he'd dropped the key. I went in. Tried to give it to Pardew. That's when he said, 'Keep it.' He said I could stay if I wanted. He left me his food. Some things to wear. His tent. All he took was his bed."

"When was this?"

The guy's fingers moved as he counted. "Few

days ago. Could be more. Numbers aren't my thing."

"Where did Pardew go? Did he say where he was headed?"

The guy shrugged. "He just went away."

Chapter Twenty-one

I CAME DOWN THE NEXT MORNING AND FOUND Robson waiting for me in the kitchen. On the table there was a large coffee he'd brought from my favorite shop. It was in a cup he'd bought specially. A china cup, with a saucer. There was a slice of raspberry Danish—my favorite kind of pastry—on a china plate he'd also bought. And between the breakfast goods there was a copy of *The New York Times,* folded neatly.

I stood for a moment and looked at him. "I haven't got a car, so you can't have crashed it. I haven't got a dog, so you can't have lost it. We're in my house, so you can't have burned it down. So, John, what's this all about?"

Robson shrugged. "I wanted to do something nice."

"Well, this certainly is nice. But why?"

"To let you know how sorry I am."

"Sorry for what?"

"The whole thing with Pardew." He held up his hand with his finger and thumb half an inch apart. "We were that close to finding him. What are the odds now? His trail will be stone cold."

I shook my head. "If we're honest, John, we were days away from finding him. And that's my fault. If I'd acted faster after finding the file, maybe we'd have had a chance. In the event we only got close because you figured out the connection between Rooney and the abandoned stores. You're the only one to come out of this thing with any credit. You certainly have nothing to apologize for."

Robson looked away. "So. What are you going to do now?"

"First I'm going to enjoy this outstanding breakfast." I sat and picked up the coffee cup. "I'm going to read the paper. Then I'm going to call Atkinson. Set up a meeting. And give him everything we've got on Rooney's bribery ring."

"What about Pardew?"

"There's nothing to do about him." I took a sip of coffee. "I've let it go. I'm over it. I'm glad we did what we did. Look what we got out of it. A judge. A clerk. A lawyer. A retired detective. They'll all be seeing the inside of a jail cell, soon. And they'll be joined by thirty-two—well, thirty-one, since Pardew's in the wind—people who cheated their way out of getting convicted before. That's a pretty good return on our effort. It's better than finding Pardew, actually. What would I have done to him? My father was a pacifist. Do you think he'd have wanted me to hurt the guy? If he'd had a choice, he'd probably have turned the other cheek, anyway. All things considered, I'm pretty sure he'd have been happy with the result."

"Maybe." Robson poured some tea and took the other seat.

"Danish?"

"No, thanks."

"Part of the paper?" I picked up the *Times* and unfolded it. "Wow. It feels much thinner than it used to be."

"You know how it is these days." Robson took a sip of his tea. "They don't put everything in the print edition. There's more online, if you subscribe."

"Maybe there's a section missing? Was it the last one left at the store?"

"No. There was a stack. I'm sure it's complete."

I started to leaf through the pages. "Yes. Look. Business isn't here."

"Oh, all right!" Robson levered himself out of the chair, stomped over to the fridge, and pulled a section out from between it and the wall. "Here."

"Thank you. But why did you hide it?"

"I thought today we should aim to avoid all sources of aggravation. There's a story in there you might not like."

"You read my paper?"

"Well, I bought it, and I hadn't given it to you yet, so technically it was my paper. But yes."

I scanned the front page. "Which story?"

"It's on page three. It relates to Klinsman. Another of his holding companies. He's mentioned briefly at the end. The headline's about sleeping sickness."

I opened the cover and found the article. It started with a lot of detail about how there's a cure for the disease that kills thousands of people, mostly in Africa. The medicine for it is very effective, but making it depends on being able to source one key ingredient. It's very rare. And there's competition. It's also used in cosmetics. In Europe. And North America. There's been tension for years over the allocation of supplies. Recently, the scales have tipped—in favor of makeup. Pharmaceutical access has dried up. Because one company has secured almost all the reserves. It shifted its strategy to focus only on the more profitable market. As directed by its new owner. Klinsman.

I put the paper down and drained my coffee. "You know what I think? It's a shame Klinsman wasn't in his house when Hendrie burned it down."

"He has other houses." Robson looked at me. "He could have other fires."

"He could. But maybe that would be too quick. Maybe we could snatch him, infect him with sleeping sickness, and when the disease reaches its height, take him to Bergdorf's, tie him to a pillar in the cosmetics department, and make him watch people having makeovers using the cream that contains the only substance that could save him."

"That would be poetic."

"It would be satisfying, it's just . . ."

"What, a bit passive? You want something a bit more hands-on?"

"Not really. I'd be happy to watch him go that

way, knowing he'd brought the end on himself. I just can't shake the feeling—the bike company, the way he abuses his employees, this Africa thing. Could it all be noise? A smoke screen, to divert attention?"

"You're not circling back to China, are you? The telecom contracts?"

"You know the saying. No smoke without—" My phone rang. I checked the screen. "Sorry. This is Carrodus. From the courthouse. You don't mind?"

I hit Answer. "Hey, Frank. Is everything OK?"

"Where are you?" Carrodus sounded out of breath.

"At home. In Hell's Kitchen. Why?"

"I need help. It's Cynthia. My little girl. She's missing."

I was on my feet before I realized I'd moved. "I'm on my way. I'll help you look. Don't worry. We'll find her."

"No. That's not it. Rita's family's here. Our neighbors are all helping. We've got the search under control. I need you at the courthouse. To cover my shift. I know it's your day off, but I'm desperate. I've got to stay here, and I can't lose my job."

"It's not a problem. I'll head over there now. Let me know when you find her."

Centre Street was clogged with people when I arrived, thirty-five minutes later.

That was nothing new. The courthouse is a

magnet for tourists, snapping selfies in front of the columns and gazing up in awe at the pediment before rushing off to tick the next box in their guidebooks. Eager spectators flock to the place, too, high on schadenfreude, hoping for a glimpse of someone famous—or infamous—taking a sorry climb up the steps of justice. But there was something different about this crowd. It was less animated than usual. Quieter. No one was splintering off or drifting away. Even the regular stream of commuters was giving it a wide berth rather than angrily forging through.

I figured I could spare a few minutes, so I joined in at the back and started to ease my way forward until I saw that the front row was being held at bay by a police officer. He looked young—barely out of the academy, I guessed—with a neatly pressed uniform and the kind of still-shiny cap badge you wouldn't want to be wearing in certain neighborhoods, late at night. His partner was a couple of yards behind him. He was wearing latex gloves and crouching over a body—a woman's—like he was cautiously checking her vitals. He straightened up and I saw that the victim was probably in her thirties. She was wearing a tan trench coat, belted tight against the drizzle, and she was lying on her back. Her right leg was bent under her left at an unnatural angle. Her arms were stretched out and her black hair was splayed in a dark halo over the shiny gray stone.

Was it a robbery? Had someone been trying to steal confidential documents? That was unlikely. She still had her purse and two briefcases. Had she been attacked? It could have been a warning of some sort. It probably wasn't a murder attempt—not so close to a road that was full of much safer bets like the crazy cabs, and even the bikes.

A baleful siren cut through the traffic sounds and a few seconds later an ambulance arrived and swayed to a halt. People shifted for the paramedics to squeeze through, and I noticed that the woman who'd fallen had one shoe missing. I could see the seam in her pantyhose around her toes. I pushed a little closer and saw the shoe, lying on the bottom step. Its heel was broken. The stone was wet. The explanation was suddenly obvious. She was hurrying. She slipped. She hit her head. My old habits—old instincts, always looking for something sinister—had almost steered me wrong. Maybe they were steering me wrong regarding Klinsman, too. Maybe there was a simpler, civilian explanation to his involvement with the telecom company. Maybe there was a simple, civilian solution. And maybe there was an ambulance in his future, too.

I was in the locker room, about to fasten the last button on my overalls, when Carrodus called back.

"Frank. Tell me it's good news."

"It is." I could hear the relief in his voice. "We found her. She's safe."

"That's fantastic. I'm so happy for you guys. Where was she?"

"You'll never believe it. She was in her bed."

"No one thought to look there before?"

"No. Not since Rita got her up and dressed,

first thing. After that she had breakfast and five minutes to play before school, like always. That's when she disappeared. We searched the apartment. The building. The roof. The basement. The furnace room. The street. The alley. The dumpsters. Our friends' houses. Then Rita had the idea she might have run away, so she went to see if any of her toys were missing. The toys were all there. And so was a big bulge in the comforter."

"What was up with her? Was she sick? Tired?"

"Neither. She was just smart. She didn't want to go to school, and figured her bed was the last place we'd look since her mom had already found her there earlier. And it worked."

"That is smart." It actually reminded me of something my grandfather had told me about WWII. About naval battles. He said that if you came under attack from a bigger enemy vessel, you were in major trouble. The opponent would have longer-range guns, so you couldn't get close enough to attack. And you couldn't run, because the other ship would have more powerful engines. The only option was to evade the enemy's fire until help arrived. And the most effective way to evade was a technique known as *follow the splashes*. Each time an enemy shot missed, you plotted a course to the spot where the shell hit the water. The assumption was, he wouldn't aim for the same place twice. "Frank, thanks for letting me know. I'm glad you're all OK. But now you've found Cynthia, will you be coming in? There is actually something I need to do."

"Sure. I'll be there in an hour and I'll make up

the time. There's no need to wait. Thanks for stepping in."

I hung up, then called Robson.

"John, this is important. You told me there were three locations where Pardew might be. The Village, SoHo, and the Bronx. Is that the order Rooney cased them?"

"No. It was based on their distance from the brownstone. I was thinking about an efficient search pattern."

"OK. In that case, what order did Rooney have them in?"

"Wait one." I heard footsteps, then the rattling of computer keys. "Rooney went to the Bronx first. Then the Village. Then SoHo."

"That's what I was hoping you'd say. I have an idea. Pick me up at Foley Square, as soon as you can."

The storefront in the Bronx was in an even sorrier state than the other two we'd visited. I guessed it had been abandoned for longer. Shingles were missing from the roof. Glass in two of the second-floor windows was cracked. Mortar was missing in several places and many of its bricks were crumbling. The graffiti was layers deep with bright fresh paint overlapping with faded older shades. The metal screen was in three sections—wider on the outsides, covering the windows, and a central section over the door that had been pried open at some point and then inexpertly bent back, leaving parts of it not quite flush.

The building was on a corner lot, so the entrance to the apartment was at the side. It had a wooden door, which had once been white. There was a new lock, the same as at the other places. There was no need to pick this one, though. A bar had been shoved between the face of the door and the jamb at some point to lever it open, wrecking the frame and leaving nothing for the tongue to engage with. I pushed the door, and it moved. Less than an inch.

"It's wedged from the other side." I looked at Robson. "Someone's home."

"I guess after they busted it open someone took a piece of the frame and braced it against the stairs." Robson slammed his shoulder against the door. It gave a fraction, then bounced back. "There's nothing too solid holding it." He slammed the door again and it gave slightly more, but there was no sign of it opening. "Wait here. I have a better idea."

Robson was back two minutes later, in the Cadillac. He slalomed across the mouth of the side street to line up with the apartment door, then reversed, bumping over the curb and stopping eighteen inches from the side of the building. He popped the trunk, removed the spare wheel from its carpeted enclosure, and centered it in the doorway. Then he jumped back into the driver's seat and reversed again until the rear fender made contact with the spare wheel. He gunned the engine; the car swayed for a moment, then lurched backward as the door gave way. He slammed on the brakes and the car stopped, wallowing on its soggy suspension, two inches from the wall. He pulled away, bounced down from the sidewalk, and stopped at the side of the street.

We stepped over Robson's spare wheel and a few pieces of broken frame and ran up the stairs. Surprise was out, so we had to hope for shock and awe. And for no one to be waiting with a gun. Or a deep fryer full of boiling oil, if they were continuing their improvised security regime.

I came face-to-face with Alex Pardew in the living room at the front of the apartment. It was the first room I tried. He was standing in front of a camp chair, which was bizarrely the same brand as the ones I'd picked out to use at the brownstone. He also had a camp table. A lamp attached to a long wire trailing down from the ceiling. An air mattress. And a sleeping bag.

"Hello, Paul," he said.

Chapter Twenty-two

IT TOOK ME A MOMENT TO PROCESS WHAT I'D walked into. It wasn't just the sound of him saying my name that was unsettling. It was the sight of him. He was standing there, stooped, his arms hanging loosely at his sides. His hair was lank. He was unshaven. Deflated. Defeated, even. When I'd imagined this moment, I'd pictured Pardew as a cornered tiger, ready to rip out my throat. A worthy adversary putting up a valiant fight as I avenged my father. Instead he looked more like a half-starved prisoner or a brainwashed hostage who'd lost all hope of rescue and was now wondering whether he had the will to survive the journey home.

"You know who I am?" I was struggling to continue looking at him.

"Of course." His voice was quiet and wheezy. "Your father showed me pictures of you, hundreds of times. He was very proud of you."

"I guess you knew my father well?"

Pardew nodded.

"He trusted you."

He nodded again.

"Did that make it easier to plunder his life's work? Or harder?"

Pardew held his hands up in surrender. "If you're here to hurt me, or kill me, fine. Go ahead. I can't stop you. But before you do anything, you should know . . . what the cops say? What the ADA says? It's wrong. If you kill me, you'll be killing an innocent man."

"So you didn't steal from my father?"

"Oh, yes. I did that. Attempted to. Kind of. Technically." He took a moment. "What I did was make it look like some of his assets were worth less, so I'd owe him less when I bought the company. It was more fraud than theft, honestly. But that was in the past. I stopped doing it ages ago. Your father knew all about it. I confessed what I'd done. Tried to do. And he forgave me."

"Cut the weasel talk. You mean you got caught, you fought, and my father dropped dead."

"No. Well, I guess he did die, but that had nothing to do with me. When I last saw him he was smiling, healthy, sitting at his desk, drinking tea. I only heard he'd died when I got arrested. I was shocked."

"When did you last see him?"

"The night he died. At his house."

"The night you fought."

"There was no fight."

"I saw the crime scene photos. His study was trashed."

"I saw those photos, too. All I can tell you is that it was fine when I left. There wasn't even a coaster out of place."

"So what happened? My father wrecked the place himself?"

"I have no idea what happened. If I had to guess, I'd say the police did it. So they could hang his death on me, in case they couldn't sell the jury on the fraud thing."

"Why did you go to the house that night?"

"Your father asked me to. He'd found out what I was up to. I figured he would, sooner or later. He asked me, and I told him everything. It was a weight off my chest, in the end. And it was the strangest conversation I ever had. I was confessing to defrauding him out of millions of dollars and yet we were sitting there, quiet, calm, polite, like friends chewing over childhood memories. I told him I had a record of everything I'd done, and a plan to put it all back the way it was. He accepted that, and forgave me. He said he took an element of the blame on himself for making the valuation formula too harsh, and giving me such an incentive to cheat."

"How did he catch on to you?"

"He said he'd been tying up loose ends, getting ready to retire. He owned a house in Hell's Kitchen. A brownstone. Worth a fortune. It was one of the first things I devalued. I thought it was a sweetener in an old deal, long forgotten. It turned out he'd bought it deliberately. Something to do with your mother. He said he'd left it alone for years because the interior was important to her, for some reason. Now it was time to finally get everything cleared out, and put the past behind him. I guess he meant he wanted to renovate, then sell it? Anyway, he saw its value in the books had fallen when it should have risen—a lot—and he got suspicious. It was easy to join the dots after that. But it was my own fault. I put myself in the frame."

"Go back a second. My father said he wanted to get everything cleared out of the brownstone?"

"Right."

"Those were his exact words?"

"As far as I can remember."

"What did he mean?"

"Well, I assumed the house was full of junk."

"Did you see it?"

"No. I can't even remember the address. It was just a number on a balance sheet to me."

"OK. So you promised to put everything right. What then?"

"We drew a line under the business and just chatted for a while. His housekeeper brought his tea, like she did every night. I passed, like I did every night I was there, because I only drink coffee. It got late, and I left."

"The tea. Did Mrs. Vincent serve it in a mug? Or a cup with a saucer?"

Pardew thought for a moment. "A cup and saucer."

"What pattern were they?"

"White, with red roses. The cup was a kind of a fluted shape, with a bouquet on all four sides."

"Good. Now, one last question. You said you stopped devaluing my father's assets a while ago. Why?"

"The plan wasn't working. There were too many assets, and it was obvious I didn't have enough time because he kept talking about retirement. I needed an alternative."

"Which was?"

"I'm still looking."

"Don't lie to me. Lie about this, and I won't believe anything else you've said. That would lead to a bad outcome. For you. Like my friend here, who has poor impulse control, throwing you out of a window of his choice."

"I had the idea to challenge the valuation formula in court."

"That sounds totally reasonable. Why try to hide it?"

"Because I asked a lawyer. He said there was no hope of winning a case like that. And now you're really going to hate me. I floated the idea of offering the judge an . . . incentive."

"So your lawyer set you up with a bent judge?"

"No." Pardew shook his head. "He dismissed the idea out of hand. Said he'd never be party to anything like that. And that I'd be wasting my time anyway, because the judges in New York are too straight. I found out he was wrong about that, though. On my own."

"Oh yeah? How?"

"Around the same time I got a DUI. I was in a high-stress situation. You can understand that, right? Anyway, I'm at the gym and a guy approaches me. He says he's an ex-cop, and that he has contacts who could make my problem disappear."

"You were using the same lawyer for the DUI as you asked for advice about challenging the formula? Steven Bruce?"

"That's right. But he wasn't involved with getting the DUI case dropped."

"Moron." Robson's whisper was audible clear across the room.

"It didn't occur to you that Bruce knew you were open to bribes, because you raised the idea yourself? So he denounces the concept publicly, and sends the ex-cop to see you on the quiet?"

"No." Pardew shook his head. "That never crossed my mind."

"Moron." Robson's voice was no quieter. "Do you believe in fairies, too?"

"Ignore him," I said. "So you paid?"

"I did. My case got thrown out. And I asked the cop if he'd be up for helping me in the future, if I was ever in need. He said yes, if the price was right and they could get the right judge. I was thinking that could be the perfect solution for my formula issue."

"Only you wound up on trial for fraud and murder two. Why didn't you try to use him to beat the charges?"

"The murder charge was bogus. It was only the fraud I was worried about. I wanted to use the guy. Obviously. But I couldn't contact him. I was in jail. I couldn't get bail because the ADA said I was a flight risk. My case was tanking, and I got desperate. I told Steven Bruce what had happened with the DUI thing and asked him to try and cut a deal. Oh my goodness. What an idiot I am. I told a guy I was willing to testify against a conspiracy he was part of. I thought word of the possible deal had just leaked. No wonder my file was taken and the case went south."

"That's what led to the mistrial. But how did you end up here?"

"The minute I got released the ex-cop—his name's Brian Rooney—got in touch. He said he knew something that could help me. So I met him, and he brought me here. He said I had to stay until all the evidence about the DUI thing had been destroyed. And that I was lucky he didn't kill me for trying to roll on him. He wanted to, but JD wouldn't allow it."

"JD?"

"Judge Dredd. It's what they call the bent judge they work for. Because of his temper. The plan was to expunge the evidence so I'd have nothing to deal. Return the file. Then let me go, and I'd either have to run or get arrested. Only the process took ages because JD insisted on fixing the file himself, and he got sick before he could finish it. In the meantime they kept moving me from one hovel to another."

"Why did you come back to this place?"

"What else could I do? Run, Rooney said. But how? Where to? I'm just a regular guy. I don't have money stashed away, or contacts who could smuggle me out of the country. I don't even have a passport. I had to surrender it. I couldn't risk going to my house after the police had the file back, because they'd be watching for me. I figured this was the safest place until I came up with a plan. No one would look, because it had already been abandoned."

"We should go." Robson had crossed to the window. "We've been here too long, and that business with the car and the door was hardly discreet."

"You're right." I scanned the room, then turned to Pardew. "Grab the sleeping bag and the mattress. Leave the rest."

"Where are we going? What are you going to do with me?"

"Don't worry. We're not going to hurt you. But I'm not going to lie. After all you've done, with my father and the DUI thing, your account is seriously in the red. I have an idea that might bring it back into the black. I need to iron out some details. And get some information from you. I can't guarantee the police won't become involved. But for there to be any chance of this ending up OK, you need to come with us and do exactly what we say."

Robson was in the kitchen when I came down. The newspaper was in the trash, the dishes were in the sink, and he was making tea.

"Did you put him on the third floor?"

I nodded.

"Do you think he'll stay there?"

"Probably. I took his clothes and pointed out

that if he wanders the city naked, he'll get arrested and the police have the file."

"But the police don't have the file."

"I know that. He doesn't. And just in case, wired his door handle to the electricity."

"What are you going to do with him?"

"Depends on how much of what he said is true. I'm not bothered about the fraud. What he did's a weird crime. Nothing was actually taken. It would have been, if he'd bought my father's company on the cheap. But he didn't. The assets are all still there, and they're in the process of being revalued. So it's no harm, no foul, as far as I'm concerned."

"What do you make of the rest of it?"

"I have mixed feelings. Some of it rang true. My father was more likely to forgive someone than to fight them. And he did like his tea, last thing before bed. Earl Grey. The cup Pardew described, that was from his favorite set. My mother picked it out on their honeymoon, in Paris. As for the other things, the jury's out. Like with this place. Why would my father say he needed to clear it out? Clear what out? Remember when we first set foot in here, we both said it felt like a safe house, it was so clean and sterile."

"Maybe your father made the decision to call a cleaning service, then found the discrepancy with the value, but after the ball was already rolling. There'd be no need to cancel the appointment because of some accounting questions, if he really wanted the place taken care of. That would explain why it was so spotless when we arrived."

"That's possible, I guess. I'll ask Ferguson, his

lawyer, to dig through the bills. See if there's any record."

"What about his office getting trashed?" Robson added some milk to his tea. "That's the biggest discrepancy, if you ask me. If Pardew didn't wreck the place, who did? And when? Do you believe the police would really do that, just to pad a case they didn't even know they were making yet? Could someone totally unrelated have sneaked in after Pardew left, but before your father collapsed?"

"You can rule out anyone else sneaking in. That's too coincidental." I helped myself to tea from Robson's kettle. "I could believe the police would tamper with evidence—some of them, in some circumstances. But I don't see the motivation here. And I trust Atkinson. No. I think Pardew's lying. And I think there's an easy way to find out."

"Time for the window?"

"Something less dramatic. More scientific. Mrs. Vincent told me she heard arguing coming from my father's study and things getting smashed while Pardew was still there. That's in her statement, too. She also said my father wouldn't let her back in the study after Pardew left. If Pardew's telling the truth, there'd be a cup and saucer—or at least broken pieces of china—in the crime scene photos and the officer's log. I don't remember seeing any. But to be sure I'll get copies from Atkinson and double-check."

"What if Pardew is telling the truth, and your father took his cup to the kitchen himself when he'd finished his tea. That would explain why it's not in the photos."

"My father would never do that. You don't buy a dog and bark yourself, he used to say. But just in case, I'll talk to Mrs. Vincent and confirm whether she brought my father's tea, assuming she can remember that kind of detail after all these months. I'll also ask if she remembers finding his cup in the kitchen, later. Then, if we figure my father's death was an accident, I'll be satisfied to make Pardew help with my idea. If he's lying, and he riled my father up, trashed his stuff, and caused his collapse, the story will have a different ending. I'll still make him help. Then I'll make sure he winds up in a place that makes those storefronts seem like Caribbean resorts."

Chapter Twenty-three

LIFE'S A GAME OF GIVE-AND-TAKE. THAT'S WHAT Mrs. Vincent used to say when I was a kid and didn't want to do something. Her words have stayed with me. Only, over the years I've learned that things often work out better if you do the taking before you do the giving.

"No!" Atkinson's voice echoed around the courthouse's dome. The early rush of lawyers and clerks and jurors had passed, but plenty of heads still turned. "How many times? It's just not possible."

"It must be possible." I tried to keep my voice reasonable, and above all, quiet. "You showed them to me before. It stands to reason that you can show them to me again."

"You were a suspect before. You're not one now. There's no reason to show you again."

"Think of a reason."

"Give me a reason. Why do you want to see them again, anyway?"

"They could help me shed new light on the case."

"How? You've got to understand, access to crime scene photos is controlled, and for good reasons. The events we're talking about happened more than six months ago. The case became inactive, officially, so everything was archived. A record's made of every request to see them now. I'd need justification."

"Hypothetically speaking, if Pardew's court file was found, would that reactivate the case? Give you justification to request your own archived files?"

"Have you—"

"I'll take that as a yes to the justification. So. Once the Pardew file is back on your desk, an untraceable copy of the photos could fall into my hands, guaranteed never to see the light of day?"

"Are you saying—"

"I'm not saying anything until I know how quickly those photos could hit my inbox."

Atkinson was silent for a moment. "Not on email. That's too easy to trace. But hypothetically, if Pardew's file was returned to me, an envelope containing copies of the photos could be at your brownstone—if I have your word they'll be returned, and not copied—within twenty-four hours."

"Detective, why don't you stay here awhile. Give me five minutes. Let me see what I can find."

Atkinson grabbed my arm. "You know where

the file is? Is there anything in it about Pardew's whereabouts? That's what I really want."

"I doubt there's anything in the file that would reveal where he currently is. He might still be in the city. Or we might never see him again. I have a feeling we'll know one way or the other, very soon."

I felt a little bad misleading Atkinson over the file. I knew I'd feel worse, though, if I found that he'd been involved with faking a crime scene. Or embellishing one. I watched him head out of the courthouse with the bulky envelope under his arm and wondered whether he was walking into a trap. Or setting one for his partner, Kanchelskis. I wouldn't have minded that so much. Kanchelskis had rubbed me wrong from the start.

I made my way to the basement. I figured there was no point trekking all the way to Westchester to talk to Mrs. Vincent unless she returned my call and confirmed she was home. In the meantime, I could work. I enjoyed it, and I didn't know how much longer I'd be at the courthouse. I came to find the file. I'd done that. It felt strange now that it was out of my hands. The Pardew chapter would soon be resolved, one way or the other. I still had to tie up the loose ends with Hendrie and Klinsman. Then I'd have a decision to make. To quote The Clash, should I stay or should I go?

I heard laughter coming from the janitors' room and when I went in I saw three guys sitting at one of the tables. Carrodus was standing by them. He nodded to me, slapped the nearest guy on the back, then hurried over, put his arm around my shoulder, and steered me into the corner.

"I need to ask you something, Paul. Where were you last Thursday?"

"I was here, working. Then I went home. Why?"

"Where were you working, exactly? Which floor?"

"I was allocated to the third, all last week."

"Did you go up to the fourth, for any reason? Particularly on Thursday?"

"Is someone accusing me of doing extra work?" I winked at him. "I'm ex-army, Frank. You know the rule. We never volunteer."

"I get that. But there's been a complaint. Some kids. They said that one of the janitors took their keys, threw them in a toilet, and made them clean a bathroom."

I shrugged. "So?"

"The description they gave matches you to a T."

"I'm sure I'd remember if I'd done something like that. Did the kids say what they'd done to deserve such treatment? I can't imagine anyone would respond that way without a good reason."

"Even if there was a reason, you can't go around hurting people and keeping them in bathrooms against their will."

"That goes without saying. Although, thinking about it, are there any guidelines in the employee handbook? Things like this are best spelled out, to avoid any misunderstandings. I could take a—"

My phone rang and I checked the screen. "I'm sorry, Frank—this is my father's lawyer. I need to take it. There are still some details I need to iron out."

Carrodus nodded and drifted back to the table. I stayed in the corner. There's something about lawyers that makes me feel the need for privacy whenever I have to talk to them.

"Mr. Ferguson, thanks for calling back. I have a question I need your help with. It's to do with the record of an expense for a service my father may have ordered a few weeks or months before he died."

"I'll certainly help if I can, Paul. That's not the reason I'm calling, though. I'm afraid I have some sad news. It regards Mrs. Vincent. I'm very sorry to have to tell you this, but she passed away. I'm sure this comes as a blow, because I know the two of you were very close for many years."

The room floated out of focus for a moment, and the others' voices seemed muffled, as if they were underwater. "When did she pass?"

"Last Wednesday. She was visiting with friends in California. It was very sudden. Turned out she had a rare heart condition that must have finally caught up to her."

I hadn't known Mrs. Vincent had any friends in California. I hadn't known if she had friends anywhere. A sudden pang of guilt jabbed me in the chest. "Who's making the arrangements? We'll have to bring her home. Sort out some kind of funeral."

"There's no need. She's already been cremated.

There was a note in some papers she left with me for safekeeping, years ago, that explains how she had a horror of mortuaries and couldn't stand the thought of her body being kept on ice for an extended period. It's a little strange, but not the strangest thing I've seen over the years. All that's left is to secure the house against intruders—and from the cold, since winter will soon be on its way—until you decide what you want to do with the place. Would you like me to send someone over?"

"No." I shook my head even though I knew he couldn't see me. "I'll go. I'll take care of it myself."

Carrodus must have seen the look on my face, because as soon as I hung up the phone he hurried across to check on me. "You OK, Paul?"

"I'm fine." The reality was at odds with my automatic, conditioned response, and it took my brain a moment to take the reins from my tongue. "Actually, I'm not. That was bad news. Someone's died. My . . ." How could I explain Mrs. Vincent to him? What word was big enough to describe the role she'd played in my life? *My father's housekeeper* didn't come close, yet I didn't know what else to say. "Someone I cared about. There are some things I need to take care of, now."

"Take the rest of the day, Paul." Carrodus took hold of my arm. "Take as long as you need. Go. Do what you need to do."

I shook my head. "It can wait till after my shift."

"That's your grief talking." Carrodus steered me toward the door. "Go. Be where you need to be. I'll cover for you here."

I figured there was no particular rush—I'd been at the house on Sunday and everything seemed pretty well squared away—but I felt the need to be doing something. I started by heading to the brownstone and picking up the keys to the rental car that I hadn't gotten around to returning. Robson offered to come to Westchester with me, but I told him to stay. Someone had to watch Pardew. And if Atkinson came through with the crime scene photos, I wanted the envelope to fall into safe hands.

I found myself passing the botanic gardens and realized I had no memory of driving through Manhattan, let alone heading up the Saw Mill. I wondered if I should have let Robson drive, after all. I was on autopilot, strangely numb, with a head full of weirdly practical thoughts. I'd be free to take the furniture from the house now. Where had my father's car ended up? In California, with Mrs. Vincent's friends? Who were they? Where did they live? How would I get it back? Would it be worth the trouble? They were all impersonal, trivial details, but they were tripping over one another in my head and degrading my ability to think.

When I arrived at the house and climbed out of the car I was struck by how quiet the area was. There was no equipment roaring away in anyone's yard. No traffic noise. No aircraft overhead. That was unusual, like the neighborhood was lying low in an instinctive show of respect. As I stood there it struck me that my mother had gone. My father had gone. And now Mrs. Vincent had gone, leaving me with no living relative or close human connection. The house was no longer a home without her. It was just a large wooden box full of memories. Most of them distant. Not many of them warm.

I was right by the gate but found myself reluctant to go through. And as if I needed more reasons to hesitate, I started to worry that I wasn't the best man for the job. What did I know about house maintenance? I'd only owned a house for a few weeks. If I wanted to blow it up and make it look like an accident, I could do that. If I needed to leave a body inside and stage it like a suicide, that would be no problem. If I had to wire the place for sound and pictures, that would be a piece of cake. But what do you do about shutting off the water? Dealing with the appliances? Do you need to close the drapes? Honestly, I was clueless.

I pushed the negative thoughts away, opened the gate, and made a plan as I walked up the path. I didn't need to leave everything in perfect shape. In a situation like this, *good enough* would do. I'd just make sure everything was locked and powered down. Take care of any flood or fire risks, and secure the place against intruders. Then we could locate Mrs. Vincent's next of kin, unless Ferguson already knew where they were, and ship her possessions to them whenever it was convenient. The same thing applied to the books and the furniture. And maybe the kitchen stuff. That could all be shipped to the brownstone when I had more time to deal with it. Along with my father's personal possessions, if there were any I wanted. There was no need for any drama. I should be in and out within ten minutes, maximum.

I unlocked the front door and stepped into the hallway. It was a wide space with a high, angled ceiling that I was used to hearing echo with the sound of footsteps or voices or Mrs. Vincent's radio. Today it was silent, as if the house itself was in mourning. I shivered and glanced through the doorway on the right. It led to Mrs. Vincent's bedroom. I realized I'd never been inside. I pushed the door a little wider open. The air still carried a hint of her soap—she never wore perfume. The bed, with its head against the far wall, was neatly made. The closet wasn't closed all the way. Inside, I could see spaces on the hanging rail and shoe rack, presumably left by the things she'd packed for her visit to the West Coast. Her bathroom door wasn't closed, either, and I could see an empty toothbrush mug on a shelf above the sink. I crossed to the window, checked the lock, and pulled the drapes. I took another glance around, then went back out to the hallway. I checked the rest of the first-floor windows. Unplugged the TV in the living room, and the coffee machine in the kitchen. Opened the dishwasher a little wider, just in case Mrs. Vincent had been right about the mold. Then I headed up the stairs. Looked in my father's room. And my old bedroom. I paused there for a minute. There were tiny marks on the walls from where the corners of my posters had been attached. I could still picture the way they were set out. I lay on my bed, and remembered staring up at the ceiling, all the nights I couldn't sleep. I remembered thinking of Marian. But never about the army. Never about all the places in the world I'd end up serving in. And never about returning here under circumstances like these.

I made it halfway back along the landing, and stopped. I'd checked every room except one. The room I'd always been forbidden to enter. The one where my mother had died. I was standing by its door. There was no one to tell me to stay out now. But the question was, did I want to see inside? Was it a picture I wanted in my head, after all these years? I reached for the handle, expecting it to still be locked. Then I could tell myself I'd tried. I'd have the opportunity to withdraw with my honor intact.

The handle moved. The door opened. Before I could stop myself I stepped forward. The room was dark. The shades were drawn. As a kid I'd had little understanding of the reality of dying in childbirth, though it always conjured nightmarish visions of blood-soaked sheets, torn flesh, lifeless eyes. There didn't need to be a lock to keep me out. My imagination did that job on its own. Horrible pictures rushed back, filling my head and making me hesitate to turn on the light. I took a breath. Reached for the switch. Flicked it up. And saw no evidence of carnage at all. Just a crib and a stroller that had been mine, lined up by the wall, ready to be reissued. Half a dozen cardboard boxes with the words *Baby Clothes* stenciled on the sides. And a bed. It was neatly made. There were no signs of blood or gore. Just an alarming 1970s turquoise flowery comforter.

I crossed to the bed and stopped at the side, near the pillow, where you might stand to say good night to someone. Or chat with them. Or stroke their forehead if they were sick. My mother had died right there. So had my sister. I knew I should feel something for them, now that I was so physically close to the spot where they'd drawn their final breaths. I tried to feel something. But I didn't. I couldn't. They were theoretically two of my closest relatives, but in reality they were just ideas. I'd never known one of them. I didn't remember the other. Not in any meaningful way. I was used to living with the knowledge that they were dead. That was normal to me, like knowing that snow was cold or you get hungry if you don't eat. I guessed that was sad, but there was nothing I could do about it now.

The far wall in the room was dominated by a fireplace, with a mirror hanging above it and a closet on either side. I started with the one on the left. It was full of my mother's clothes. Outdoor wear mostly—coats, boots, nothing too personal. I recognized a ski suit, from a photograph that had been in a frame on my father's desk. That was the only picture of my mother he ever displayed. I'd often gazed at the image, growing up, so now it felt strange to see the outfit she'd been wearing, full-sized, hanging where I could reach out and touch it.

The right-hand closet was filled with shelves, making it more like a bookcase with doors. They were lined with rows of bankers' boxes. I picked one at random and lifted it down. It was full of books. They were my mother's, from grade school. The other boxes held all kinds of other academic souvenirs, from her high school days through college. She'd gone to MIT and majored in electronics. Or so the documents showed. I'd had no idea. My father had never mentioned it, and I'd never asked him.

It was strangely intimate to be suddenly poring over my mother's things, like I was finally getting to know her through the items she'd chosen to keep. There were circuit diagrams. Articles. Research papers. Pages and pages of handwritten notes and sketches and ideas for inventions and projects and experiments. I couldn't follow all the science—it was simultaneously outdated and too complicated—but it seemed like her specialty was sound engineering. She'd been working on new techniques for eliminating interference from live recordings, and had drawn up a bunch of detailed plans for fitting out some kind of advanced studio. Advanced for her times, anyway. Now I'd bet you could do more with your phone. I couldn't help wondering how she'd have felt about that. And whether, if she'd had the chance to continue her work, my teenage years would have been spent sitting in on sessions with Lucinda Williams and Alanis Morissette rather than enduring lectures about profit and loss and cash flow from my father.

I stayed in the room, reading for another hour, then repacked the boxes and put them back on their shelves. I closed the door I'd never expected to open, went back downstairs, and was about to leave the house when a final thought crossed my mind. It was too late to ask Mrs. Vincent about my father and whether he had tea on the night he died. But the next best thing was waiting for me in the kitchen. The cups, lined up in the cabinet. With a telltale space among them. Or without.

Chapter Twenty-four

THE NEXT MORNING ROBSON WAS IN THE KITCHEN when I came down. He was sitting at the table, drinking tea, with a sheaf of photographs in his hand. It reminded me of the days as a kid when we'd come back from a trip and my father would send his roll of film away for processing, then jump on the prints the moment they arrived in the mail. Only, the pictures Robson was holding were larger, and they'd come special delivery from the crime lab.

"Seen these?" He held up the pictures.

I nodded. "Looked at them last night when I got back."

"I just went through them again." He shook his head. "There's no sign of any cup, or any fragments of china. Not in any of the photos. And not in the inventory. I have to say, that doesn't augur well for Pardew."

"That's true. But I checked in the kitchen when I was up at the house. One of the cups is missing."

"That doesn't prove his story. It could have been broken at any time. By anyone."

"In theory. But you have to understand how sentimental my father was about those cups. You had to treat them as if they were filled with weapons-grade plutonium, only more carefully. If you grew up in that house—if you spent any time there at all—you'd rather hack your own head off with a blunt potato peeler than chip one. Let alone break one."

"It's still possible. Cups can break however much care you take with them."

"Maybe. But the theory's moot now, anyway. We needed Mrs. Vincent to corroborate the details. If we'd been able . . . Wait. Pass me that photo."

Robson handed me the photograph from the top of the stack. "It's not one of those magic pictures, you know. The image you want won't appear if you stare for a while."

"I'm not looking for the cup." I took out my phone and opened its magnifying app so I could study one section. "This is weird."

"What is?" Robson came around behind me and looked over my shoulder.

"See the picture frame on the floor? It's broken. The picture's fallen out. It was of my parents, on a ski trip. It was cute."

"How can you tell? It's facedown on the floor."

"I recognize the frame. And my father only had one picture on display in his study. He only had one anywhere. But that's not the point. Out of its frame, you can see part of the photo is folded back. Why would he have done that?"

"To make it fit in the frame?"

"No. It actually looked too small for the frame. He made a cardboard surround to fill the gaps at the sides. I thought the picture must have been some odd '80s format, or that they'd had it developed in Switzerland, or wherever."

"If those are your mother's hands, it looks like she was holding a trophy. A big one. Could your father have been jealous?"

"No. Definitely not. Jealousy wasn't in his nature."

"Then I'm out of ideas."

"Look at this. It's even weirder. See, there's something engraved on the trophy? On the plate on its base." I handed Robson my phone.

"It says, 'Women's Downhill, Open. First Place. 15th August 1983.' She won. Awesome. What's wrong with that?"

"What's wrong is that in August '83 my mother was seven months pregnant with my sister. How was she winning a downhill skiing competition?"

"Paul, you caveman. Life doesn't have to stop just because a person's pregnant."

"Sure. Early on. If you're talking about working. Driving. Swimming. But downhill skiing? At seven months? That's recklessly irresponsible."

"You've been known to do the odd reckless thing yourself from time to time. Maybe it runs in the family."

"I've never been reckless when someone else's life is at stake. And here's another thing that doesn't add up. I saw my mother's ski suit yesterday, at the house. I recognized it from the picture. It was regular-sized, not maternity."

"You're reading way too much into this, Paul. She could have had another ski suit from the same brand that she didn't keep. The one suit could have been baggy enough for her to wear it, anyway. Not everyone swells up to the size of an elephant when they're expecting a baby. I actually think it's quite cool to ski one day, give birth the next."

"Except that my sister was stillborn, and my mother died in delivery."

"Oh. I'm sorry, Paul. I didn't realize. No. That's not cool. Maybe it's why your father hid the trophy part of the picture? Maybe he resented it, if he thought the race played a part in the outcome."

"But why—" My phone beeped. Robson passed it back and I saw an email had arrived. From Harry. I opened it and quickly scanned the text. "All right. Forget all that sad stuff. Some news is in and it's just what the doctor ordered. How do you fancy a trip to Albany?"

"Have you got anything sharp I could stick in my eyes, instead?"

"No, you're going to like this. It's going to be fun. Harry found something in Klinsman's contacts. One of them did business with Rooney."

"The same kind of business Pardew did?"

"Correct. So I'm thinking we should have . . . shall we call it an elevated discussion with the guy?"

Chapter Twenty-five

Howard Wilkinson was at his desk when I opened the door to his office on the twelfth floor of a clunky van der Rohe rip-off building, tucked into the elbow where State Street meets Broadway. He was adding numbers to a spreadsheet, and smiling greedily as he watched his projected profits rack up at the bottom of the screen.

"Wrong office." He barely glanced at me. "Get out."

"Right office." I took one of the faux antique dining chairs from the mini conference table near the right-hand wall, moved it closer to the window, and sat down. "Wrong answer."

"I don't know who you are"—his hand tore itself away from the keyboard and reached for the phone—"but I'm calling the police."

"Very good." I nodded. "Very civil-minded. I like that in a felon. It'll save them the trouble of calling on you. Again."

Wilkinson froze with the receiver halfway to his ear. Slowly, he replaced it.

"Allow me to introduce myself." I summoned a brief smile. "My name's Paul McDonnell. I'm an attorney. I work with a friend of yours. Steven Bruce."

"With Steve? That's excellent." He was speaking slowly, playing for time. "I haven't seen him in I don't know how long. How's he doing?"

"Health-wise, he couldn't be better. Professionally, not so well. In fact, to use a legal term, he's in deep shit."

"Oh dear. I'm sorry to hear that. Is there anything I can do to help?"

"To help Bruce? No. You know how resourceful he is. The process of him digging himself out is already well under way. But to help yourself? Yes. Absolutely. That's actually why I'm here."

"I don't need help, from myself or anyone else. I'm not the one who's in trouble."

I shook my head. "Are you familiar with the term *myopic,* Mr. Wilkinson? It means *short-sighted,* which is what you're being right now. Can you guess the nature of the trouble that Bruce is in? Its origin?"

Wilkinson closed his eyes and sighed. "What do you want?"

"We're both busy men, so I'll keep this concise. To avoid an extended stay in jail, Bruce needs to provide the DA with the names of six people he facilitated bribes for to have their criminal cases dropped. Some were relatively trivial, so they're off the table. Yours, however—solicitation of minors—fits the bill nicely."

"This is a shakedown, right?" Wilkinson opened a drawer and took out his checkbook. "How much to leave my name out, and move on to the next on the list?"

"The actual number will be Bruce's call. My job was just to see if you were amenable."

"Of course I'm fucking amenable, given the alternative. I'm not happy, though. Tell the bastard I'll be in touch and we'll set a time and place to meet."

"I can tell you the time and place." I looked at my watch. "In twelve minutes, at the Egg. Bruce has a nice private space lined up for you two to chat."

"Twelve minutes?" Wilkinson slammed his checkbook closed. "That's too soon. I need time to compose myself, think this through, before I see him in person."

I gestured to Wilkinson's computer screen. "I can see you like numbers, Howard, so here are some to think about. The DA wants six names. Bruce has ruled out all but eight. You're one of those. So imagine it this way. You're on the *Titanic.* The water's rising. Fast. There are two spots left in the final lifeboat. Do you want to get on board? Or would you prefer to take your chances with the icebergs?"

Wilkinson clenched his fists, pressed them to his temples, and closed his eyes. Then he banged the desk with both hands. "Fine. Where in the Egg?

That place is huge, and it's like a maze inside. And how am I supposed to get there?"

"You're supposed to walk. It's not unusual. People have been doing it for millennia." I stood up. "Come on. If we leave now, we'll make it on time. I'll show you which elevator you need."

The Egg's concrete shell seemed a little paler than the last time I'd stood on it because the sun was higher in the sky. Wilkinson blinked as he took his first couple of steps out onto the crunchy surface, then dropped to his knees when it dawned on him where he was. He spun around and tried to scuttle back to the elevator, but Robson stepped across and blocked his path to the hatch.

"I hope you're not one of those pedantic-type guys who gets all bent out of shape about being taken places on false pretenses." I waited for Wilkinson to stop moving. "That would just make everything take longer, and I don't know about you, but I'd like to get back down to the ground as quickly as possible. And as safely as possible."

"I hate heights." Wilkinson's voice was strangled and tight. "I'll pay whatever Steve wants. Just let me go back down, right now."

"Pay attention, Howard. You're not keeping up. The Bruce thing was just a ruse to get you up here. Now that we are here, we're going to discuss something else."

"Anything. Just make it quick."

"I understand you're friends with Jimmy Klinsman?"

"Yes. So?"

"He shorted some stock, recently, in a company that makes things for telecom networks. Why did he do that?"

"I can't tell you."

"You seem like an educated kind of guy. I wonder if you could clear something up for me that I've always wondered about. People say that if you fall from a great height, like the height we're at now, for example, you're dead before you hit the ground. Is that true, do you think? I kind of hope it is, given the speed you'd fall. How hard you'd hit the ground. The mess you'd make. Imagine if you were conscious when you smashed into the sidewalk."

"I can't tell you. Please, let me go down. I'll pay you."

"Are you one of those guys who thinks there's a certain cachet to being the first to do something? Because I'm not sure that anyone's ever committed suicide by jumping off from here, before. Think of the splash—or should that be splat?—you'd make in the newspapers, and online. People would wonder why you'd done it. All your secrets would come out. It would be embarrassing for your family, but I'm sure the public would understand. The whole underage thing being about to come out—who could live with that? And you never know, your name might even be immortalized. In the future, any time a pervert kills himself out of shame, people will say he's done 'a Wilkinson.'"

"OK! I'll tell you. It was just a game."

"Klinsman short-sells shares as a game?"

"Shorting's one way you can play."

"What are the other ways?"

"Anything you can think of. There aren't any rules."

"So what's the point of this game?"

"Each person nominates a company. The one who causes the biggest fall in its value wins."

"Why?"

"What else is left? Anyone can spot shares that are going to rise. We've been doing that forever. We needed a new challenge. Something different."

"How do you make money from it?"

"We don't. It's just for fun."

"Who's involved?"

"Six of us. We meet every quarter or so."

"And you don't care about the damage you do? The harm you cause?"

"Who to?"

I was struggling with the irony. I'd finally found something that wasn't about pure profit, and it was just as disgusting. If not worse. And I was struggling with Wilkinson's position on the surface of the Egg. One little push with my foot and he'd be rolling inexorably toward the edge . . .

I took a moment to refocus. "OK. You said there were no rules to this game you play. Meaning no one would balk at using information that wasn't common knowledge?"

"Of course not. We do that all the time."

"So you know where to get that kind of information?"

"I have my sources."

"Good. In that case, we're going to try a different kind of game. There's a real prize to be won with this one. Something you can't put a price on. A ride down in the elevator."

Wilkinson whimpered.

"Concentrate, now. This isn't hard. To win, all you have to do is give me the correct answer to one simple question. Ready? Are you going to (a) introduce me to your friends; (b) get me the name of a company whose shares you know for sure are going to rise, but the others don't; (c) tell no one about our arrangement; or (d) all of the above?"

1978. Forty-two years ago.

Anna Valentina strode into the motel room like she owned it.

It was the way she'd been taught. It was an entire concept she'd been taught. And it still felt strange to her—alien—after twenty-five years of life with her mother and her sisters in an apartment that was generously provided by the state. That apartment was much nicer than the place she was in now. She hoped she'd see it again, but she knew deep down how unlikely a prospect that was.

Things would be different if she'd had the same aptitudes as the rest of the family. Then she'd have been free to walk to the factory with them. Have lunch with them. Walk home again, as part of a group. Do things together, in familiar surroundings. She wouldn't be waiting, alone, in a foreign land. Not that she resented it. She accepted her fate happily. You take according to your needs, and you contribute according to your abilities. Anna had few needs. But she had prodigious abilities. That wasn't a claim she made for herself. She hadn't even realized, at first, that it was the reason the people from Moscow started coming to watch her ballet lessons. Sitting in on her language classes. Why they sent her to camp to learn geography. To speak English with an American accent. And to kill without breaking a sweat.

Her skills meant moving to a new continent. Adopting a new identity. Never speaking her real name. Never revealing the truth to anyone she met. And she was content with all that. Happy, in fact, because she knew she was helping to make the world a better place.

She crossed to the air conditioner and switched it on. She knew how. She could have operated it in her sleep. Or sabotaged it. Or used it to conceal weapons, or matériel. She knew the controls and inner workings of every make and model by heart, though she had no desire to chill any air. She despised the machines. They were for the weak. But a westerner would use it, so she had to as well. It was vital to fit in. She moved to the mirror hanging over the dresser. She knew that vanity was bad, and she rejected it. But honestly, this was the worst part. They wouldn't allow her to cut her hair, so it was now impractically long with a stupid center part. Her face was so plump she hardly recognized herself after all the months of being forced to eat hot dogs and hamburgers. Her makeup was gross and slutty. Her blouse was flowery and cut so low as to be immodest. Her mother would be shocked. No wonder unwanted pregnancy rates were so high here. And then there were the jeans she had to wear. They were tight at the top, which was fine, but lower down there was a ridiculous amount of fabric. The more efficient factories at home could have used it to make three pairs. They looked ridiculous, too. And people here wore them out of choice! She supposed she shouldn't be surprised, though. It was simply another step on the path toward the inevitable collapse that every decadent society must face.

She carried her bag to the bed. It was a Yankees duffel. She could name every player on the roster for the last decade. Discuss the key points in all the most contentious games. Offer opinions on managers and opponents. List the food for sale in the concession stands. Justify her preference for certain seats. Bemoan the shortfall in public transportation. She'd learned all of this without ever setting foot in the state, let alone the stadium. And she'd done it in record time, because her original posting was supposed to be Washington. It had been changed at the last minute. She didn't know why. But she did know better than to ask.

She unzipped the bag and took out a book. *The Thorn Birds,* by Colleen McCullough. She'd bought it at the airport after she landed. She had no personal interest in reading it whatsoever—give her Bulgakov or Leonov, any day—but she knew it was important to be thorough. It was evidently the sort of thing that was popular, so she'd need a working knowledge in order to not stand out. She lay down and plowed through fifty pages in half an hour. The speed-reading technique she'd learned was finally coming in useful, and it was nice not to have a test at the end, like with the tractor maintenance manuals they'd practiced on. When she felt she'd built a decent foundation, she put the book down and crossed to the window. She wondered how long she'd have to wait. For her equipment to be delivered. And for her "husband."

Anna had grown up without a father, so she'd given little thought to ever having a husband. She was aware of them. Most women had one. Some did not. The ones who didn't seemed no less satisfied in life. She'd never really cared which way it would work out for her, though on balance she'd assumed it was more likely that she would end up with one than she wouldn't. She'd never spared much thought as to how she'd acquire one. Though she'd certainly never imagined a husband would be issued to her, like a gun or a cyanide pill. Mikhail—or Misha, as he said he liked to be called—was introduced to her during the final phase of her training in Leningrad. The couple was required to spend two weeks together, so that they wouldn't look like strangers to other people when they were finally deployed.

They spent fourteen days together, anyway. They returned to their barracks at night. Their segregated barracks. Anna wandered across to the bed now, flopped down onto her back, and stretched out her arms. They barely reached the sides. It was the biggest bed she'd ever been in. She wondered if it would be the first one she wouldn't sleep in alone. Not counting her sisters, of course. She wondered if

Misha would try anything. He better not. She had been trained in certain arts, naturally. She'd received high marks. But she was clear that she was only going to use them when it was necessary to further a mission. Not for the pleasure of a pimply asshole from Ukraine whose breath stank of potatoes.

II

1980. FORTY YEARS AGO.

BRIAN ROONEY WAS DROWNING. THAT WAS CLEAR.

It was so clear that eight weeks into the program, the academy instructors had him down as third favorite out of a class of seventy-eight to drop out. Rooney didn't know it, but there was enough money to buy a small car or a long vacation riding on his woeful performance. It wasn't just one area that was letting him down. In isolation he could post satisfactory scores in his fitness tests. Or with firearms. The proper operation of his vehicle. Even the basics of criminal law. The problem came when he tried to put all these things together. The volume of work was overwhelming. And he wasn't helped by the academy's study requirements. Specifically, note taking. All the cadets were required to maintain their notebooks in a particular way. The format had to be neat. And the content, comprehensive. Rooney had big hands. That was good when it came to punching people. Good for wielding a nightstick. But bad for handwriting. He was very slow. When he tried to keep up in the classroom, where he was supposed to record everything verbatim, his clarity suffered. If he concentrated on his presentation, he fell further behind. It made him dread their random notebook inspections. He was on edge all the time. The stress was killing him. And this was only coursework. The exams were still to come.

One instructor—a guy named Thomas Brolin—bucked the trend. He did have money riding on Rooney's fate, but he was backing him to pass. Not because he was an optimist. Not because he was hoping to send good vibes out through the universe. Not even because he'd been seduced by the lopsided odds. But because he'd been watching. He'd spotted a characteristic that he believed would enable Rooney to turn his performance around. A willingness to cheat.

Rooney wasn't up to anything outrageous. He wasn't breaking into the office and stealing papers. He wasn't bribing anyone to get better grades. The things he was doing were more subtle. Looking over a classmate's shoulder when he was falling behind. Sneaking another cadet's notebook back to his room to copy after a particularly fast session. Volunteering to clean the chalkboard, but only wiping half at the end of the class and creeping back later in the evening to transcribe the rest.

Brolin watched, and he knew that outside the classroom there was a particular bar that Rooney liked. It wasn't popular with the other cadets, which was the reason Rooney chose it. He didn't like being surrounded by people who made him feel stupid. One evening, when things in the course were nearing a crisis point, a woman approached him. She said she had something special to offer him. Rooney felt a flutter of excitement. Then a hint of fear that the stress he was under might affect his performance. Then a major dose of embarrassment when he realized that wasn't the kind of *special* she was talking about. He asked for details, and she explained that two options were available. Silver. And gold. Silver would see his notebook completed, neatly—but not too neatly—for the rest of the year. Gold would give him the same thing, plus sight of the questions and answers two weeks before the date of the exams.

Rooney finished the program third. From the top. All the instructors lost their money, except the one who was running the book. And Brolin. He won his bet. And he pocketed the fee for the *special*. Gold doesn't come cheap. So when he approached Rooney, right after the graduation ceremony, and offered him commission for visiting various bars from time to time, and explaining certain packages to any cadets who might benefit from a discreet leg up, the new officer was more than happy to accept.

III

1981. THIRTY-NINE YEARS AGO.

"MOM! WILL MY FRIENDS BE HERE SOON?"

Mrs. Klinsman couldn't look her son in the eye. It was the kind of moment that every parent dreads. What should you do? Lie? *Yes, honey, I'm sure they'll be here any minute.* Like you want to, so you don't break their heart. Like you have done three times already. Or do you tell them the truth? And if you go with the truth, how do you explain what's changed? How you honestly believed everything you said before uprooting your family and transplanting them to New York.

Last year, when Jimmy turned five, all the local kids came to his party. There were too many to fit in the house. They had to rent a marquee for the yard. They had a magician. A clown. As much pizza as anyone could eat, cooked fresh in a wood-fired oven imported from Italy. Not that the kids cared where it came from. Or that the freezer for the ice cream—all seventeen flavors—needed its own generator. Then there was the disco, with genuine quadraphonic sound and a mirror ball. A table for the presents, which almost collapsed under the weight of all the packages. And a separate tent, complete with beanbags and a margarita bar, for the adults.

That was back when they lived in Pittsburgh.

When Jimmy was in preschool, on Fridays he'd always ask his friends over to play after the session had finished. Half a dozen showed up every week, minimum. Often there were more. Always it was bedlam. There were toys everywhere. Kids shrieking and racing around. A movie blaring on the VCR. Mrs. Klinsman would seek sanctuary in the kitchen with the other moms, under cover of baking cookies. They'd talk. They'd laugh. Sometimes there was even a glass of wine.

Back when no one cared about the size of your house.

On the weekend, if Jimmy wanted to go to a museum or the pool, his mom would make a few calls. There were always plenty of volunteers. She'd swing by the kids' houses, scoop them up, and usually stop somewhere for burgers and shakes on the way home.

Back when no one cared about the badge on the car you drove.

Mrs. Klinsman enjoyed the ritual of packing Jimmy's lunch, and standing outside with him and the other moms as he caught up with his friends and waited for the bus.

Back when people didn't send their kids to kindergarten in a limousine.

Mrs. Klinsman used to get some time with her husband when Jimmy went to the neighbors' to play. She used to get some time she especially enjoyed, if Jimmy was feeling brave enough to sleep over somewhere.

Back when kids didn't pick their friends by how much their parents earned.

This year, when Jimmy was turning six, Mrs. Klinsman sent out a bunch of invitations. More than she'd sent the previous year. On fancier paper. She called the other moms to confirm. She mainly got their machines. No one turned her down. But she knew how it was going to be. She could read the signs. So she didn't get a tent. She convinced Jimmy he was too grown up for a clown or a magician. And as much as she felt she needed it, she left the margarita mix on the shelf at the store.

"Mom! Will they be here soon?"

"No, honey. They won't. They're not coming."

"Why not? They're my friends. It's my birthday!"

"I can't explain, Jimmy. It's something you'll have to figure out on your own. When you're older."

IV

1983. THIRTY-SEVEN YEARS AGO.

ANNA VALENTINA WAS NOT A FAN OF MANHATTAN ARchitecture. She felt that the buildings were ugly and gauche when compared with the magnificence of Leningrad. And she felt entitled to her opinion. She'd happily wager that over the preceding five years she'd looked at more buildings through her camera and taken more pictures of more structures than anyone else in the city. The fact that the buildings only played a supporting role in her photos made no difference to her. Her mind was made up on the matter.

Anna's real subjects were always people. She'd been capturing their images with her trusty Zenit since her second day in America. It was a special model. It had two lenses—a dummy one at the front, in the regular place, which was connected to the viewfinder, and a real one hidden at the side, which operated blind. It enabled her to take anyone's picture, completely undetected, and if the police or the FBI showed any interest, it would seem absolutely normal unless they took it to pieces. It was a powerful tool. There was only one problem. It wasn't easy to use. It took great skill; otherwise you ended up with photographs of blank walls, or the sky, or a subject with no head. Expert operators were rare, and Anna was one of the best.

For four straight years her routine had been consistent. She was directed toward politicians. Diplomats. Businessmen. She followed them to the UN. To their embassies. Their offices. Their homes. The park. To restaurants and clubs and bars. She kept a meticulous record of everyone they met, and that helped the KGB resident stay current with the local players and their roles. Occasionally Anna would be sent on spicier assignments, to hotels. She only needed a regular camera for those jobs. She didn't enjoy them. She found the business of kompromat distasteful, although she understood it was necessary. And she was glad she wasn't required to be on the other side of the mirror, exercising an entirely different set of skills she'd learned in training.

During the last twelve months a new priority had emerged. In Afghanistan the Mujahideen had managed to get their hands on a supply of Стрела missiles—or Strela-2s, as the Americans call them. Moscow suspected that the CIA had bought them in Egypt and smuggled them into the mountains via Pakistan. They weren't great weapons, Anna knew from her studies. The design was fifteen years old, so they were fairly primitive. They were no use against MiGs, for example, because they were too slow and had no answer to the latest countermeasures. They could, however, be effective against slower, more basic aircraft, like helicopters.

Helicopters are attractive targets because they're used to carry troops. The Mujahideen had enjoyed some success against them. The problem, Moscow believed, was that the rebels lacked the skill to operate the Strela-2s on their own. They must have been getting help. Deserters from Ukraine were suspected of providing it. Anna was disgusted when she heard about this. To her, Russians and Ukrainians were part of the same single Soviet people. To betray one's brothers was appalling. Then Anna learned that some of the vile traitors had found their way to the United States. The KGB believed that four had settled in New York. A team was formed to find them so that they could be sent home and made an example of. Anna was assigned, and her pictures were pivotal in locating two of them. They were caught and successfully exfiltrated. To help find the others—and as a kind of reward, her handler hinted—Anna was to be the first operative on foreign soil to be issued a new kind of camera. It could take regular photographs. Moving pictures. And even record sound.

Anna was going to need to know how to use the new equipment, as well as assume responsibility for its maintenance and provide feedback on its performance in the field. Accordingly, an in-depth training session was arranged. A developer from the lab in Zagorsk was to handle the briefing personally. He was flown to New York specially, and a KGB safe house was lined up for the event so that no one—not even Anna's handler—would be able to overhear the strictly classified details.

The safe house was located in a neighborhood known as Hell's Kitchen. That was appropriate, Anna thought, given that the city was full of capitalist devils who were obsessed with nothing but filling their stomachs. She arrived with her "husband," Misha—her backup since the day she'd arrived in the United States—at the appointed time and used the code she'd been given to open the door. She stepped inside and was hit by a wave of unexpected nostalgia. The house was old and unreasonably large, and it was contaminated with abhorrent trappings of decadence, such as conspicuous displays of rare wood and swaths of degenerately decorated tile work, but the furniture was pure Soviet. It was solid. Functional. Reassuring. Their comrades in the Establishment Bureau must have brought it over specially to provide a psychological boost for any burned-out operatives in need of sanctuary. Anna stood for a moment, moved by the purity of its aesthetic, then sank gratefully into the corner of a green vinyl couch and gestured for Misha to join her while they waited for the expert to arrive.

Twenty minutes had passed before Anna and Misha heard the front door open again. They stood and greeted the expert when he bustled in. He was carrying a case—hard-sided, made of some kind of composite material rather than the canvas bag Anna used with the Zenit—and launched into his briefing without apology or preamble. Anna and Misha watched his demonstration. It was long and comprehensive—not too complex, though made harder to follow than it needed to be by the guy's dull monotone delivery. But they were professionals, so they kept their focus. They memorized the procedures he outlined. Asked questions where appropriate. And finally reached the only part Anna was truly looking forward to. The hands-on test.

Anna picked the new camera up from the lid of its closed case, which the expert had been using as a table. She held it still for a moment, surprised by its weight. It was considerably heavier than her Zenit, which itself was by no means a light piece of equipment. That shouldn't be a problem, she thought. She was confident she could adapt, given time. She examined the controls, replaying the expert's instructions in her head. There was a regular-looking shutter release for stills. A button to activate the more advanced features. And a slim lever that worked with it to set the mode. There were three positions. Up was for video and audio. Center was for video only. Down was for audio only. It was a bit like the fire selector on the side of an AK-47, she thought, only her targets didn't know she was taking shots of them. The pain they felt—if any—came later.

Anna raised the viewfinder to her eye, pointed the camera at Misha, flicked the lever up with her thumb, and hit the button. The room was instantly filled by a high-pitched, piercing shriek. It wasn't loud enough to hurt her ears, but it was certainly a shock. It seemed to be coming from the wall behind the couch, just a few feet away. Anna didn't know what was going on. The expert was on his feet, instantly, shouting at her to switch the camera off and not to say another word. He had a gun in one hand. He tore open the case with his other, grabbed the camera, and jammed it inside. The room was quiet now—the howling had stopped as soon as Anna released the button—and the crack of the case slamming shut echoed like a gunshot.

The expert snapped the locks and grabbed the handle. He ran for the door, ducking and twisting and jerking his body from side to side as he went. Anna saw another man rushing toward them from the corridor. He had a gun, too. He raised it and fired two quick shots. Both missed the expert. Behind her Anna heard Misha grunt and fall. She felt a burning in her arm, high up near her shoulder. The expert fired and the guy in the corridor pitched backward and crumpled onto the floor. The expert fired again. He was aiming at a woman. She was farther away, just passing the bottom of the staircase. He fired again and the woman clutched her neck and slumped to the side, leaning against the wall. Then the expert ran to the front door, clawed it open, and dashed out into the street.

Anna watched the woman stumble forward. She kept coming, sliding her shoulder along the wall for support, until she reached the living room doorway. She paused and the two women locked eyes for a second. Then Anna was aware of a green ball falling to the floor by the other woman's feet. It bounced a couple of inches into the air, and the world turned a blinding, burning white.

Anna woke up on the living room floor. Her eyes were stinging from the smoke. Her ears were ringing. Her right arm was wet and sticky, but strangely warm. She touched it with her other hand and realized she was bleeding. Heavily. She raised her head and did her best to take stock of her situation. The expert was gone. Misha was lying to her side with a hole through his chest. He was clearly dead. The other man had been hit in the head, and half his brains were sprayed across the wall in the corridor. He was clearly dead. The woman was lying just inside the doorway. She had no visible injuries. She might not be dead. Not quite.

Anna tried to crawl across the floor. She found it hard to move. Her right hand was numb. Her arm couldn't take any weight. Her head was swimming. She forced herself forward, and after what felt like hours of exhausting effort she reached the woman's side. And immediately wished she hadn't moved. The woman's eyes were open but they were dark and empty, and the floor around her was slick with the blood that had drained from a neat, innocuous-looking hole in the flesh above her collarbone.

Anna's handler visited her in the sick bay at the Soviet embassy two days later. He told her not to worry. The expert and the secret camera were safe. The mole who'd betrayed the briefing had been found. His character had evidently been weak, as he'd fallen prey to the advances of the FBI's counterintelligence division, but he'd have plenty of time to work on remedying that defect in the gulag to which he was currently en route. Misha was dead. And so were two American operatives. One of them—the man—was known to the KGB. He was a veteran, and had survived postings all over the world. His time had come. The other—the woman—shouldn't have been there at all. That was a mistake on the Americans' part. She was a developer, not a field operative. She'd designed the monitoring system—which was old by Soviet standards, and unacceptably prone to feedback—and had evidently insisted on supervising the installation. An asset like that should have been pulled out of the house before the briefing began, but there'd apparently been a screwup over the timing.

Anna herself had been luckier. Relatively speaking. Her eyesight had been slightly degraded by the gas from the percussion grenade because she'd been so close when it exploded, and there was minor nerve damage to her arm from the bullet that grazed it. Her injuries could have been much more serious. She was expected to recover to the point where she could function to average standards. But nonetheless she wasn't being returned to her previous posting. She was being given a different assignment. The researcher's widower also had connections to American counterintelligence. He was a consultant for them now, semi-retired, using his business as a cover. Not much was known about him, and the KGB had been looking for a way to get close to him for years. Now he was left alone with a young son to raise. Maybe he'd need a nanny. A cook. A housekeeper. Whatever position he decided on, Anna was to fill it. Papers would be provided. References prepared. It would soon be time for a new role. A new place. And another new name.

1990. THIRTY YEARS AGO.

BRIAN ROONEY WAS FLOURISHING. THAT WAS CLEAR.

It was so clear that he had two commendations hanging above his desk in the cubicle nearest to the lieutenant's office. The newest of the pair had only been there for a week. It had been awarded at a press conference outside 1PP for his contribution to an operation that led to the arrest of six Japanese mobsters, plus the recovery of twenty-two AR-15 assault rifles and 52,200 Percocet tablets—a new record for both weight and quantity.

Rooney wasn't present when the detectives and SWAT team officers busted down the door to the apartment in the Lillian Wald Housing Project. He didn't get shot at, and he wasn't attacked with a sledgehammer. He didn't chase a guy through an escape tunnel running down inside the wall to the unit below. He didn't fight hand-to-hand in a bathroom to prevent vital evidence from getting flushed away. Instead, he was cited for his dedication to detail in his paperwork. He'd been instrumental in securing the warrants that had been necessary to allow the operation to succeed, which was in stark contrast to a number of recent missteps by other officers that had resulted in failed convictions, embarrassment for the department, and an erosion of public trust.

Rooney was present at the Lillian Wald apartment a week before the bust, however, when he'd gone with the lieutenant to sell the pills and the weapons to the Japanese gang. He'd also been at a warehouse near JFK another week before that, creating a diversion to distract the sentry while the other detectives smashed through a wall with a stolen SUV and confiscated the pills, the weapons, and four suitcases full of cash from a gang from Jamaica. There'd been no paperwork for him to worry about on that occasion. No arrests. And no reports. It's one thing to use police misconduct as part of your defense when jail is your only alternative. It's another to walk into a police station and complain that some detectives stole your stash of drugs and illegal weapons. You'd have to be crazy to do that. And the detectives worked hard to avoid ripping off anyone who was crazy.

Rooney was nearly finished with the last of his paperwork when the lieutenant approached his desk.

He had three packages with all the i's dotted and t's crossed, ready for the judge. They were cases where people were in danger, or any potential contraband had too low a resale value. They went in the blue tray. He also had one package in his green tray. It contained statements from informants. Surveillance reports—some official, others freelance. And a page with a list of handwritten numbers. They stated quantities and values multiplied by risk factors that were calculated by the lieutenant himself.

"What have we got in the recycling?" The lieutenant leaned against the cubicle's flimsy wall.

"One possibility." Rooney reached for the contents of the green tray. "Vikes, this time."

"Prescription stuff again?" The lieutenant shook his head. "Someone needs to do something about this before it gets out of hand. In the meantime, we may as well make hay . . ."

"The quantity's the only downside I can see." Rooney checked his page of notes. "Five thousand. Six at the most. We could cycle them twice before we go to the judge? The Russians are definitely interested. And the Irish, you can always rely on those guys."

VI

1995. TWENTY-FIVE YEARS AGO.

TO THE STUDENTS ON HIS FLOOR IN THE WASHINGTON Square Village dorm, it appeared that Jimmy Klinsman wasn't interested in making friends. He only left his room for classes, work, the library, food—he allowed himself one meal a day—and the occasional walk in the park. He never went to any bars or clubs or parties. He did nothing that involved spending money. And he never invited anyone home for break.

The impression that Klinsman gave was not entirely accurate. He avoided letting anyone see his home because he was ashamed of it. And he had nothing against making friends. It's just that he was more interested in making money. In a theoretical sense, hence his dedication to study. And in a practical way, as witnessed by the many schemes he either hatched or adapted. A week didn't go by without him trying something new. One time he figured that mail-in offers on retail products looked so attractive because corporations gamble that their customers wouldn't redeem them. So he bought cases and cases of cereal, cashed in the tokens on the boxes for airline miles, and sold them to a homesick overseas student. Another time he bought a bunch of magnetic bracelets from a trader in the park, packaged them with phony endorsements that he printed on hospital letterhead that he paid a cleaner to steal, and sold them to football team wannabes. He also tried more mainstream ways to boost his income, like when he got a job as a mystery shopper for three department stores. And when he found he could make more by taking bribes in return for writing flattering reports than he earned in wages, his eyes were opened to what he came to think of as alternative sources of revenue. He dismissed the obvious Ponzi and pyramid schemes as being too risky. But when he temped at a brokerage during his sophomore year he realized there was a way to turn the disappointment of being allocated to the mail room into an advantage, as long as he didn't pay too much attention to the regulations. Particularly the ones surrounding insider trading.

Klinsman's roommate, Howard "The Hound" Wilkinson, always asked him along on nights out. Wilkinson didn't really want the company, but he was a very superstitious guy. He'd invited Klinsman at the beginning of their year together, got lucky that first night, and was always hoping to replicate the feat. Generally he didn't succeed, and ended up disturbing Klinsman again as he blundered back into their room, drunk and disappointed. But when he stumbled home one night at around 2:00 A.M. after striking out at a party for the last night of a play one of his friends was in, he was surprised to find Klinsman not asleep. Not in bed. Not dressed—not all the way. He just had his underwear on. His briefs were alarmingly small. He was dancing wildly and listening to headphones that were plugged into a giant CD player Wilkinson hadn't seen before. There was a champagne bottle in his hand. And another empty one, discarded on the floor, spinning lazily after Klinsman had inadvertently kicked it. Wilkinson stood and watched for a moment, and it struck him that this was the first time he'd ever seen his buddy drink.

"Who are you, and what did you do with my roommate?" Wilkinson said, then he repeated himself after Klinsman took his headphones off.

"I am your roommate." Klinsman's smile was broad, and his words were slurred. "But I won't be for long."

"You're dropping out? Don't do it, man!"

"Not dropping out. Moving out."

"You're going home? Like, halfway to Canada? That's crazy. You need to chill. Party, like me, and soon you'll like the city just fine."

"I already like the city just fine. That's why I'm staying in Manhattan. I'm getting my own place."

"You're beyond crazy now, man. How can you afford a place? Have you got any idea what the rent's like? You'd be stuck in a shithole in the Bronx or somewhere. There'll be entire families of immigrants living in single rooms. Rats. Spiders."

Klinsman pointed to a piece of paper fixed to the wall above his fax machine, trying its best to curl despite the illegal pins holding it up.

Wilkinson peered at the sheet. He normally wore glasses, but left them in their case when he was out chasing girls. "What does it say?"

"It's a trading report. It says I just made $1,000,073.17. Think about that. I'm twenty years old. I needed a fake ID to buy this wine. And I'm a millionaire!"

"Fantastic news!" Wilkinson pulled the headphone wire out of the stereo and started jiggling to the sudden beat. "We can get a condo. We'll have beer delivered every night. And pizza. Think of all the girls—"

"I can't"—Klinsman hit the power switch and realized his voice was louder than he'd intended—"hear you."

"I was just saying, our condo, we'll fix it up real cool, it'll be a magnet for—"

"Wow, wait. It's not going to be 'our' anything. You're not coming."

Wilkinson sat down on his bed. "You're joking, right? We're roomies. We stick together. I'd take you with me if the foot was on the other shoe."

"But would you, now?" Klinsman glared at his friend. "Did you help me take all those Fruit Loops to the food bank?"

"No, but—"

"Did you help me address all the envelopes, to send out the vitamin packs?"

"I didn't know—"

"I could go on and on, but the answer would always be the same. I'm always working. You're always partying. Out of all the money I've made, you didn't help me make a single cent. So give me one good reason. If you didn't help earn it, why should I let you help spend it?"

VII

1996. TWENTY-FOUR YEARS AGO.

THE YEARS AFTER SHE WAS WOUNDED WERE HARD FOR Anna, in exile in her gilded Westchester gulag.

Her injuries hadn't been serious. A proper medic, like the ones in Russia, would have given her a realistic evaluation. The doctors in America were marred by decadence. Her eyesight was almost perfect. She could drive. She could see well enough to shoot. She certainly could have continued to take photographs. With her arm she could tell she'd lost a little range of movement, but not so much that anyone else would notice. She made sure to keep the scar covered up. She'd suffered no loss of strength. And if anyone said otherwise, give her two minutes with them in the dojo, her "good" arm tied behind her back, and she'd make them eat their words.

During her first months in the McGrath house

Anna found herself harboring violent fantasies. She was mad at everyone else who'd applied for the job. They must have put up a pretty poor effort if they couldn't even beat a disabled foreigner. She was resentful of her own people when it dawned on her that they must have had a hand in tipping the scales. She was driven crazy by Mr. McGrath, who'd retired altogether from espionage when his wife died and was hypocritically trying to bring his son up as a pacifist. She'd read his file. Incomplete as it was, she'd seen enough to know the kind of things he was capable of. Cabin fever set in. She had nothing worthwhile to do. And nowhere to go other than the grocery store, and that was nothing more than a temple to the worst excesses of rampant consumerism. She tried to escape via the TV, but was tortured by the mad clown who kept constantly popping up on her screen. She couldn't believe that the feeble-minded freak had somehow gotten elected president not once, but twice. It was like she'd become an unwilling participant in a live-action demonstration of the shortcomings of Western democracy.

As bad as things were in America, though, she knew they were worse at home. She wasn't supposed to show any interest, but she was very discreet. She read about the fatal blow that was struck in November '89, in her room with tears in her eyes, as her German comrades succumbed to the degeneracy of their western neighbors and dismantled the antifascist bulwark that had kept East Berlin safe since 1961. The union clung on for another eighteen months, then Yugoslavia crumbled. The Baltic states disintegrated. And finally, on Boxing

Day 1991, the unthinkable happened. The USSR was officially dissolved. She took to her bed for a week. She felt like her comrade cosmonauts who were marooned on the space station *Mir* when the terrible news was broken. One of them was from Leningrad, too. Their country had disappeared while none of them were there. At least the cosmonauts were able to land again on friendly soil. Eventually. Whereas she was trapped in a vacuum. She signaled her handler, asking permission to return home. His response took two days to arrive. *Request denied. Remain on station. Await instructions.*

Instructions that never came.

Anna considered killing herself. She considered going back to Russia and killing the traitor Gorbachev. Eventually she settled for an uneasy compromise between boredom and anxiety. She was proficient at the mundane chores that were expected of her. Mr. McGrath's son, Paul, was growing up and becoming more interesting. She was amused to see how completely he failed to buy into his father's bogus pacifist agenda. How funny it would be if Paul followed in his father's real footsteps. So she helped him, and guided him whenever she could. She continued to watch Mr. McGrath in the vain hope that he'd return to some real work. Then he might reveal something that she could parlay into a reason to return home. Or at least capture her interest. But when he did finally make a move, it wasn't anything she'd expected. He started digging into the availability of a certain piece of real estate. A brownstone in Hell's Kitchen, New York.

The property had been owned by the Soviet

Union. After the place had been compromised by the Americans it couldn't be used as a safe house any longer, so it was mothballed. It wasn't disposed of, because transactions leave trails and the Kremlin valued secrecy above all else. But now there was no Soviet Union. Its successor, the Russian Federation, was tainted by capitalism and desperate for hard currency. Who knew what it would do with all the miscellaneous assets it had inherited? Evidently Mr. McGrath knew what he hoped it would do. Sell them. But did he want to buy the place to keep it out of the hands of developers, and maintain it as a kind of shrine to his wife? Or did he hope to find some clues there about how she'd died? And who'd been present at the time?

Anna signaled her handler for assistance. She needed information. Above all she needed to know what had happened to the American monitoring system. Was it still in place at the house? Or had it been torn out for study, or disposal? She got no response. Her go-bag was ready, as always. The habit was too deeply ingrained for it not to be. So should she run? She was tempted. It's always safest to assume the worst. But where would she go? There was no more Soviet Union, after all. Leningrad—St. Petersburg, she supposed she should say now—was overrun with oligarchs, by all accounts. Maybe evacuation was premature. The house might have been sanitized. There was bound to be a lot of bureaucracy to contend with, Soviet Union or not, so Mr. McGrath may never complete the purchase. Someone else could come along with more money or better connections, who wouldn't be the same kind of threat as an owner. She should hold her position.

She should hold, but she should also raise her alert status. Find out as much as possible about the degree of risk Mr. McGrath acquiring the brownstone could pose. She should start by going back to Mr. McGrath's wife's records. The files and folders of notes and diagrams he kept boxed up in the room he pretended she died in. Anna had skimmed through everything soon after she'd moved into the house. She knew some of the papers related to the monitoring system, but she hadn't sweated the details. She knew the brownstone was bugged, because she'd been there. The presence of the invention wasn't a surprise. But now she needed to understand its operation in more depth. There was one detail in particular that was critical. Had the system been monitored remotely? Or had there been a recording device at the premises? It was the kind of difference that could determine whether someone lived or died. But it was also moot, unless Mr. McGrath bought the house.

Mr. McGrath bought the house. It took a few more years, but he was nothing if not persistent. He didn't hide what he was doing, which Anna took as a good sign. He passed it off as a business thing, which he'd developed a habit of talking about. Anna claimed to have a personal interest in the project, pretending that her father had been a joiner who'd worked in that area. She asked if she could visit the house with him the next time he went there. He agreed, and proposed one day the following week.

Anna pretended to have errands to run in the

city first, so they agreed on a time to meet in front of the house. Mr. McGrath was there early. He unlocked the front door and stood aside for Anna to go in ahead of him. She was fine while she was in the hallway, but when she reached the living room all she could smell was smoke, from the guns and the grenade that had shattered the peace more than a decade ago. Her eyes watered, and Mr. McGrath thought she must be crying over something to do with her father. She was too distracted to deny it, battling to keep on an even keel in the room where her "husband" and Mr. McGrath's wife had died, and her life had changed forever. It was a struggle not to gawk at the floor by the doorway where his wife's fatal blood had flowed. To scan the walls for a hole left by the bullet that had torn through Misha's chest. To search for traces of brains on the hallway plasterwork, where the American operative had fallen. The only encouragement Anna felt was that Mr. McGrath showed no signs of knowing the significance of the room. She thought she saw him paying a little extra attention to the wall where the green sofa had been, but he soon looked away and offered to show her the rest of the house.

When they reached the ballroom on the top floor Anna pretended she needed to use the bathroom. She left Mr. McGrath gazing out over the Hudson and hurried back downstairs. She went into the living room. Took out the current detector she'd bought at a hardware store on 23rd Street. Checked that it was set to silent. Fired it up and held it against the wall near the place where Misha had been sitting when she'd tested the camera. The needle sprang across its dial. That was one question answered. The wiring from the monitoring system had not been removed. But the query remained, how much else of the system was left intact?

There was still no need to panic, Anna told herself. If Mr. McGrath planned to keep the house as a shrine, she was in no danger. But if he brought in demolition contractors or electricians or security system installers, it would be a different story. The key would be to have enough warning. It was time to put some precautions in place.

VIII

2001. NINETEEN YEARS AGO.

BRIAN ROONEY WAS SWEATING. THAT WAS CLEAR.

What he hoped was less clear were the pains in his chest and left arm. He wanted to finish his testimony. To get the ordeal over with, once and for all. It would be a nightmare to collapse in front of everyone. To have the paramedics run in and cart him off to the hospital, only to have to come back to do it all over again. He gripped the brass rail that ran around the top of the witness box with both hands, took a breath, and focused on the lawyer's words. On the sound of them. Not the image they conjured in his head. Each syllable he pictured as a bloodhound, racing unerringly through the forest of his lies to drag the damning truth out of its fragile, shallow grave.

Let me get away with this and I swear I'll be good . . .

Steven Bruce, counsel for the defense, winked. He shot Rooney a sly smile. He knew. He was waiting to bring the hammer down. Drawing out the agony. The sadistic shyster.

"Detective Rooney, you described the events that followed your entry into my clients' apartment on the evening of September 22. But you didn't tell the court what prompted you to smash down their door in the first place. In fact, you seemed to deliberately skirt around the issue. Would you care to enlighten us now?"

I didn't tell the court about the bags of cash we removed and sent to the lieutenant's brother for laundering, either, Rooney thought. "We were acting on an anonymous tip." He could feel a steel band tightening around his chest. Bruce was closing in . . .

"How was this alleged tip received? Via carrier pigeon? Did someone hire a skywriter?"

The asshole was circling. It wouldn't be long now. "The tip came in by phone, to 911." Normally Rooney would have invited the lawyer to check the 911 recordings, but there was a problem. The idiot they'd paid to drop the dime had done it late. They should have waited for the call to come through from dispatch before taking the door, but they heard glass smashing. They guessed that the pimps were going for the fire escape. The operation wasn't sanctioned, so they had no backup. Money was at stake—a lot—so they figured they'd go for it and fudge the timing in the report. But, as Brian Rooney senior used to say, once the fuck-up fairy comes to stay, there's no getting rid of her. A stray bullet went through the wall into an adjoining apartment and took out the neighbor's clock. The guy was a gadget freak, and this was no garden-variety timepiece. It was an exact replica of the first atomic clock. Precisely accurate, and worth around four thousand bucks. The guy made a statement so he could put in a claim on his insurance. Compare that with the 911 log, and it was game over. One more question and the case would collapse. Then the rat squad would come crawling, and the whole house of cards would collapse.

Bruce tipped his head and pursed his lips. The question was coming. The final nail . . .

Let me get away with this and I'll quit the job. I'll put my papers in this afternoon. Live on my pension. Quietly. Never allow myself to be led down the garden path again. I swear!

Someone must have been listening.

Bruce twitched like he was coming out of a trance. "I'm sorry, I lost my train of thought there for a second. So the call was made to 911. Why was it that your unit was the one to respond?"

Rooney's mind was whirling, looking for the angle. Why wasn't Bruce asking about the time of the call? Setting him up to reveal the discrepancy, while his jugular was exposed? "We responded because we were the closest to the suspects' address when the call came in."

"That's not what I meant." Bruce paused, cranking up the pressure on Rooney's heart. "Given the nature of the crimes my clients are charged with, wouldn't it have been more appropriate for the vice squad to have been involved?"

"We didn't initially know the category of crimes that were being committed." Rooney was struggling to control his breathing. "The call we received only referred to a child being in distress. When we entered the premises and realized the kind of activities your clients were indulging in and the sort of matériel in their possession, we informed our lieutenant. He called his opposite number in vice, which is the proper procedure. When the vice detectives arrived, we left. This is all recorded in the log maintained by a uniformed officer at the scene."

"Thank you, Detective. We may need to examine that log in due course. Until then, no further questions."

Rooney's retirement racket was a muted affair. Not all of the detectives from the squad showed up. The lieutenant only stayed for the first half hour or so. There was no one from his time at the academy. No one from his days in uniform. No one from any of his old precincts. When it was nearly time for the bar to close he was barely buzzed. He told himself to look on the bright side. One lousy evening was better than a lousy rest of his life. Especially if all that was left of it had to be spent in administrative segregation.

Rooney decided to cut his losses and head home, but as he approached the door he spotted a familiar face at a table in the shadows. It was Steven Bruce. He was sitting on his own, and he waved for Rooney to join him.

"Come, sit for a minute," Bruce said. "I have an

idea how you could put this damp squib of a party behind you. Put retirement on hold for a while. Start a new chapter of your life. The best you've ever known."

Rooney's first thought was to tell Bruce to stick his idea, whatever it was. Then he reconsidered. He was a civilian now. It was OK to fraternize with shysters—or lawyers, as he'd have to try to think of them. Especially if by *best* they meant *most lucrative*.

IX

2009. Eleven years ago.

Jimmy Klinsman hadn't eaten any food that wasn't prepared in a restaurant or packaged from a store for as long as he could remember. That was inevitable, given the demands on his time. But he often thought that if things had panned out differently, he'd have liked to be a gardener. That could have been the perfect occupation for him, he figured, given how much he enjoyed planting things and watching them grow.

Klinsman was standing at the back of the room at the clubhouse, doing his best to look like a dutiful supporter. Or at least like he was listening. In front of him the regular furniture had been taken out and replaced with rows of chairs that were usually used for weddings. The place was full to overflowing with the city's movers and shakers. Some of them were the real deal. The kind of people who regarded $50K for a day of golf to back a cause they couldn't have cared less about—that they probably couldn't have spelled—as chump change. Others were from the *fake it till you make it* school. Many of those were stuck terminally at the *fake it* stage. But the guy up front who was doing all the talking—Dick White—had certainly made it. That didn't make him interesting, though. It was safe to say that success had gone to his head. From Klinsman's vantage point White was standing in front of a giant painting. Of himself. Klinsman made a final attempt to focus and catch some of the vapid words that were floating past him on the overconditioned air. Then he gave up and turned his attention to the massive artwork. He wondered if the abundance of hair and lack of flabby jowls was a matter of artistic interpretation. Or a reflection of the record fee that White's own charity was rumored to have paid for the picture at auction.

One hour and three—paid for—scotches later, an assistant collected Klinsman from the bar and escorted him to Dick White's private office. White was standing behind the marble table he used as a desk when Klinsman walked in. He offered him his hand, passed him a cigar, and gestured toward a transparent plastic Louis Quatorze–style chair that seemed to be floating in the middle of the room.

"Best. Event. Ever." White waited for Klinsman to sit before settling into his own, much sturdier chair. "A record number of people. More press coverage. Higher revenue than even in '06."

"I'm glad to hear that, sir."

"A lot of the credit for that is down to you."

White pointed his cigar at Klinsman like it was a miniature bazooka. "You did some very fine negotiating to squeeze so much free stuff out of our suppliers. We saw a significant uptick in donations as well."

"Thank you, Mr. White." Klinsman smiled. "And let's not forget how big a factor it is, getting the use of the course for free."

White nodded magnanimously.

"Which is why next year you should charge the full market rate."

White stopped, his cigar halfway to his mouth, his lighter poised. "And you have to go and ruin it. That's the last thing I should do."

"With respect, sir, it would be the best thing."

"No, it would be a disaster. People are so generous to us because they know that every cent they give—almost—goes to the charity. Whatever it is. They're impressed by our zero overhead. It sets us apart. Free use of the course is the key to that. Change, and we become just one of the crowd. And it's a big, noisy crowd. Two years, three at the most, we'd be finished. And all my lovely free publicity would be in the toilet."

"Here's the way I see it. The first few years, the event was smaller. That meant less wear and tear on the greens. And the course was less well-known, so there were fewer demands on it. Both of those things have changed, so you could absolutely justify introducing the charge."

"It's not about justifying. It's about being free. That's what's unique."

"What if there was a way for the course to be

free, so the event's still unique, but you charge for it, too?"

"How many rounds did you play? Were you out in the sun too long?" White made a show of sniffing the air. "How much scotch did you put away?"

Klinsman smiled and let the insults bounce off his thick skin. "It would work like this. You announce you're going to charge the charity, which is totally justifiable. The course is a business, after all. But because knowing that every cent goes to a good cause is so important to our supporters, you make a donation from your own foundation that exactly covers the charge. The uniqueness is maintained, and as a bonus you personally get to look more generous."

White shook his head. "I take, I give. The optics would be neutral. And there's no benefit to paying myself. There's no new money."

"There would be if you used the Richard J. White Foundation."

"Why that one?"

"Because it's classified as a public charity. That means you can take donations from other people, but you have no obligation to contribute yourself. Over the last four years you haven't put in a single cent. So if the course charges the charity, and the foundation covers the bill, the donors' money is effectively going straight into your own pocket."

White lit his cigar. He took two hefty puffs. Then he hit a speed dial key on his landline phone. "Bill, I need some information. Right now. The Richard J. White Foundation. What's its status? How much have I personally donated over the last decade?"

White took another puff and turned back to Klinsman. "One of two things is going to happen in the next five minutes, when Bill calls back. Either you're going to get a seat on the board. Or you're going to get fired."

Some seeds grow, and some don't, Klinsman thought. *And some bloom almost immediately . . .*

X

PRESENT DAY.

YOU CAN'T TEACH AN OLD DOG NEW TRICKS. THE PERSON who coined that phrase had clearly never met Anna Vincent. Or attended an Internet for Seniors class at the Chappaqua public library.

Mr. McGrath's death hadn't come as a blow to Anna. She'd never liked him. And in fact, once the dust had settled and she'd had the chance to reflect on it, she had to admit she'd found the whole episode very satisfying. It had proved that even after lying dormant for all those years, her instincts and her skills were just as sharp as ever. She hadn't frozen when she overheard the conversation between Mr. McGrath and his partner about getting the brownstone cleared out. She hadn't panicked. Instead her training had kicked in. Instantly. She'd dosed the tea just right despite not having handled K-2 since the poisons course she attended at Laboratory 12, more than forty years ago. She delivered the drink without arousing suspicion. Had the presence of mind to remove the cup and destroy it offsite, later. And she'd smashed up the study so comprehensively that the police hadn't doubted for a second that a man—like Alex Pardew—must have done it.

With the target of her surveillance out of the picture, Anna's thoughts turned to Russia again. She seriously contemplated going back. She'd had no contact with her handler for years, so she no longer felt the need to seek his permission. But everything she read suggested that the corridors of power were crawling with oligarchs now, who were more interested in collecting expensive apartments in foreign capital cities and buying Premier League soccer teams than in fighting for the worldwide emancipation of the proletariat. She also found that she liked the house a whole lot better now that she lived in it on her own. What she needed was a way to continue her mission, but without having to leave. The library provided that. The library, plus a new computer and a fast Internet connection. Although really she felt the new technology made the job too easy. When she began her training, back in Leningrad, changing your identity was a complicated business. Now you could create an entirely new persona with a few clicks of the mouse. In her formative days, you could only be in one place at any given time. And it used to be dangerous to operate in the same city using more than one cover story. But now you could just open multiple windows on your screen and be anyone, anywhere.

After six months Anna had cut back on her initial enthusiastic overproliferation and settled on just becoming three other people. Most of the time she was *Sophie,* a mild-mannered teacher from Detroit who was dedicated to educating teenagers about the true meaning of socialism. The movement had gained some popularity—in name, at least—in the country over the last couple of years, but it was clear to Anna that the spoiled American brats who thought that posting trite memes online was radical behavior actually had no concept of its underlying principles. That wasn't their fault, she told herself. They'd been raised in a degenerate environment, starved of the oxygen of truth, and were in desperate need of guidance from someone who did understand the true struggle. She also enjoyed the role of *Scar,* a guru of activism who operated exclusively in private groups, where he could be more forthright in encouraging workers to organize and resist. And when she was feeling playful, *Kali* would take to Facebook and Twitter where she could bait fascists and ridicule their brainwashed mantras to her heart's content.

When she put the three strands together Anna was more satisfied than at any time since she'd left Leningrad. She had a good routine. She felt like she was making a contribution. And she enjoyed the poetic justice of taking corporate America's profit-hungry products and using them to hasten its own demise. The disastrous events of the world may have pushed utopia further into the distance, but that was no reason to give up on trying to reach it.

It was a shock when Paul appeared on her doorstep. She worried that it wouldn't be safe to continue her work if he wanted to live in the house with her. It wouldn't have been an insurmountable problem—she'd chosen a laptop because it was portable, and all her passwords were safely memorized so she could easily rebuild her profiles even if it became necessary to ditch and destroy the computer—but she was still relieved when Paul opted to stay at a hotel in the city. She worried again when he found out about the brownstone and decided to move in there. Then she calmed herself down. The alert level was no higher than amber, she figured. There was no way Paul could know the significance of the house. About what was hidden in the walls. It would make sense to be extra vigilant, though, so Anna contacted the person who'd been watching the house for her since Mr. McGrath had bought it. She ordered an increase in the frequency of the reports from weekly to daily. There was a commensurate increase in the fee she had to pay, but this was America. What else could she expect? And anyway, it was worth spending a little more for her peace of mind.

The new message schedule took effect the day Paul moved into the brownstone. Every day, within five minutes of 5:00 P.M., Anna received an email: *Are you free for dinner tomorrow, say around 7:00 P.M.?* That meant there was nothing to report, so Anna just sent back her confirmation of receipt: *Sorry, I'm busy all week.* Then one Saturday morning Anna received a different message: *A slot just opened in my diary. Are you free for coffee right away?* That was an alarm. The most urgent kind. Anna replied: *What changed at your end?* A moment later an email arrived with a photograph attached. One snapped with a cellphone. There was no skill involved with it, unlike the ones Anna used to take. But she couldn't question its significance. It showed a van. Parked outside the brownstone. Navy blue, with a gold shield logo. And Paul letting two men—one with tools, one carrying a clipboard—into the house.

A picture like that could mean only one thing.

It was finally time for Anna to run.

XI

PRESENT DAY.

BRIAN ROONEY WAS SUSPICIOUS. THAT WAS CLEAR.

He used his firmest handshake, then kept a careful watch as his visitor moved his chair far enough to fit his long legs into the space in front of the desk.

"Mr. Bruce sent you?" Rooney crossed his arms.

The visitor nodded. "That's what I said."

"Why?"

"He has a new client. Wants you to meet him. Thinks the guy has a problem he needs help with."

"Why didn't Bruce tell me this himself?"

"New procedures. An extra layer of insulation, to make the deniability more plausible. It's not Bruce's idea, though. This is coming straight from JD. He's been paranoid—more paranoid—ever since the Pardew fiasco."

"I thought we were still on hiatus, because of hat."

The visitor shook his head. "Nope. No need any-nore. Pardew's file is back—"

"The file's back? Are you sure? No one told me."

"It's back. That's positively confirmed. I spoke vith someone—a reliable contact—who saw one of he detectives on the case physically holding it. Seems like you handled that situation with the in-ernal security guy perfectly."

"Good, then. Thanks."

"And you ensured that Pardew was clear about vhich path he should take?"

"Oh, the little weasel was clear. There's no way ve'll see him again."

"Excellent. In that case, there's no need to leave any more money on the table. As long as we're care-ful, and we learn from recent experiences."

"OK." Rooney leaned forward and rested his el-bows on the desk. "Who's the mark?"

"A guy named Len Hendrie." The visitor took a piece of paper from his jacket pocket and passed it to Rooney. "Here's his picture and a list of his haunts."

Rooney took a pair of reading glasses from his drawer. "What did this Hendrie guy do?"

"He's an arsonist."

"A torch?" Rooney dropped the paper. "I'm not sure we should touch him. Those guys are weird."

"Mr. Bruce OK'd it. So did JD. This guy's not a psycho. He was just getting even with some worse-type asshole who stitched him up. It was a onetime kind of thing. There's no risk of this guy getting back into the system, further down the line. He's learned his lesson, for sure."

"All right, then. I'll try to make contact tonight."

"Perfect. Let me know how it shakes out." The visitor passed Rooney a smaller slip of paper. "Here's my cell number. Call me anytime."

"Let me finish." Rooney didn't take the note. "I'll try tonight, after I've talked with Mr. Bruce and confirmed he sent you. No offense."

"None taken. Of course you should get confirmation. Mr. Bruce was certain you'd insist on it. He can't talk to you himself right now—he's in the middle of something he just can't get out of—so he said you should check directly with JD."

Rooney paused, and splayed his stubby fingers out on the surface of the desk. "I'll wait. Talk to Bruce tomorrow."

The visitor shook his head. "JD won't be happy about the delay. The disruption Pardew caused cost him big. He wants the operation back up and running right away. His wife's got her eye on a new Maserati. Better call him right away. You have his home number, right?"

Rooney folded his arms and leaned back.

"Here." The visitor took out his phone, pulled up an entry from his list of contacts, and handed it to Rooney. "His personal cell's on there, too. You're bound to get him on one of them."

Rooney pushed the phone back across the desk. "Don't worry about it. I'll call you tomorrow. Let you know if I got hold of Hendrie. And if he's up for any special assistance."

XII

Present Day.

Jimmy Klinsman slackened his pace and scanned the line of iPad screens. He spotted his name on one of them. Strode forward. Dropped his battered leather Gladstone bag at the feet of the guy who was there to greet him and continued toward the exit without saying a word. The chauffeur felt that he showed extraordinary restraint when he didn't drop-kick the bag onto the roof of the smoking shack. Instead he picked it up and followed his client, making sure never to get closer than six feet away. He wondered if Klinsman would confuse his disdain for respect, but didn't care too much either way.

"Wait." Klinsman stopped. "You're not my regular guy."

"No. I'm not."

"Why?"

"I'm sorry. I'm not here for that kind of thing."

"What are you talking about?"

"My job is to wrangle your baggage and drive you to your destination. Not to speculate about my own existential nature. That costs extra."

Klinsman's top lip wrinkled as if he'd taken a mouthful of something rancid. "I mean, where is my regular guy?"

"He was selected for astronaut training, so he's now en route to a NASA camp in the desert in New Mexico."

"Seriously?"

"Of course not. He has a gallbladder infection. He's out for two weeks, minimum."

"What's your name?"

"McCarthy. Paul McCarthy."

"I'll remember that. Are you any good?"

"I believe you'll find my performance to be satisfactory in several respects. If not, I can provide you with the number for our customer complaint hotline. Although I suspect you already have it."

"Come on. Get me to my office ASAP, and we'll see."

All the exit routes from the airport were seething with traffic, as usual, but as they were about to join the Van Wyck the driver spotted a gap between a taxi and another limousine. He hit the gas, hard, and as the car surged forward a folder slid out from beneath the passenger seat. In the mirror he saw Klinsman reach down and pick it up.

"At least you're reasonably cheerful." The driver

accelerated again to avoid getting blocked off by a minivan.

"What?" Klinsman threw the word forward like it was a physical thing with sharp edges.

"You're more cheerful than my last client." The driver forced his way into the outside lane. "I picked him up at his office, in Midtown. He seemed gloomy when he got in the car, then he started reading a bunch of papers and I swear I actually saw the will to live leave his body. I was genuinely worried he was going to slit his wrists where he sat."

"Stop." Klinsman held his hand up. "Say one more word and I'll see to it you're fired."

"One more word."

"Did you just speak?"

"Sorry. Misunderstanding." The driver looked in the rearview mirror until he locked eyes with Klinsman, then mimed that he was zipping his lips. Klinsman sneered in return.

In silence, Klinsman turned his attention to the folder. He started to read. Soon he was starting to feel a strong emotion, too, like the guy he'd just been told about. Only in his case, it wasn't despair.

The driver checked the interior of the car very thoroughly when he dropped it around the corner from the limousine depot. The folder was definitely gone from the backseat. Klinsman must have taken it. Along with all of its contents. All the documents that outlined in great detail a fatal flaw that had come to light in a well-known company's signature product. They confirmed that its regulator knew all about the problem. A confidential memo from a PR consultant suggested a range of strategies to contain the fallout when the bad news inevitably broke. The president of finance had projected the losses she expected to ensue. Their broker had forecast the hit their share price was likely to take. To ensure that these points were clear, graphs were included. They showed a series of red lines plunging relentlessly toward catastrophe. Even the most hopeful scenario ended with a total wipeout.

The driver couldn't resist a smile. He just wished he could snag a seat at Klinsman's next dinner party. *Shorting is dangerous,* Ro Lebedow had said. *The losses can potentially be infinite . . .*

Chapter Twenty-six

I'D BEEN TO MCGINTY'S BAR BEFORE AND I HADN'T hated it. They had good coffee, and when the barman saw I was there with a bunch of cops he added a generous dose of whiskey without feeling the need to ask. Or to charge. The ambience was pleasant, too. The bar itself was long, with plenty of space to sit without feeling crowded. It was made of solid mahogany, darkened over time and wearing the kind of shine that only comes from years of polishing by hand. Its wide array of dings and dents weren't hidden or disguised. No one had tried to repair them, either. Rather than being shunned as signs of age or disrepair, it was like they were welcomed as distinguished witnesses to all the scenes that had played out there over the last three quarters of a century.

I hadn't hated the place when I last visited. It was different this time. Sheets of coarse, heavy plywood had been dropped on top of a few rows of upturned beer crates near the wall between the bar and the door. A microphone stand had been thrown on top. A few multicolored lights on wobbly tripods were set up on either side. A battered speaker cabinet perched on each corner. And a computer monitor was fixed to each one.

It was Hell. Otherwise known as Karaoke Night.

Someone had once told me that in Japanese, the prefix *ka* meant *without*. That was plausible for karate—without weapons. The guy claimed that on the same lines, *karaoke* was *without instruments*. I wasn't so sure about that. I might have believed him if he'd said *without shame*. *Without self-respect*. *Without the opportunity to relax without some idiot plaguing you to make a spectacle of yourself despite an utter lack of talent*. Robson evidently didn't feel the same way, though. He'd put in a request before even ordering a drink, and the instant his song started he leaped onto the stage, a whisker away from smashing his head into the air duct that was suspended from the ceiling. He'd chosen "Freedom! '90" by George Michael. And he did a good job with it. I didn't want to walk out in the middle of his performance, so I ordered a second cup of coffee and stayed in my seat at the bar. Robson soaked up the applause when he reached the end of his final chorus, then jumped down and came across to join me, still radiating heat and energy.

"You should try it." Robson waved for a beer. "You might enjoy it."

"I'm out of here." I slid a twenty under my coffee mug and stood up. "If Atkinson ever shows, tell him I got sick of waiting. Or that I got sick. Your call."

A crowd had gathered in front of the stage to watch a woman I recognized as a vice cop from the fifteenth precinct singing "Like a Virgin," and that delayed me long enough to bump into Atkinson just inside the doorway.

"You're not leaving?" Atkinson looked genuinely surprised.

"I say this with love, Detective, but if you ever trick me into visiting a karaoke bar again, I'll kill you and your entire family."

"You should sing something. Shake this horrible mood you're in." Atkinson grinned. "How about 'Eye of the Tiger'? Can't you see yourself, stalking your prey in the night?"

I glared at him.

"Maybe a duet, until you're more comfortable. 'Out in the Fields'? 'Dancing in the Streets'? No? OK. I get it. No singing. But at least let me buy you a drink." He nodded toward an empty table near the door. "I want to thank you for the tip about the bent judge. Him, his crew, it's huge."

"Sure. That would be nice. I'll have a coffee."

"So how did you find out about the whole bribery thing? An operation like that, there's a lot of moving parts."

"It was no biggie. Hang around the courthouse long enough, you hear people talking. Do you think you'll be able to make the case?"

"Definitely. Rooney was on the job a lot of years. He knows how the game's played. He's giving us chapter and verse. And we got another lucky break. A guy came forward, said he'd been approached by Rooney, and volunteered to wear a wire. The weird thing is that he's not one of Steven Bruce's clients—but gift horses, right?"

"You've got to love it when a citizen chooses to do the right thing."

"You do. It certainly makes my job easier. And talking of doing the right thing, I owe you an apology. About the Pardew file. I never really believed you'd find it. I made that clear a few times, and I wasn't subtle. But I was wrong. You came through. I never should have doubted you."

"I'm happy I was able to help."

"You never told me where it was."

"I found it shoved in a closet."

"A closet you just happened to look in?"

"You know how it goes. Better lucky than good."

"You're not going to tell me where it really was, are you?"

"And lose my air of mystery?"

"Oh, is that what you have? But all right. The hint is taken. I'll say thank you and leave it at that." Atkinson paused and drummed his fingers on the tabletop. "Strange coincidence, you finding Pardew so close to your house."

"Small world."

"I'm glad you turned him in. Imagine the scenes if my partner, Kanchelskis, had found him floating in the East River."

"Like you once said, that guy has an oversuspicious nature."

"Be honest a second." Atkinson leaned in close. "Weren't you tempted to take care of things for yourself? Not even for a second? I kind of thought that might have been your goal all along."

I shook my head. "When I got back from the army and found my father was dead, it looked like Pardew wasn't even going to stand trial. That's what I couldn't live with. But is he guilty? Did he cause my father's heart attack? I don't know. The evidence isn't clear. As far as I know. Better to leave that kind of a decision to a jury."

"I'm glad you feel that way. Can I get you another drink?"

I was about to accept when Robson started singing again. "I Will Survive." "Another time?"

"Sure." Atkinson stood and we shook hands. "One other thing. I nearly forgot. Here's another coincidence for you. That guy Klinsman, who you thought was hooked up with Chinese Intelligence? He's been arrested. Insider trading. He bought a whole bunch of shares that were in the process of skyrocketing. A buddy in the SEC told me about it. He said they got a tip to check the computer at his apartment in some fancy building on Billionaires' Row. They found an email on it—a trace anyway, because Klinsman had tried to wipe the disc. It was full of confidential details about a patent the company had just won. Klinsman denied all knowledge. He claimed he'd been forced to buy the shares—and make a huge loss—because of a failed attempt at short-selling. He even produced a stash of documents showing the company was in all kinds of trouble. They were forgeries, of course—

real good ones—but they wouldn't have helped anyway. He bought the shares. That's a fact. Sc either way he was acting on illegal information. It's still a crime, even if you screw up and burn a loac of cash."

I couldn't hold back a smile.

"What's so funny? I thought you'd be disappointed that he turned out to be a rogue trader, not a spy or a secret agent."

"It's just that when I first heard of the guy, he was pissed because someone had burned down his big house. Now he's going to a different kind of big house. I feel like that brings a little balance to the world. It restores my faith."

Chapter Twenty-seven

MRS. VINCENT HAD BEEN CREMATED A WEEK AGO, but now she was back. She was thinner than I remembered. Her hair was longer. Her skin was chalky white. She was surrounded with a pale, glowing mist. And she was smashing holes in my living room wall.

"What kind of ghost uses a hammer?" I turned on the light and flapped my arms in a vain attempt to dispel the plaster dust that was already starting to cling to my clothes. "I thought you guys could walk through walls."

Mrs. Vincent suppressed a sneeze, lowered her hammer, and turned to look at me. A hint of a smile played across her face. We stood in silence for a moment, comfortably sharing space at close quarters as we'd done a million times before, then she leaned down to switch off her camping lantern. When she straightened up again she had a small pistol in her right hand. "Hello, Paul. You're home early."

I'd seen that kind of pistol before. In a glass case. It's known as a PSM, because *Pistolet Samozaryadny Malogabaritny* is such a mouthful. Although the name isn't as exotic as it first seems. It translates as *compact self-loading pistol.* It was designed for officers of the Red Army high command but quickly became popular with other branches of the Soviet military. It was admired for its compact dimensions. And for its ability to propel one of its special bullets through fifty-five layers of Kevlar.

One branch of the military had adopted the gun with particular enthusiasm. The KGB.

"Do I need to call the Cold War Museum?" I gestured to her pistol. "Tell them one of their exhibits is missing? Or did you get that thing someplace else?"

"Have you found it?" Mrs. Vincent gestured toward the wall. "Do you have it?"

"If you go all *Marathon Man* on me, this is going to take ages. So stop with the pronouns and tell me what you're looking for."

"The recording device."

"Why would there be a recording device in my wall?"

"Your mother put one there."

"She couldn't have. She never set foot in this house. My father didn't buy it until after she was dead."

"There's a lot you don't know about your mother. She designed a listening system that the

FBI used in this house." Mrs. Vincent reached around and tugged at a mesh of copper wires that was visible through one of the holes she'd broken in the wall. "She helped them install it here. And she died here."

"She died at the house in Westchester."

Mrs. Vincent shook her head. "In this house." She walked to the doorway and pointed to a spot on the floor with her foot. "Right here. She was shot in the neck. She bled to death."

"Did you shoot her?"

"No. But I was here when it happened. I saw."

"How on earth did you come to be here?"

"That's a long story."

Very slowly, and with an eye on her gun, I moved across and lowered myself into one of the chairs. The one Robson normally uses, because it was farther away from her. "I'm not going anywhere. Are you?"

Mrs. Vincent hesitated, and shifted her weight between her feet. "I just want the device. Then I'll go."

"Do you know what it looks like?"

"No."

"Where it is? There are lots of walls in this house."

Mrs. Vincent didn't answer.

"Do you really think you'll find it?"

Mrs. Vincent stayed silent.

"What's so important about this thing, anyway? Whatever's on it, whatever it reveals about you, no one would come looking. You're officially dead. Why wouldn't you stay that way?"

"And go where, Paul? And do what? I'm sixty-seven years old. I don't want to start my life a over again. I've done that too many times already And how would I find a place to live? Where would I get the money for food? I realized I just want to be back in Westchester, doing what I was doing."

"So why run in the first place?"

"Protocol. A little bird told me you'd hired a security company. As soon as they started work they'd discover the monitoring system. They'd find the recorder. You'd listen. I couldn't be around when that happened. So I pulled the rip cord That's what I'm trained to do."

"Then why come back?"

"I got to California, where my fictitious friend are supposed to be. I had the pre-prepped documents dated and sent to Ferguson. And that's when everything started to unravel. I'm a relic, Paul. My motherland's gone. My handler's gone. The rest of my escape route was gone."

"So you thought you'd resurrect yourself?"

Mrs. Vincent nodded. "I figured I'd claim there'd been an admin screwup. Mistaken identity It would be easy to prove I was alive, after all. But first, I needed the recorder."

"What's so important about it?"

Mrs. Vincent didn't respond.

"If you're worried about admitting you were a KGB agent, I have news for you. That rabbit's out of the hat. And I knew my mother was an electronics engineer. I just didn't know who she was working for. So what happened? This place was a Soviet afe house, and the FBI bugged it with her sys-em?”

“It was still experimental. Your mother houldn’t have been here. The whole thing was—ow do you say it?—a cluster fuck. There was hooting. A grenade. You lost two. Us, one. Plus I vas injured.” She rolled up her sleeve and revealed er scar. “Here. And I almost lost the sight in one ye. I couldn’t work in the field after that.”

“I understand cluster fucks. I’ve been on the vrong end of a few myself. But why were you ere? Was your cover blown? Were you running?”

Mrs. Vincent shook her head. “I was called here for a briefing. New equipment.”

“Why would you care about that being re-corded? Everything from the eighties has been ob-solete for years.”

“I don’t care about the briefing. It’s my voice. It’s on that tape. Speaking English, to the other agent before the technician arrived. That was the rule. We were never allowed to talk in Russian. If anyone else heard that—Joe Public, the authorities—who cares? But you? You were in Military Intelligence. You were trained how to lis-ten. You’d recognize my voice. Know it was me.”

“And now I’ve found out, anyway.”

Mrs. Vincent nodded. “Which is a problem. And there’s only one solution, as far as I can see.”

She raised her PSM. Looked me in the eye for ten hour-long seconds. Then reversed the gun and handed it to me. “I’m throwing myself on your mercy, Paul. One professional to another. I’ve said enough. Do what you think's right. I won't fight you."

The gun nestled comfortably in my hand, reassuringly solid and heavy.

"After my mother was dead and you couldn't return to the field, how did you end up at our house? The KGB wasn't known for its child-raising program."

"I wasn't sent there because of you. Your father was the target. Close surveillance."

"My father was a businessman. He had nothing to do with counterintelligence."

"There's a lot you don't know about your father. A lot I could tell you, if I have the chance."

"My father was a pacifist and—" I was interrupted by another voice in my head. Pardew's. He'd said my father wanted to *clear the place out* . . . "Wait. My father knew about my mother's monitoring system being here?"

"Of course."

"He knew she died here?"

Mrs. Vincent nodded.

"That's why he bought the place?"

She nodded again.

"OK. Some pieces are falling into place, but I need to think for a moment. Make sure I'm seeing the full picture. So, come. Sit."

Mrs. Vincent took the seat I normally used, but within a couple of minutes she was fidgeting like a two-year-old. "I need to do something. How about a cup of tea?"

"No, thanks."

"Your father always liked tea at times like this, when he needed clarity."

I thought about my father for a moment, and the predictability of his habits.

"Actually, that's a good idea. We should have some tea. I'll make a pot."

"No, I'll do it." She reached across and touched my arm. "You have a lot to process. And I looked after you for lots of years. I've missed it."

"I don't know. There's a door leading out of the kitchen. What's to stop you from running?"

"What would be the point?" She stood up, stretched her arms out wide, and turned a full circle. "I don't have the recorder. That's the time bomb I came to defuse, and it's still ticking. Unless you decide to stop it."

"OK. Fair point. Let me help you, then. It's my buddy's kettle, and it's really weird."

"I can manage! I think it's fair to say I've used more kettles and made more cups of tea in my life than you ever will."

"All right. But one other thing. There's only one real cup, and it isn't clean, so you'll have to use disposable ones. And me, I don't take milk."

Mrs. Vincent returned ten minutes later. She was using the glass turntable from the microwave as a tray to carry three paper cups. Two were full of tea. The other, some milk.

"You choose." She set the tray on the table between us and sat back down.

I started to reach for the cup that was closer to

me, then changed my mind and stretched across t
take the other. "I'll leave you the one with roor
for milk."

"Thank you, Paul. Always the gentleman." Sh
topped up her cup, and as she was about to replac
the makeshift pitcher I nudged the table over a
inch. That shifted the rim of the turntable jus
enough to end up under the pitcher and cause it t
overbalance, tipping the last of the milk all ove
the floor. Mrs. Vincent yelped and hurried to he
purse to grab a pack of Kleenex and mop up th
mess.

We sat in silence for the next ten minutes whil
we drank our tea. I was the first to finish. I set m
cup down on the table and saw Mrs. Vincen
glance inside, checking it was empty.

"You were right," I said. "The tea did help m
think. It clarified something about your problem
There are two dimensions to it. The recorder. An
me."

Mrs. Vincent didn't answer.

"You only need to neutralize one."

The ghost of a smile played across her face.

"The recorder's hard to find. I'm not."

"You should have thought faster."

"Did you put the same thing in my tea as in my
father's? It stands to reason, if you couldn't risk me
recognizing your voice on that tape, you certainly
couldn't risk him listening to it. And you'd just
overheard him telling his partner he was going to
have this place cleared out."

Mrs.Vincent nodded. "I used K-2."

"Good choice. Old school. Effective. If the victim was a diplomat in Moscow or some such place, the navy would have known to screen for it. But with a civilian and a suburban doctor, you figured an old KGB favorite would slip through unnoticed."

"I did. And I was right."

"But you disposed of the tainted cup, anyway."

"Of course. I was trained to be thorough."

"And when it was my turn you couldn't shoot me, because then the police would investigate. Instead you'd make it look like I was doing some vigorous DIY and collapsed just like my father had done. Weak hearts must run in our family."

"That was the neatest solution. I like neat."

"Let me ask you one other thing about your thorough training. You studied the culture of the nation you were assigned to?"

"Of course."

"That was smart. Helps you anticipate people's moves."

"The battle won is won in the mind."

"You learned that men in America tend to be chivalrous."

"Or as we call it, sexist."

"Before you came to the United States you knew that would be true of people in general. You found from experience that it was true of my father in particular. I showed signs of it myself, just now. So it was a reasonable assumption that I'd leave you the cup with the space for milk."

"It was less suspicious to let you pick your own cup, but I needed you to choose the right one."

"Did I choose the right one, though? Have a closer look."

Mrs. Vincent glanced down, her face suddenly creased with doubt.

"I saw you check just now when I put the cup down." I pointed to it. "You were focused on whether it was empty. But what you should have been looking at is the color of the dregs."

She picked up the cup and stared inside it.

"That one was left by the guy who shares the house with me. It's one of dozens he leaves strewn around. He takes milk." I reached down to the side of my chair and produced a full cup. "Here's the one you brought for me."

Mrs. Vincent's expression hardened and she scowled at the empty cup as if it had personally betrayed her. Then she crushed it and dropped it on the floor. "So." Her voice was soft and barely audible. "Where do we go from here, Paul? After everything? All the years? We're like family, you and me, now."

"You've done a lot for my family. That's true. You murdered my father. You watched my mother die. You just tried to kill me. History aside, that limits our options."

"I was only doing my job." She grabbed my arm. "We're both professionals. You of all people should understand."

"About my mother, maybe. If you're telling the truth. You didn't know us then. But my father? You lived under his roof all those years. And then killed him to save your own skin."

"No. Everything I did was an act of war. I was

doing my duty. Your mom and dad were hurt. I regret that. But they chose their paths, the same way I did. The same way you did. How many people have you hurt over the years? How many have you killed?"

I pulled my arm free and crossed to the window.

"What are you going to do, Paul?"

I looked at the houses on the other side of the street and wondered which neighbor had told Mrs. Vincent about seeing Rooney's van. Whoever it was, something needed to be done about them.

"Can you forgive me, Paul? If not as one professional to another, then for all the meals I made you. The clothes I washed and ironed. The times I didn't tell your father when I heard you sneaking into the house after curfew."

I could feel the weight of my phone in one pocket. Her gun in the other. I knew which tool I wanted to use to end this.

"Whatever you decide, Paul, please, let's settle things between us. Whether I walk out of this room or not, I don't want to get locked up. I don't want to be disgraced. I don't want to be deported to a country that doesn't want me back."

Triggering a police investigation wouldn't be a problem for me, if I put a bullet in her head. She was an enemy agent, and she'd just tried to kill me.

"Please, Paul. Let me go."

I closed my fingers around the grip of her gun and felt the textured aluminum warm up under my skin.

"If you can't do that, then shoot me. Please. Just don't turn me in."

I pulled my hands out of my pockets, turned t
face her, and held up my phone. "I can't do that
It's not my decision. I have to make a call."

"I knew you'd say that, Paul." Mrs. Vincent pu
the cup back on the table. The one she'd intende
for me. It was empty. "I don't know how you ca
drink tea without milk, though. It's disgusting."

"No!" I reached her chair in two strides. "Yo
shouldn't have—"

"I told you, Paul. I couldn't go to jail here.
couldn't get sent back there. You couldn't turn
blind eye. So this was the only option."

I held up the phone. "Shall I call 911? There'
still time, if I tell them what they're dealing with."

She shook her head. "No. I've made my choice
This is the way I want to go. But you can sit wit
me. So I'm not alone when . . . you know. It won'
be long."

I sat and took her hand. "Remember when
was little, and I couldn't sleep? You'd sit with m
for hours."

She shrugged. "I didn't want to go back down
stairs. The mask didn't feel so tight in the dark
with just a kid to fool."

"You used to sing to me. You said they wer
songs your father taught you, back home in Mis
sissippi. I guess you were fooling me then, too."

"I learned those stupid songs from cassett
tapes. In a classroom. In Leningrad. I've never bee
to Mississippi. And I never knew my father."

"I'm beginning to think I never knew mine. Yo
said you could tell me things about him."

"There's no time." Her voice was tightening. "

can feel it. It's close. Later, go to the house. My bedroom. Inside the drapes. At the bottom, where they're hemmed. I kept copies. All my notes. I wasn't supposed to, but the radios. Couldn't rely on them."

"I'll do that."

We sat in silence for a minute—or it could have been an hour—then she turned to look at me. "It was my mother who liked to sing." Her voice was barely above a whisper. "I wanted to sing her songs. I couldn't sing them here. Too dangerous. I should have stayed home. Sung to her. My sisters. Their kids."

"You can sing those songs now, if you want. There's no danger."

"There's no time." She gripped my hand tighter. "It's coming. I can feel it. Goodbye, Paul."

"Прощай, Mrs. Vincent."

"No. Call me by my real name. Just once, after all these years."

"I don't know it."

"My name—oh. It's strange to say out loud, after so long. I thought I never would again. It's Anna Alekseyevna Vasiliev."

"Then farewell, Anna Alekseyevna Vasiliev. I wish we'd met under different circumstances."

"Really? I wish we'd never met at all."

Chapter Twenty-eight

ROBSON WAS NOT HAPPY ABOUT THE BODY IN HIS trunk.

"Come on." I slammed the lid. "What are you complaining about? It's clean."

"It's covered in plaster dust."

"That's no big deal. You can hoover that out. It's not like we've had to tape a bag over her head to keep the blood and brains off the carpet."

"That's not the point. This is a Cadillac."

"That's exactly the point. Anna—Mrs. Vincent—is not taking her last ride in a rented Chevrolet."

We made sure to dump the body outside the boundary of the Fifteenth Precinct. I didn't want there to be a chance of Detective Atkinson catching the case. Not because I thought he might trace the body back to me. Anna Alekseyevna Vasiliev was the definition of untraceable, destined to spend eternity as Jane Doe even though I finally knew her real name. It was more that I liked the guy and didn't want to be responsible for adding an unsolved case to his record.

Robson dropped me at Foley Square when we were done and I stopped after a few yards to gaze up at the courthouse. It looked magnificent in the low fall sun. I figured I had a little time to kill, so I strolled over to the steps and sat for a while, enjoying the warmth and the view. I found it was also a good place to think. About Pardew—how to keep him out of jail now that I knew he wasn't responsible for my father's death, rather than to make sure he stood trial. And about Marian. Maybe it was time to take Harry's advice and ask her out to dinner. Maybe sometimes it was better not to give in to old habits.

I took out my phone and was about to text Harry and ask him to track down Marian's cell number when I felt someone watching me. I looked up and saw a familiar face. It was Len Hendrie. The guy who'd burned down Jimmy Klinsman's house. I stood up and nodded a greeting.

"Paul, how are you doing?" Hendrie hopped up a couple of steps and we shook hands.

"Good to see you, Len. Are you heading in? Working on your defense?"

"No need." Hendrie smiled. "My case is over. I'm a free man."

"Fantastic! What a result. I remember you thought you didn't stand a chance. You must have made one hell of an argument."

"No. I didn't have to. The lawyer you recommended to give me some advice? Di Matteo? He reached out to me. Then a weird thing happened. A guy approached me and said he had a way to nix my case, if I paid him."

"Did you take him up on his offer?"

"Are you crazy? No way. I went to the police. Offered to wear a wire on the guy. It turned out he was part of some really big thing. Even a crooked judge was involved. So this di Matteo, he picked up my case. Got me a plea deal. Guilty—because I did set the fire—but sentenced to time served because of my cooperation with the bribery thing."

"That's tremendous, Len. You stood up when it counted, so I'm glad you came out of this thing all right."

"Thanks. You want to hear something even weirder, though? Di Matteo told me that Jimmy shorted the shares in the deal that hurt me as part of a whacked-out game. He's in some kind of legal trouble himself now, but when the guys he played with found out the consequences of what they'd done, they all threw some cash in a pot. Enough for me to buy back my house. Can you believe it? I have a roof over my head again."

"That's wonderful. It's not often you hear about guys like that doing the right thing."

"It is wonderful. And none of it would have happened without di Matteo."

"I told you he was good. Didn't I tell you that?"

"You did. But there's one thing I still don't understand. How did he know to contact me?"

"The law's a business, just like any other. Attorneys are always looking for new clients."

"But how did he pick me, specifically?"

I shrugged. "Luck? Good fortune?"

"No." Hendrie shook his head. "Do you know what I think? I think he pays people at the courthouse to find him leads."

"He could do that, I guess. That would actually be smart."

"But the thing is, Paul, you're the only person I gave my cell number to. You're the only one who could have sold it to him."

I shook my head. "Absolutely not. I didn't sell him your number, or anyone else's. You have my word on that."

"Look, if you did, if you work for him on the side, that's totally cool. I'm not here to cause you trouble. I'm here to thank you."

"I appreciate that, Len. But there's nothing to thank me for. I don't work for di Matteo, or any other lawyer. I'm just a janitor. I work for the city of New York."

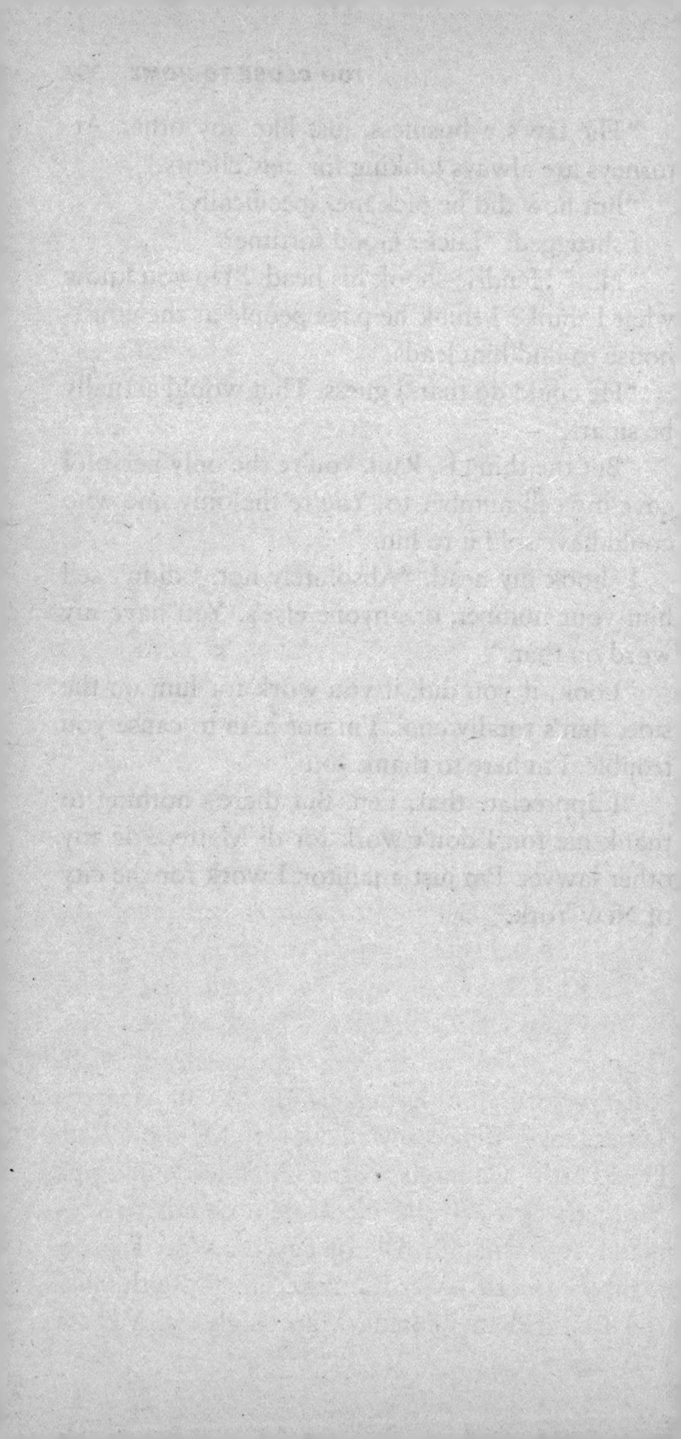

ACKNOWLEDGMENTS

I WOULD LIKE TO EXTEND MY DEEPEST THANKS TO the following for their help, support, and encouragement while I wrote this book. Without them, it would not have been possible.

My editor, the excellent Kara Cesare, and the whole team at Random House.

My agent, the outstanding Richard Pine.

My friends, who've stood by me through the years: Dan Boucher, Carlos Camacho, Joelle Charbonneau, John Dul, Jamie Freveletti, Keir Graff, Kristy Claiborne Graves, Tana Hall, Nick Hawkins, Dermot Hollingsworth, Amanda Hurford, Richard Hurford, Jon Jordan, Ruth Jordan, Martyn James Lewis, Rebecca Makkai, Dan Malmon, Kate Hackbarth Malmon, Carrie Medders, Philippa Morgan, Erica Ruth Neubauer, Gunther Neumann, Ayo Onatade, Denise Pascoe, Wray Pascoe, Dani Patarazzi, Javier Ramirez, David Reith, Sharon Reith, Beth Renaldi, Marc Rightley, Melissa

Rightley, Renee Rosen, Kelli Stanley, and Brian Wilson.

Brendan Vaughan.

Everyone at The Globe Pub, Chicago.

Everyone from Fish Creek Ranch Preserve, Wyoming.

Jane and Jim Grant.

Ruth Grant.

Katharine Grant.

Jess Grant.

Alexander Tyska.

Stacie Gutting.

And last on the list, but first in my heart—Tasha. *Everything, always . . .*

I'd also like to extend extra-special thanks to Ruth Troyanek for generously bidding on a character name which she dedicated to her mother—the real Patricia Lee Spangler—in support of the wonderful Albany County Public Library.